S0-ANG-724

St. Martin's Paperbacks Titles
By Tamara Sneed

You've Got a Hold on Me

All the Man I Need

The Way He Makes Me Feel

All
the Man
I Need

TAMARA SNEED

St. Martin's Paperbacks

ALL THE MAN I NEED

Copyright © 2004 by Tamara Sneed.

ISBN: 0-312-98730-7
EAN: 80312-98730-5

Printed in the United States of America

St. Martin's Paperbacks edition / August 2004

St. Martin's Paperbacks are published by St. Martin's Press, 175 Fifth Avenue, New York, NY 10010.

10 9 8 7 6 5 4 3 2

To my cousin Marlo,
who imparted her love for romance novels and
the written word to me at a young age

Acknowledgments

I would like to thank fellow author Reon Laudat for always being a voice of reason and a voice of encouragement when I doubt myself or my writing.

And, as always, I would like to thank my family for being supportive, loving, and the best promoters a writer could have.

CHAPTER ONE

Lana Hargrove had spent half of her life running from men. Men who either wanted more than she was willing to give—like a second date or a returned phone call or E-mail, or men who wanted to give her too much, like the key to their house or a kidney. But, after spending five months in a self-defense class that she had initially taken because the instructor looked like a shorter, darker version of Boris Kodjoe, she had vowed to never run from a man in fear. Not that she ever had before, because Lana Hargrove was scared of no man, but she didn't want there to be a first time, either, which was exactly why Lana decided to confront the man who had been following her for the last half hour on the crowded streets of the Georgetown shopping district.

Lana turned down a quiet tree-lined street that branched off from Wisconsin, the main street in the heart of Georgetown. She hurried on her tiptoes—so that her three-inch stiletto heels didn't make noise against the pavement—to the opening of the alley. She set her three shopping bags on the ground, then waited. Sure enough, she heard the steady rhythm of footsteps on the sidewalk. It had to be the pervert.

Lana balled her right hand into a fist and patiently waited, remembering to breathe evenly and deeply. She was following her training perfectly, except for the part where she planned this confrontation. Her self-defense instructor, Raj—who later turned out to be married with two kids and, more important, a personality as exciting as a package of tofu—had always taught the other smitten and subsequently disappointed women in his class to avoid confrontation and to only engage "the enemy" when forced to. Lana had never liked avoiding anything.

She tensed as the footsteps grew nearer; then as she was about to jump out and attack, a short white man walked past her, yelling into his cell phone. Lana stared past the man, confused. There was no one else on the sidewalk. Where was the tall black man in the baseball cap and sunglasses? Lana had been certain that there had been a tall black man, with impossibly broad shoulders, following her. Men usually followed her, because she was an attractive black woman in Washington DC, where black men followed any black woman as if she held the Holy Grail. The following thing didn't bother her. It was the fact that the man never made his move. He just followed her. The lurking stalkers she didn't like; the open and obvious stalkers she could deal with.

Lana was so preoccupied with her disappointment that she wouldn't be able to kick some pervert's butt today that she didn't notice the man with the baseball cap and sunglasses until he stood almost in her face. Her training took over. She grabbed his hand and tugged and pulled with a warrior yell that would have made Raj proud. The man flipped over like a Hollywood stuntman and landed in the middle of the sidewalk with a loud groan that made Lana smile in satisfaction.

She placed one thin heel squarely in the middle of his chest and stared down at him, feeling mildly triumphant, even though common sense told her to just run. Unfortunately, a lack of common sense was one of the traits she would actually admit that she had inherited from her father.

"Why are you following me?" Lana asked coolly, as if she had all the time in the world.

Then she noticed his face, which was fully visible, since his cap and glasses had flown off during the fall. The majority of his face was chocolate brown perfection, a perfect nose and full lips, almond-shaped eyes, and eyebrows as dark as midnight and silky smooth. But then there was the portion of the left side of his face, which was very far from perfection. It was as if a section of his face had melted, and brown tangled, scarred tissue was frozen to preserve the injustice of it compared to the majority of his dark, unblemished skin. Only a small portion of his face was horribly scarred, but it was enough to draw her attention, and enough horror and sympathy flowed through her body to make her take her foot off his chest.

The man took the opportunity that her obvious shock provided to push her off him and scramble to his feet. She almost lost her balance but wobbled on her feet only for him to grab her shoulders and slam her into the brick wall behind her, hard enough for her to wince in pain and berate herself for feeling sympathy for him. His hands were rough on her shoulders as he pinned her to the wall. It was a strange time to notice it, but she observed how dark and intense his eyes were. If his hands hadn't been digging in her shoulders at that moment, she would have thought he was easily manipulated, like most men she met.

"Are you scared, Lana?" he demanded in a husky voice as his mouth hovered inches from hers.

Lana's gaze unwillingly lowered to his wet, full lips. She was grateful for the sudden pinpricks of pain in her back from the sharp edges of the brick wall through the thin material of the dress. She winced and it could have been her imagination, but it felt as if his hands loosened on her shoulders. She cursed herself. She refused to have lust-filled thoughts about her attacker.

She forced herself to swallow the lump of fear and arousal in her throat and demanded, "How do you know my name?"

"Nice outfit," he said, his gaze raking over the lilac-colored sundress she wore. It was too short and cut too low and those were the two main reasons she had bought it, except she had not pictured this scenario when she had. When lust flashed openly in his eyes, she struggled against his hold on her shoulders, but his grip was too strong. His gaze lingered on her breasts, on the cleavage visible there, and he actually licked his lips. His very beautiful and full lips. He finally met her eyes again. "With that dress, I'm surprised half of the men in DC aren't following you . . . or throwing dollar bills at your feet for a lap dance."

Rage flowed through her body and she rammed a knee into his groin with enough force to make him scream in pain. He immediately released her and fell into the wall as he cradled his private parts, his face contorted in agony. He slid to the ground with a whimper. Lana smiled at him, then spotted his sunglasses nearby and purposely ground one heel into the designer shades. Then she crossed her arms over her chest and watched him.

"We were about to get to the part where you tell me who you are and how you know my name," she said cheerfully.

His eyes rolled in their sockets as he continued to grimace in obvious pain. Lana sighed in impatience, then examined her fingernails while she waited. It was definitely time for another manicure.

"You're insane," he finally managed to gasp.

"That's creative," she said dryly, then demanded, "Now, who are you?"

"You could have caused serious damage," he said.

"Hopefully, I have. I guess we won't know for certain until you take the equipment for a test run. I would volunteer for the job, but I think it's probably too small to hold my attention for long," she said cheerfully, then pointedly stared at the spot in his pants where the equipment resided, until he cleared his throat.

She was surprised she didn't internally combust from the look of hot anger he directed at her. She actually took a step back to place more distance between them before she reminded herself that she was scared of no man. He obviously tried to calm himself as he took several deep breaths before he said, "My name is Justin Larkin."

"That's a good first step, Justin," she said in a soft, soothing voice. "Next question: Why are you following me?"

"I'm not going to hurt you," he said, then slowly and carefully pulled himself to stand, although she noticed with satisfaction the flicker of pain crossing his face with the movement. She never before wanted a man to think about her while he used the bathroom, but she hoped that Justin Larkin would be thinking about her while he painfully tried to take a piss for the next few days.

She laughed, amused, then said dryly, "Thanks for the reassurance. I feel much better now."

"I work with your father," he said flatly.

It was Lana's turn to lean against the wall for support. She tried to breathe but suddenly forgot how. Her father. She looked at Justin again, but his face was a blank mask as he watched her. When her gasps for air intensified, a flash of concern crossed his face before he hesitantly approached her, almost as if he were waiting for her to knee him again. Then he placed a hand on her back, a large, warm hand that felt nice. There were no ulterior motives, no demands from him, just comfort. It had been a long time since any man had touched her without any ulterior motive, and she had forgotten how nice it could feel.

"Breathe, Lana," he instructed in a surprisingly gentle tone.

"My father?" she whispered, confused. That word "father" hadn't existed in her life in years. Twenty years, to be precise, since her father left her with his mother and never made any attempt to contact her. "If you work with him, then . . . then you're a—"

He smiled and the sight was almost out of this world, showcasing beautiful even white teeth. It was a shame that a pervert had to have such a nice smile.

"I'm a thief," he supplied the word for her, his smile fading only slightly. "Or as your father likes to say, we commandeer and exchange artwork for a fee."

"But you're . . . How can you . . ." Her voice trailed off, but her gaze remained glued to the scarred side of his face.

His smile instantly disappeared, and she realized too late that she had touched—or, more accurately, looked at—a sensitive spot. "One of the only jobs, outside of Disneyland, where wearing a mask is a prerequisite. You can see why I'm perfect for it."

For some reason, she didn't like the self-loathing she heard in his voice. Once more she had to shake herself from feeling sympathy for her attacker, or even worse, since he was no longer her attacker but one of her father's colleagues. Lana abruptly moved away from his touch, all too aware of the feelings being awakened by it. She could have told herself that any man could make her body hum like that, but it would have been a lie. She had never reacted to a man like she had to this one.

"Why are you following me?" she demanded, finding her voice again.

"Because your father asked me to," he said simply, then retrieved his cap and broken sunglasses off the ground. He placed the shattered sunglasses in his shirt pocket and sent her a look that was designed to make her feel guilty but instead made her want to stick out her tongue at him. "I've been following you for a few days—"

"No, you haven't," she said, shaking her head in disbelief. "I would have seen you."

"Yes, I have."

"No, you haven't."

Justin sighed impatiently, obviously stopping himself from arguing with her again, then said, "The point is you're in danger and your father wants me to take you somewhere safe."

"You?" She snorted in disbelief. "I'm supposed to voluntarily follow a strange man to God knows where, all because my father, whom I haven't seen in twenty years, supposedly wants me to? Maybe your head was damaged in the fall, but I . . ." Her voice trailed off when he held up his hand, from which a familiar small sapphire pendant on a white gold chain dangled.

She snatched it from his hand and studied the sapphire. On the back of the pendant LH was engraved and her birth date. It was hers. Her father had bought it for her the day she was born and gave it to her the day her mother died. Lana hadn't seen it in twenty years, since her father had dropped her off at her grandmother's house in Oakland, and she had given it to him with a foolish innocence that said he would return and give it back to her. Her heart beat wildly as she glared at Justin. "Where did you get this?"

"Your father wanted me to give it to you so you'd know that you can trust me."

She snorted in disbelief, but her gaze returned to the pendant. She couldn't believe that he had kept it. Twenty years. She abruptly slipped it into her purse, then said to Justin, "I don't trust him and I sure as hell don't trust you. He disappears for the majority of my life—not even bothering to attend his own mother's funeral—and then you show up saying I'm in danger and I'm supposed to follow you without question—"

"You weren't supposed to see me yet. I was supposed to wait to talk to you after your father contacted you," he grumbled reluctantly.

"You're hard to miss," she snapped. He went completely still and Lana rolled her eyes in exasperation. "I'm not talking about your face; I'm talking about you. Have you looked in the mirror lately? You're a big guy."

She would die before telling him that with the way his shoulders filled out a shirt and the square line of his jaw, any woman would notice him. That's what she had noticed. Lana liked to think that she had radar when it came to fine men, and she had spotted him blocks ago.

"You just noticed me today," he obviously felt compelled to add.

She rolled her eyes, then asked, with feigned boredom, "Why am I supposedly in danger?"

"Your father has some enemies in DC. He doesn't want you to get hurt, and he thinks that they'll use you to get to him."

"What did he do this time? Steal something from the most violent criminal in America?" She felt an uncharacteristic flash of fear when she saw the distinctly uncomfortable look on Justin's face. "I was being sarcastic, but that's it, isn't it? My father took something from the wrong person and they want it back."

Justin ignored her question and glanced up and down the quiet street. "It's not safe here. Let's go to your house so you can grab a few things, and then we're going for a drive."

Lana laughed in disbelief and shook her head. "I'm not going anywhere with you."

He sighed as if he were a long-suffering martyr. "I'm not going to hurt you, Lana."

"I know you aren't going to hurt me, because I won't let you," she said simply. "But I'm still not going anywhere with you. If you are telling the truth, that someone is trying to use me to hurt my father, then you could be the exact man that I should be avoiding. And if you aren't telling the truth, then you're crazy and if you make any sudden moves I'll make sure the family jewels are permanently out of commission."

Silence stretched between them as Justin glared at her. She could tell he was half-tempted to throw her over his shoulder and take her where he wanted her to go, and she wasn't entirely certain that she could do anything to stop him besides scream a lot. And there was that small part of her that didn't want to scream at all.

Justin abruptly threw up his hands in surrender and said, "I give up. I'll tell Frank that I tried." He turned and began to walk down the street.

"Where are you going?" she demanded, surprised.

"I don't like to waste my time, and talking to you is a waste of my time," he called over his shoulder, without breaking his stride.

"What about all the danger and my father's enemies and . . . and stealing?"

He ignored her and continued walking until he rounded the corner of the building and disappeared from her sight. Lana tried to tell herself she was glad she had gotten rid of the man, but then she pulled the sapphire pendant from her purse and studied it. The fact that he had it told her that he really knew her father or . . . that her father was dead.

CHAPTER TWO

Three hours after being accosted and shocked by a man whose smile should have been bronzed in a dentist's museum, Lana stifled a yawn as she sat across from Bruce Longfellow. She was in one of the most exclusive restaurants in DC, enjoying delicious food and expensive wine, which normally would have been enough for her to at least enjoy herself, despite the company, but tonight she felt anxious. Out of place. As if everyone in the restaurant was watching her. She couldn't blame herself for being paranoid. The reappearance, the mere mention, of Frank Hargrove in her life was cause for alarm in an image-conscious town like Washington DC.

She had spent a long time making certain that her father's infamous past would not affect her reputation in public relations. After college, she had spent the requisite few years in a large PR firm, grinding out the hours and landing the major accounts, and for the last two years she had been running her own company, Lana Hargrove Public Relations, Inc. Her company was just beginning to reach the level she had envisioned; she had hired a secretary to come into her office—which was the converted bottom floor of her brownstone in Dupont Circle—only a few months ago to handle the ever-increasing administrative duties that she didn't have time to deal with anymore. The mention of her father reminded her how fragile her house of cards was. Being known as the daughter of an art thief did not fit into her carefully crafted image.

"Lana, are you feeling well?" Bruce asked, his handsome cinnamon brown face reflecting the perfect amount of compassion and concern.

Lana noticed how perfect and smooth his skin looked under the soft light before she forced a smile and murmured, "I'm fine."

"I was beginning to think that I was boring you," he replied with a laugh of disbelief, as if he could ever bore anyone.

Bruce Longfellow was another part of her life that was falling into place. She had decided that after years of playing the field or, as Mae West would have said it, "enjoying the company of men," she needed a steady companion to make her reputation in the social circles where pedigrees and respectability mattered. Bruce fit the bill. He was handsome and rich and, most important, came from a respectable family. The two had been dating for almost a month. It was the longest relationship Lana had ever been in, and she was starting to remember why she didn't last in relationships very long.

Except Lana felt like she had invested so much time in researching and then recruiting Bruce that she had to hang in there. She had spent considerable energy finding someone who knew Bruce, so they could casually introduce her. She and Bruce had shared a few dinners and even fewer dry kisses. She could only imagine what having sex with him would be like, but he hadn't mentioned it and Lana wasn't pressing the issue herself.

Lana now realized that Bruce's good looks, very fat wallet, and Georgetown home could not make up for his irritating habit of only being able to talk about himself. She had almost talked herself into ending the charade with him, but then he had invited her to a family dinner next month where she would meet his mother, Clarice Longfellow, who threw parties weekly for her congressman husband. Securing a woman such as Clarice Longfellow as a client would be a great coup for Lana Hargrove Public Relations, Inc. But tonight Lana couldn't even use that reason to make herself act personable with Bruce.

Lana blamed Justin Larkin. If he hadn't breezed into her life only a few hours before and made her dream about his mouth or wonder how he got his scars—when she wasn't thinking about her father—she would be enjoying her dinner with Bruce. Although even she admitted that she couldn't blame

Justin for Bruce's choice of conversation topics, or lack thereof.

"I was about to tell you what happened at the club today," Bruce continued, as he cut his steak into tiny exact pieces. Lana restrained the urge to grab his fork and knife so that he wouldn't cut the pieces anymore. "You remember I told you last night that I was going to play tennis with the boys from the firm? Don had to cancel at the last minute, but we needed a fourth or we would have lost the court, so I asked one of the waiters at the club to join us. You should have seen the other members when they saw a waiter on the court. They were horrified. I had to give him some tennis whites to play in," Bruce said, with a laugh of shock. "Can you believe it? A waiter playing tennis with us?"

"I can't believe it," Lana murmured, not even bothering to make herself sound remotely interested. Bruce never noticed if she was interested or not, as long as she made the appropriate sounds of agreement.

Bruce suddenly took her hand across the table and Lana actually prayed that he wasn't on the verge of proposing. It wouldn't have been her first proposal, but it would have been the first one that she couldn't turn down. A woman did not turn down a marriage proposal from one of the most eligible bachelors in the District.

Bruce said seriously, "Lana, I'm glad that Pauline introduced us. I've had my eye on you for a long time."

She tried to sound surprised. "You have?"

"Don't pretend you didn't know. Women as beautiful as you always know."

She smiled because it was true. She had noticed him noticing her, but now she made herself look wide-eyed, innocent, and flattered all at once. "I honestly didn't notice, Bruce."

Bruce winked and said, "I didn't want you to know, not at first. I've found that when women know I'm interested, it leads to complications."

"Complications?"

"And let's face it, Lana, we've had our understanding from the beginning. Nothing too serious, your modus operandi, from what I've heard."

"What is that supposed to mean?" she asked tightly.

Bruce laughed and held up his hands in self-defense. "I'm not trying to insult you, but your reputation for being discreet and mature about . . . things that a lot of women aren't normally discreet and mature about was the main reason I allowed Pauline to set us up on a date. I needed someone to take to a few functions and to make me feel a little less lonely."

Lana thought her head would explode, from either anger or relief; she wasn't certain which. The more she thought about how she had been using Bruce and, truthfully, feeling more and more guilty about it, the more annoyed she became that he had been using her.

Bruce's voice lowered as he said, "I'm thirty-three

years old, Lana, and I'm beginning to realize that I couldn't be with the most recent Spelman woman my mother always tries to set me up with every year. I needed someone who would accept that the occasional indiscretion should be expected—"

"I don't know whether to be insulted or flattered," she said in disbelief.

"It's a good thing, Lana," he said sincerely; then he appeared slightly distracted as his gaze focused on something over her shoulder. He leaned forward and murmured, "I don't mean to alarm you, but there's a very large man with a very unique face across the room watching you a little too closely."

Lana froze in her seat, feeling the strange mixture of anger and relief because a very large man with a unique face was in the restaurant. She turned in her chair and was not surprised to see Justin Larkin sitting at a table alone in the shadows of the large room. And despite her irritation, Lana's heart pounded a little faster against her chest and her palms became sweaty as their gazes met across the restaurant.

Justin didn't bother to pretend that he wasn't staring at her. Instead, he held her gaze. He didn't smile or nod or even shrug in apology and it should have pissed her off, but instead Lana found her body reacting. Her breasts grew heavy and her stomach dropped and she subconsciously licked her lips in anticipation of whatever the man could offer. She realized that she was acting like the "loose woman" that so many people thought she was.

"Do you know that man, Lana?" Bruce asked, breaking into her thoughts. "Should I alert someone?"

Lana turned to Bruce and forced a smile. "I know him, unfortunately. Excuse me for a moment."

She ignored Bruce's confused expression and stood. She straightened her powder blue dress, then walked across the room, for once not noticing or caring that every man followed her progress. All of her attention was focused on Justin, who still didn't bother to pretend that he wasn't watching her. For some reason, knowing that he watched her progress made her feel self-conscious and made her hips sway less than usual. In fact, she felt awkward and ungainly, like she was back in high school trying to blend in and not be so tall and big compared to the other girls. She told herself that Justin should have felt awkward, but as he lounged in the chair, he seemed the most comfortable man in the room.

She stopped at his table and watched him calmly sip from his glass of red wine. "You look bored," he said.

She gritted her teeth and decided to ignore his accurate take on the evening. "How did you get reservations here? This restaurant requires at least two weeks' advance notice."

"Who is that man?" Justin asked, staring past her to Bruce. He actually ignored the plunging neckline and high slit of the dress she wore to dinner. No man had ever done that, especially a man she wanted to notice her. Lana clenched her jaw in anger. "He looks like he does something boring and predictable. Lawyer? Accountant? Or, even worse, a politician?"

"His name is Bruce Longfellow, and he's a lawyer with one of the top firms in the District. His grandparents were the first black—"

Justin looked at her and asked, amused, "And that is who you were shopping for earlier today? The stop in the lingerie store on Wisconsin?"

"Jealous?" she asked, lifting one eyebrow.

"Not in the least," he said, and he actually looked like he was telling the truth. She glared at him and he took another sip of wine.

"I want you to leave this restaurant right now."

"I'm allowed to eat dinner, aren't I?"

Lana wanted to scream but glanced over her shoulder at Bruce, who continued to watch them, concerned. She would not be the starring player in a scene while Bruce watched her, although she thought he would have enjoyed it because it would have cemented her in his mind as a wildcat. She leaned across the table and kept a pleasant smile on her face but said through clenched teeth, "Not in this restaurant, not tonight. You walked away from me earlier, remember?"

His expression turned somber as he said, "I shouldn't have left you."

The concern on his face momentarily made her anger subside. She sighed heavily, then said, "Justin, I know you think that you're doing the right thing here because of some strange misplaced allegiance to my father, but whatever my father told you is going on is not. He has a way of making people believe things that aren't true. It's the reason he's so successful at what he does. I don't know where you're from or what you do, when you're not stalking poor, unsuspecting women, but go back there and forget my father."

Justin actually smiled and held up his glass in salute. "The kind, magnanimous role doesn't fit you, Lana. It must be the designer shoes and dress."

"You're impossible," she declared, frustration making her voice rise. She forced a smile and a slight nod at the nearby diners who made no pretense that they weren't gawking at the two. She smoothed her hair toward the chignon at the nape of her neck; then, without another glance in Justin's direction, she turned and walked across the restaurant to her table.

She sat down and neatly arranged the cloth napkin on her lap. She noticed the concerned expression on Bruce's face but decided to ignore it and concentrate on the spinach salad in front of her.

"Lana, are you all right?" Bruce asked, sounding worried, as he glanced across the room at Justin.

"I'm fine."

"He's leaving. Who is that man?"

"No one." She gulped down the full glass of wine in front of her, then announced, "This is delicious."

From the corner of her eye, she saw Justin walk out of the restaurant. She tried to remember to feel relieved.

• • •

"You were supposed to call me three days ago!" Clarence Baxter screamed loud enough to make his cousin and partner in Baxter & Baxter Investigations, Justin Baxter, hold the telephone a short distance from his ear. "Where the hell are you?!"

Justin rolled his eyes at the lecture he knew was coming. He loosened the buttons on his shirt and picked up the telephone to pace the large hotel room that he had rented under his alias, Justin Larkin. Justin Larkin lived in style. Only the best hotels, the best food, the best clothes. Justin Larkin had an expense account that very worried museum boards of directors paid for. Justin Baxter, on the other hand, did not. Justin Baxter could barely afford the mortgage payments on his house in the renovated section of Southeast every month and rolled out of bed and threw on the closest pair of pants and shirt that appeared clean every morning. After living as Justin Larkin for the last six months across Europe and New York, Justin Baxter was glad to be back home in DC. Even if that meant his cousin's screaming sounded louder on the telephone.

"I'm in DC," Justin confessed tiredly.

"You're in town? Come to the agency. We need to talk—"

"I can't. I shouldn't even be calling you now. It could blow my cover, but I knew you were probably chewing on your eyeglasses and drinking too much coffee, so I called."

"We're partners, Justin. Being a partner means communicating and sharing information. The museum has been calling me every day after the debacle in Paris, and I have nothing to tell them because our man in the field hasn't called in over two weeks."

"Things have become complicated," Justin muttered, and his prime complication had worn a dress tonight that was probably very similar to the one Helen of Troy wore when scores of men supposedly killed and died for her. Besides the dress, there were a lot of other complications with Lana Hargrove. Like her heart-shaped mouth that begged a man to kiss her, the smooth honey-colored brown skin that she displayed just to tell a man he could look but not touch, the large brown eyes with impossibly long eyelashes, and the brownish-black hair that fell in a tumble of perfectly arranged waves to her shoulders. Her breasts had bounced softly with each step and her swaying hips and her rap-video–worthy behind were all more than complications. Thinking about Lana and that dress made Justin notice the sudden discomfort in his pants.

"Of course it's complicated," Clarence shot back. "The priceless ancient Egyptian artifact that our client agreed to use as bait to catch Frank Hargrove is gone! Where is the miniobelisk, Justin?"

"I don't know."

There was a long pause, then another explosion: "You don't know?!"

"Frank doesn't have it, and I don't have it. As planned, we posed as workers at the warehouse where the obelisk was waiting to be shipped to DC. As planned, I lured the security guards to the opposite end of the warehouse while Frank went inside for the obelisk. However, not as planned, by the time Frank reached the holding cell, the obelisk was gone."

"What?!" Clarence's exclamation left a small ringing in Justin's ears.

He shook his head, then said, "I think Frank's right, Clarence. Someone is trying to frame him. The police showed up before they were supposed to. They were supposed to come and catch Frank with the obelisk, but they got there too soon and they weren't our guys. I barely got out of there with my own neck. I didn't even have time to look for Frank. So I went to our rendezvous point, but he never arrived. I thought the police got him, but then he called me on my cell and told me that someone was trying to set him up and he knew who it was. He told me to come to DC, grab his daughter, and wait for him at a safe location."

"His daughter? Lana Hargrove?"

"Frank thinks that if someone wants to hurt him, they'll go straight to Lana if they can't find him. Lana is a good target . . . although nothing but a cross and holy water could hurt that woman."

Clarence sounded resigned as he asked, "You've met Lana Hargrove?"

"Yes."

"The museum did not authorize surveillance or contact with Hargrove's daughter."

"The first person Frank plans to see when he comes to DC—if he's not already here—is his daughter. Right now, we don't have Frank or the obelisk, but if I stay with Lana and wait for Frank to contact her, we'll have him then."

The silence on the other end of the telephone was too heavy. Clarence said quietly, "You're in too deep with this assignment, Justin."

"The Smithsonian hired us because we go deep on our assignments. Frank Hargrove has been a thorn in their side—in the side of every major museum for years. I can finally get him. His attempt to take the obelisk has been the first warning the museum has ever gotten."

"It's been six months and you've been living and breathing as Justin Larkin and we're no closer to catching Frank Hargrove in the act and now we're partially responsible for the missing obelisk."

"We're not responsible for that," Justin protested hotly. "The French police were supposed to keep their eye on the obelisk. I was supposed to keep my eye on Frank. Someone jumped the gun too soon—or was paid to jump the gun too soon—and everything got ruined."

Clarence ignored his outburst and said, "Let's cut our losses while the museum still has a shred of trust in us. We'll give all our information to the FBI and

Interpol and they can find Frank and the obelisk, and we'll still get our fees paid."

"We're so close, Clarence," Justin said, shaking his head. "If we can bring in Frank Hargrove, and end his reign of terror over these museums, our agency will have the best reputation for fine art recovery in the nation. Any assignment we want, we can get."

"I don't need that. We've always been a family business," his cousin said. "I like our agency the way it is now."

"I promise you'll like it a lot better when more and more people come to us for answers first, when we get the fat bonus for a successful assignment from the museum and you can buy that house in PG County you've been talking about for the last two months."

He heard Clarence's heavy sigh over the telephone, then silence. They had had this conversation numerous times since Justin joined the agency with his cousin and uncle six years ago. Justin's uncle had liked the idea of expanding, but he had retired to leave the work to "the boys" last year. Now Justin and Clarence each had an equal vote in the agency's future, which meant they frequently never came to any kind of mutual understanding.

"You have one week, Justin," Clarence said simply.

"We're partners, Clarence, not employee-employer," Justin snapped, his patience gone.

"The Hargrove case has run its course, and I've been more than patient. This case is bleeding us dry. The Smithsonian is balking about the bills, and, frankly, we need you on other matters. You have one week to bring in Hargrove and the obelisk or we turn over all of our information to the FBI."

Justin clenched his jaw in anger but knew that his cousin had been more than accommodating. He had given Justin all the leverage he needed. A part of Justin knew that Clarence's sudden and unexplained generosity was only because Frank Hargrove had been the first case, first anything, that Justin had shown interest in since he had returned to work after the fire that had permanently scarred him. And Clarence had felt guilty. Stealing a man's wife while he was in the hospital covered in bandages from third-degree burns probably did that to a man, even one as cold as Clarence.

As for Justin, he had liked the idea of creating a new persona, of living life on his terms, without a past, where his scars were just a part of him, not a reminder of his past. And Justin had known that Clarence had been reluctant to take that from him. But, apparently, his mourning period was over.

"OK," Justin said, with a heavy sigh.

He heard Clarence's sigh of relief before he asked, "What's the plan for today?"

"Frank was supposed to reach DC today and call me, but I haven't heard from him. I'm going to try a few places around town that he likes and ask around. I don't think he suspects me, so I expect he'll call at some point."

"Do you really believe that he doesn't have the obelisk?"

"He told me it was gone by the time he reached the room. He said that he didn't have a chance to look around because he heard the police coming."

"And you believe him?" Clarence asked doubtfully.

"Yes."

Clarence once more sighed like Justin's father had when Justin threw an errant pass on the football field or forgot to take out the trash on his night. His father had never yelled, he always sighed, and it was those sighs that Justin dreaded more than anything else. When he woke in the sterile surroundings of his hospital bed after the fire, the first thing he had heard was his father's sigh.

Clarence said, "I know you think that Justin Larkin and Frank Hargrove have this bond, but remember, Justin, it's not real. Frank will turn on you the moment it suits him, and you're supposed to do the same."

"I know that, Clarence," he snapped, then sighed, because the truth was, at times, maybe he had forgotten it.

He had never been particularly close to his father, and he had been surprised to meet a man like Frank Hargrove, who was like his father in so many ways but not like his father in the ways that counted. Justin could talk to him; he could laugh with him.

"Keep safe, Justin. You get on my damn nerves, but I still worry about you." Justin heard the hesitation in Clarence's voice before he muttered, "We both do."

Justin's hand tightened on the receiver at the

disguised reference to Clarence's wife, who also happened to be Justin's ex-wife. He said stiffly, "I'll call you when I can."

He hung up the receiver before Clarence could respond.

CHAPTER THREE

"I heard that you and Bruce Longfellow were at Bebe Smith's last night?" Pauline Stanton said with a secret smile as the two women sat across from each other in a sandwich café the next afternoon. "That's the third spotting for you two this week. Are things getting serious?"

Lana had publicized a social event for Pauline's publishing company two years ago, and the two women had been friends ever since. As was the case with most of Lana's "friends," though, she didn't know much about Pauline's family or her past and Pauline didn't know anything about hers. Lana had a wide circle of such friends and acquaintances. Her personal phone book was almost the same size as the yellow pages. Most of her women friends were intelligent, beautiful and successful. They were also all independent and solely used one another as company for meals and drinks and for the exchange of expensive clothes. And that arrangement suited Lana fine, because she had found in the past that when a friend shared her history or feelings with Lana, Lana was expected to share the same with her, which Lana could not do or it would lead to awkward conversations involving her father. Except she now realized that she had no one to have an awkward conversation with about her father.

"Bruce is fun to be with," Lana replied casually, then bit into her tuna sandwich. She looked up when she noticed that Pauline was suspiciously silent. Pauline usually had a comment for everything, and judging from the calculating expression on her latte-colored face, she did have one. She was just holding it in.

Lana sighed tiredly, then said, "What, Pauli?"

"I'm sitting here eating my salad, not saying a word," Pauline said innocently.

"And looking like you're about to explode. What is it?"

Pauline tossed her long black tresses over her shoulder, then said, "You made it your mission for the last few months to get your claws in Bruce Longfellow. You made me call a woman, who I lost my seventh-grade boyfriend to, just to get invited to her party so I could invite you and you could meet Bruce. I now have to meet Delores McPhee for coffee this weekend and listen to her taunt me about my ex-boyfriend, who became a millionaire in the Internet craze. I don't think I've ever seen you this determined, not even when you went after Douglas Maxwell. You can at least give me a few more details besides this."

Lana set down her fork and said reluctantly, "I think he has something more long-term in mind."

Pauline clapped excitedly and said, "Isn't that what you want? Long-term with a Longfellow?" She laughed at her own phrasing while Lana frowned. When Lana continued to frown, Pauline rolled her eyes and said, "I knew this would happen. If I believed in betting, I would be rich right now."

"What are you talking about?" Lana asked irritably.

"It's not a secret. You date a man until he accidentally mentions the possibility of a future or tells you that his feelings run to something more serious than dinner and whatever you do after dinner, and then you dump him. Immediately."

Lana shrugged, because Pauline was right. She had never wanted a serious relationship in the past and she still didn't, but now she needed one if she wanted to take her business, her reputation, to the next level. She told Pauline, "I told you that things would be different with Bruce."

"Why? Because he's the One?" Pauline asked dryly, then laughed in disbelief. "Women like you and me don't believe in the One, Lana. Besides, I've met Bruce, and the only One he believes in is himself."

Lana was surprised that she was annoyed Pauline placed them in the same category. Pauline had dated a different man every week and probably slept with a few more than that, with no apologies to anyone, before she landed her own version of a Longfellow. Now Pauline was engaged and took every opportunity to flash the diamond rock on her finger.

"Bruce and I understand each other," Lana said simply. "Apparently, I'm acceptable enough for his mother and freaky enough for him."

Pauline looked disgusted as she asked, "Did he really say that?"

"In a much more poised, Bruce Longfellow manner."

"Asshole," Pauline snapped, then asked excitedly, with a crooked grin, "Exactly how freaky is he?"

Lana rolled her eyes but couldn't stop her laugh. At least Pauline was predictable. "I'll admit it, Bruce's days with me may be numbered."

"Are you kidding? Bruce is rich, gorgeous, a Longfellow, and—did I mention rich already?" Pauline stopped talking, then demanded abruptly, "Why do you keep doing that?"

Lana looked up from her food, surprised. "What?"

"You keep looking around. Are you expecting someone else to join us?"

"No," Lana answered Pauline while shaking her head.

Lana thought of Justin and realized that she did half-expect to see him lurking in a corner of the café. After he left the restaurant last night, she had spent the rest of the evening looking for him—mostly to add excitement to the evening. Then she had realized that maybe Justin had actually listened to her and he was gone. And she had spent this morning and afternoon looking for signs that it wasn't true. She had barely known the man one day and she already missed him or, at least, missed looking at him. It irritated her.

Pauline shook her head as if to dismiss the topic; then she grinned again and said, "When are you going to dump Bruce?"

"I'm not dumping him . . . at least not soon. Besides, tonight I'm going with him to a reception at the Natural History Museum."

"Xavier Lattimore is sponsoring that event," Pauline said, sounding amazed. "I've been trying to get an appointment with that man for months to convince him to write his autobiography. One word from Xavier Lattimore and a person's reputation is set in this town—for good or bad. The people who attend his events . . . Lana, you have to be excited about that. You could make excellent contacts tonight. You're always excited about making contacts."

"I am excited, but—"

"But what?" Pauline prodded.

Lana stared into Pauline's expectant brown eyes. She thought about telling Pauline about her father, about Justin, but then she looked down at her food. She couldn't tell Pauline; she couldn't tell anyone. As usual, when it came to her father, Lana was alone.

Lana pasted a smile on her face and said, "Actually,

I can't wait for the reception tonight; I just didn't want to make you jealous."

"How surprisingly kind of you," Pauline said while rolling her eyes; then she squeezed Lana's hands across the table and said, "Lana, you have Bruce Longfellow, and as boring and self-absorbed as he is, he's a Longfellow. Tonight, you're going to a reception given by Xavier Lattimore, where you're going to meet a lot of people who will want to give you money. Don't blow it."

"I didn't know you could be so firm," Lana said, surprised.

Pauline smiled and held up her left hand where the engagement ring with a diamond the size of a small rock rested on her finger. "That's exactly what you told me when I first started dating Ethan. Now we're four months from our wedding date. You give good advice; I just want to give it back to you."

Lana frowned because the advice didn't sound good; it sounded cold.

Justin considered it a special form of torture to have to watch Lana Hargrove. He was not obligated to watch her; in fact, he had expressly told her that he would not. But he had. All day long, from when she woke, got ready, and walked downstairs to begin work in the converted bottom-floor office of her house, to lunch with another woman whose skirt had been impossibly shorter than Lana's and the multiple errands that had driven him crazy, to more shopping, then back to work. And now here he still was. Sitting in a truck down the street from her house in Dupont Circle in the middle of the night, watching her silhouette through the window that he knew belonged to her bedroom, since he had entered her apartment earlier that day to make certain no one or nothing was waiting for her.

He could still remember the sweet smell that perfumed the air in her apartment from the numerous flowers, the bright colors, and the many pictures on the walls. There hadn't been one family photo. She had framed newspaper clippings with photos of her and famous clients that had gotten in the paper, but there was no picture of family, besides one framed photograph of an old woman who stood with her legs planted and her hands on her hips in a wild empty field. Even though the woman wasn't smiling, there was life dancing in her eyes, and Justin had smiled at her.

Without her knowledge, Frank Hargrove had been watching Lana her whole life. He told Justin all about her. From her first tooth to how pretty she looked at her high school graduation. When Justin saw the fully grown Lana with the short skirts and tight shirts, he had expected a spoiled, superficial, materialistic princess, and that was exactly what he had gotten at their first meeting. Except that when he had stood in the middle of her town house he had felt a strange connection to her.

His gaze was once more drawn to Lana's town house. She had moved to stand in front of the gauzy curtains at her bedroom window. The light provided a full-scale peep show for anyone who looked long enough. Justin decided that the first thing he would do if he ever spoke to her again was tell her to invest in some heavier curtains. And then through the curtains—which he suddenly decided weren't so bad—he watched her slowly and sensuously pull off her dress. Justin gulped down the sudden lump in his throat at the outline of full breasts, indented waist and flared hips. Maybe heavier curtains was a premature idea.

The cell phone in his shirt pocket rang and he quickly answered it, turning away from a view that could possibly get him arrested.

"Bubba," came the familiar greeting on the other end of the telephone.

Justin was surprised by the relief that flooded his body at the sound of Frank's familiar gravelly voice. It wasn't until that moment that Justin realized he had been worried about Frank.

Justin mentally shook himself. Frank Hargrove was an assignment, an assignment that Justin was not completing very well at the moment.

Justin asked, "Frank, where are you?"

"Standing in front of Lincoln's statue. Do you think I'll have a statue like that one day? Maybe in a retired thieves' museum somewhere?"

Justin laughed and said, "I wouldn't be surprised if you did."

"Of course, nothing would be in the retired thieves' museum—including my statue—because everything would be stolen by the nonretired thieves."

Justin smiled in response. "You're right once more."

He heard Frank's hesitation before he asked, "How is she, Bubba?"

Justin shot a quick glance at the curtains, then looked away when he realized that Lana was brushing her hair, giving him a nice X-rated outline of her breasts as she raised her arm. He felt the sweat bead on his forehead and he quickly turned to the more boring view of the parked car in front of him.

"There was an incident today," Justin said hesitantly.

"What do you mean? Is Lana all right?"

Justin had never heard panic in Frank's voice. In the six months he had known him, Justin could count on one hand how many times Frank had been serious. If Frank told Justin one more time, "Easy come, easy go," about anything, Justin planned to hit him.

"Lana is fine," Justin assured him. "In fact, if you want my opinion, you don't have to worry about her at all. She spotted me following her and . . . we had a talk. She knows about me and you."

Frank's panic became nervousness, another first that Justin had never heard before. "She knows that I sent you to watch her?"

"Yes, and she's not happy about it."

"I had no doubt she wouldn't be," Frank murmured, sounding suspiciously like he was laughing.

"You could have warned me," Justin grumbled, then said, "She doesn't believe there's any danger. She doesn't trust you and she sure as hell doesn't trust me. She told me not to follow her, not to talk to her, basically, not to sully her existence with my shadow."

"Sounds like my girl hasn't changed at all," Frank said, not bothering to hide his laughter. "Just like her mother."

"Seriously, Frank, you don't have to worry about her. She can take care of herself. We should concentrate on finding the obelisk."

"I'll admit that Lana can be tough to take—"

"My ears are still ringing, Frank."

"She's had it rough, Bubba. You have to cut her some slack," Frank said. Even though his tone was light, Justin could hear the sincerity on the edges. "How does she look, Bubba?"

Justin refused to glance at the window again. Once was an accident, twice was human nature, but a third time would be a misdemeanor.

"She's gorgeous," Justin muttered begrudgingly.

"Also like her mother," Frank said gravely. "You have to keep her safe, Bubba, until I can figure this whole thing out. No one else was supposed to have access to that Paris warehouse, but someone else did. I heard that the police have a videotape of me entering the warehouse, but not of whoever took the obelisk."

"Why would someone set you up?"

There was a long pause and Justin almost thought that Frank had hung up until he said, "There's a lot about me you don't know, Bubba. Maybe one day . . . Tomorrow I'm going to see the man who I think is responsible—"

"Alone? I should go with you." Justin realized only after the offer left his mouth that it was not for the agency or for the case. He wanted to do it for Frank.

Frank snorted in disbelief. "It's not his style to dirty his own hands. Lattimore likes to hit low and when you least expect it. It's the only way he'll win."

"Lattimore? You mean Xavier Lattimore, the millionaire?" Justin asked, coughing on his surprise.

"I think he's a billionaire now," Frank grumbled.

"Why would Xavier Lattimore want to frame you for taking the obelisk? He's one of the most successful businessmen in the District. You're . . . You're nothing compared to a man like that. He was one of the most frequent dinner guests at the mayor's and—"

"Thanks for the Xavier Lattimore update, but I know he's rich," Frank said dryly.

"What is it? What's between you two?"

"Even a man like Xavier Lattimore, frequent dinner guest at the mayor's dinner table, has a past."

"And that past involves you?"

Justin heard Frank's impatient sigh before he said, "All you need to know is that Xavier Lattimore is dangerous and he hates me about as much as I hate him. If you really want to help me, Bubba, you'll protect my daughter, because if there's one thing that I do know about Lattimore, it's that he doesn't play fair. If he can't find me, he'll go after Lana."

"She doesn't want me around, Frank," Justin said. "I've been following her around all day like a pervert, after she tried to make me a eunuch—"

"She did what?" Frank asked, sounding amused.

Justin continued his protest, ignoring Frank's interruption, "I had to sit in a restaurant and watch her pretend to enjoy herself with some guy who . . ." Justin cleared his throat when he realized that he had gone too far.

"Justin. Please."

Justin had known Frank Hargrove for six months, had probably grown to like him the last three months, and had never heard that one word come out of Frank's mouth. Not once. It had surprised Justin how much he missed hearing his real name. "Bubba" did not have the same ring to it as "Justin."

Justin sighed, then promised, "Lana will be safe."

"I have to go. Watch your back, Bubba."

Before Justin could make Frank swear to do the same, the dial tone hummed in his ear. He pressed the disconnect button, then turned to Lana's window. The window was dark, along with all the other windows in her town house. Apparently, she was asleep in that nice, big bed. Then Justin thought of Lana lying in bed, all of that brown skin waiting for his touch. He groaned and shifted uncomfortably in the truck cab. It was going to be a long night. And an early morning when he told his cousin to research everything he could find on Xavier Lattimore.

CHAPTER FOUR

"And the prodigal son returns," Clarence Baxter greeted Justin as he walked into the appropriately bland lobby of the offices of Baxter & Baxter Investigations, which were housed in a low-rise office building on K Street close to the White House. "Dad is here today. He wants to talk to you."

Justin held back a groan. He should have known that Clarence would call in the big guns. Justin's Uncle Dwayne had opened the agency thirty years ago. He had gone from helping people in "trouble" after working a full shift at a steel plant in Maryland to opening his own office. Justin had visited his uncle as many times as his father would let him when he was a kid. His uncle had been his hero. Justin had never wanted to do anything else in his life besides help people in "trouble," like his uncle. His father, who managed one of the largest banks in Atlanta, had not been happy with Justin's career choice.

So Justin had done the banking route after college. For four long and torturous years after graduating from Clark University, he had risen in the Atlanta bank management world until after one too many disappointed sighs from his father and too many promotions—he was really good with numbers and bank management—he left. Justin had packed everything into his truck and driven to DC, and he had never returned to Atlanta. And his father had never forgiven him. Clarence had probably never forgiven him, either, because the family jokes about Justin being Dwayne's true son and Clarence being Robert Baxter's only became more frequent.

"Hi, Justin," said the cute receptionist whose name Justin could not remember. She sent him the type of gentle smile that really pretty women sent him when they spotted his scars.

He heard Clarence's groan before he pointedly motioned for Justin to follow him into his private office, which adjoined the reception area. Justin forced a smile at the receptionist, whose vanilla cheeks flushed with color when she got caught staring at Justin's face. He walked into Clarence's office and Clarence followed him.

"We have a major problem here," Clarence said as he shut the office door.

"Hello to you, too, Clarence," Justin muttered as he took off his sunglasses and baseball cap.

"Justin," Dwayne greeted from his position at a round table in the corner of the large office.

Justin couldn't help but smile at the older man and he crossed the room to give Dwayne a manly, affectionate slap on the shoulder. Dwayne Baxter patted the unmarred side of Justin's face, then folded his newspaper and set it on the table.

"How are you, son?" Dwayne asked, watching him carefully. Justin dropped into the chair next to Dwayne while Clarence paced the length of the office.

"I'm good," Justin lied. His shoulders and back ached from sleeping in the truck the night before, but he could only imagine Clarence's reaction if he told him that he had slept outside Lana's apartment.

"You look tired," Dwayne said plainly. "I'm worried about you."

Justin's uncle never minced words and never said what he didn't mean. It was his best quality and the reason clients trusted him. It had also been the biggest drawback to his career, because he couldn't go undercover. A propensity for layered words with hidden meanings was a characteristic on Justin's side of the family.

"You don't have to worry about him. Right, Justin?" Clarence said dryly, stopping in front of Justin.

Clarence wore his usual uniform of neatly pressed slacks, a startling white dress shirt, matching tie, and suspenders. Clarence hated dirt, he hated wrinkles, and he hated late expense reports. He was tall and slightly plump and had brown skin. Justin would have considered his cousin attractive if he didn't know him. Unfortunately, the two men needed each other. Clarence despised fieldwork, having been dragged into the family business by his father, while Justin despised sitting behind a desk eight hours a day, but each enjoyed being his own boss. The agency paid its own bills and allowed each a semicomfortable existence and they rarely had to see each other. It was the perfect work arrangement.

Clarence handed a thin binder to Justin. "That's everything on Xavier Lattimore that I could find in the last few hours. Are you going to tell me what this is about now?"

Justin flipped through the neatly typed pages in the binder and said, "Frank called me last night."

Clarence's eyes grew round as he demanded, "What? Where is he?"

"He's in town, and he thinks that Xavier Lattimore is behind all of this. He thinks that Lattimore has the obelisk and is trying to frame him and that he'll hurt Lana at the first opportunity."

"That is insane," Clarence announced, rolling his eyes. "As if one of the most respectable men in DC would waste his time on a two-bit thief—"

"Frank Hargrove may be a lot of things, but he's not a two-bit thief. He's one of the best thieves in the world."

Clarence's eyes narrowed as he said tightly, "You say that as if it's a compliment."

Dwayne held up his hand to stop the brewing

argument, then asked quietly, "Why does he think Lattimore is responsible?"

"When I asked him that, he said that even Xavier Lattimore has a past," Justin said, shrugging. He looked at Clarence and asked, "Is there anything in here that would hint at a connection between Lattimore and Frank?"

Clarence sighed and said, "Of course not." He paused, then said reluctantly, "But this is just a basic credit and last place of residence report. I'll need more time. Maybe interview some people from Lattimore's hometown in California."

Justin's heart skipped a beat as he looked at Clarence. "Lattimore is from California?"

Clarence nodded. "Oakland."

"Frank is from Oakland," Justin said, staring at his uncle.

"Oakland is a big town. I doubt these two men ever met," Clarence said, sounding almost hopeful.

"They're the same age," Justin retorted. "It's too much of a coincidence. Come on, Clarence; you're the most paranoid person I know. You have to see the coincidence."

"Dad, this is ridiculous," Clarence said, turning to face Dwayne. "If Xavier Lattimore wanted the obelisk, he could have bought it. He doesn't need to steal it."

"He couldn't have bought it. That's the point," Justin snapped in return. "Scholars think that this miniobelisk was made as a model for a larger, more traditional version to go in front of Nefertiti's tomb, except no one knows where she's buried."

"Nefertiti?" Dwayne asked uncertainly.

"Researchers have searched for her tomb for years. If this miniobelisk exists, then the real obelisk had to have existed somewhere, too. Scholars in Cairo were still examining the miniobelisk for clues, hoping it would lead to her tomb. Do you know how important and invaluable this thing is? It's not for sale. Lattimore could not buy it, so he had to steal it."

"Thanks for the history lesson, Justin, but it still doesn't prove to me that Xavier Lattimore would risk his wealth and his reputation to steal some bauble that may or may not have belonged to some woman—"

"That bauble has been appraised with a market value of millions of dollars and for a man like Lattimore—who bid millions on that Egyptian scepter last year just to say he could—this would be perfect for him."

Clarence sighed heavily. "I still think this is insane."

"Enough, boys. You two are worse than a married couple," Dwayne said wearily. "Clarence, don't be so certain that Lattimore is not involved. Just because he's rich doesn't mean he's good. And, Justin, don't be so certain that everything Frank tells you is true."

There was a long moment of silence; then Clarence nodded and said, "I'll dig deeper into Lattimore's background. I'll look for a connection between him and Hargrove."

Justin scanned the contents of the binder. Then his blood turned cold and he ripped one page from the binder. He stared at Clarence and demanded, "Lattimore is sponsoring a reception at the Natural History Museum tonight?"

"Yes. A pianist from Sweden is giving a performance."

Justin held up a sheet of paper that contained a guest list. "And Bruce Longfellow is invited?"

"What's wrong, Justin?" Dwayne asked, instantly aware of Justin's rising panic.

Justin ignored his uncle and asked Clarence, "Who is Bruce taking? Is there any way to tell?"

"It says 'plus one.' I don't know who it is. . . . Why—"

Justin jumped to his feet and shoved his sunglasses and baseball cap in place. "Lana . . . she may be going with Bruce, and if what Frank says about Lattimore is true, then it could be dangerous for her."

Dwayne stood and grabbed Justin's hand. Justin inwardly sighed when he saw the concerned look in his eyes. At least in Atlanta Justin didn't have to deal with fatherly concern.

"We're in this together, Justin," Dwayne said quietly. "Clarence is here to help you. And you know that if you ever need me, I'm here. No one expects you to bring down Frank by yourself."

"I know."

Dwayne patted Justin's face again, then nodded. Justin glanced at Clarence, simply held up a hand, which was the closest thing to a good-bye Clarence could manage. Justin grimaced in return, which was the closest thing to a good-bye *he* could manage; then he left.

Lana sipped champagne as she stared at the display of jewels in the glass case. She had seen the multicolored jewels numerous times before. It was no surprise that the museum that displayed the diamonds, rubies, and emeralds was her favorite. Whenever she needed to think, she came here to stare at the precious stones and to imagine the lives of the people who had once owned them, before donating them to the museum's priceless collection.

She had been raised by two art lovers. Her mother had painted, and her father had vast knowledge that he had freely shared. Lana had always appreciated beautiful things, but a long time ago when she first found out about her father's career choice, she had stopped going to traditional art museums, perhaps to atone for her father's sins, maybe to protest her father's career choice.

Lana heard a burst of mingled laughter from the hallway. She was by herself in the precious stones display room. Everyone was still enjoying the closing talk by the Swedish pianist on the ground floor lobby. Normally, Lana would have been in the thick of the crowd, hunting for potential clients, reconnecting with old clients. The power elite of Washington DC stood in the lobby of the museum, gathered around the famous gargantuan stuffed elephant, and Lana found herself alone in this room. This wasn't like her, not the Lana Hargrove who made it a mission to make three new contacts at every party.

Lana inwardly cursed and drained her champagne glass. She knew exactly why she was in this room. Justin Larkin. She could not stop thinking about the man. She had dreamed about him last night, and not just about grinding her favorite pair of spike heels into his hand. She had dreamed about him watching her from the dark shadows of her bedroom while she undressed. She had dreamed about him coming to her and touching her and making her feel things that she hadn't felt in a long time, that she was scared to feel. It wasn't like her. Men had always been low on her priority list. But not Justin. It was unsettling.

Lana turned to rejoin the party, and it was as if her unspoken dreams came to life. As if he were a part of the shadows, Justin Larkin emerged from nowhere and walked directly toward the Hope Diamond, which stood behind protective glass, under a spotlight, on a velvet stand.

He wore the traditional black tuxedo that the other men wore, but on him it looked more dangerous, more sexy. She leaned against the door frame in the inner room and watched him. She had a feeling that Justin didn't allow people to watch him too closely. He was a striking man, as her grandmother would have said, even without the added air of mystery from his scars. From his height to the way he moved with such authority. She had never met another man like him. Nor had any man made her feel such lust just from looking at him.

She refused to allow herself to be attracted to such a rude, mannerless man, but she found herself walking toward him.

"If you're planning to steal that, I'm going to have to call security," she said as she walked into the small circle that displayed the diamond.

Justin didn't appear surprised to hear her voice, nor did he turn toward her. He continued to stare at the diamond and said, "It would be a challenge, wouldn't it? To get this out of the case and out of here with all of these people standing around."

"You wouldn't make it out of this room."

He turned to her then and she withheld her gasp at the intensity burning in his eyes. Her palms suddenly grew damp and her heart began to pound against her chest. It wasn't fear, because she wasn't scared of anyone. It was some emotion that she didn't want to name.

Justin took two steps closer to her and she couldn't withhold the gasp of surprise and arousal this time. He towered over her, his mouth close to hers, his breath mingling with hers.

"And why are you so certain that I wouldn't make it out of this room, if I wanted to?"

"Because I wouldn't let you," she answered in a whisper that didn't sound as firm as she meant for it to be.

He smiled, but instead of making her feel better, it made her feel more scared, not of him but of herself.

"You're going to stop me?" he asked, his mouth forming a crooked smile.

"I'd make it my life's goal."

He moved even closer, until her vision filled with him, until she could only think about and feel him. His gaze went to her hair for a moment and then he fingered a few strands. She allowed him to. He finally met her gaze and asked in a low, husky voice, "Do you really think you could stop me from doing whatever I wanted to do?"

She stared at him, unable to tear her gaze from his, unable to move. It was the first time in her life she had ever been frozen. As if Justin knew it, he smiled. A smile that told her he had her. And normally that smile would have pushed Lana into action, would have made her send him a cool smile or a sharp retort, but instead she tried not to collapse in a boneless mass of pliant flesh at his feet.

"Lana."

Lana jumped back from Justin and turned toward the entrance of the precious jewels exhibition to see Bruce standing there. Bruce looked from Lana to Justin, a confused and suspicious expression on his face. Lana quickly moved around Justin to cross the room and stand at Bruce's side.

"I've been looking all over this museum for you," Bruce said to Lana, sounding distracted as he looked from Lana to Justin. He pointed at Justin and said, "I know you. You're the man from the restaurant last night. I remember your face. . . . What are you doing here?"

"The same thing you are. Enjoying the party," Justin said calmly, his expression blank.

Lana placed a hand on Bruce's arm, mostly to show Justin that she wasn't affected by him, rather than to show any allegiance to Bruce. She said, "Bruce, this is Justin Larkin. He's a friend of the family."

"First the restaurant and now this party," Bruce murmured suspiciously. "Either it's a coincidence or there's something else going on."

Justin's eyes hardened and Lana thought he would actually hit Bruce. Bruce must have thought the same thing, because he took a subtle step behind Lana.

"What else could be going on, Bruce?" Justin asked, his voice low and dangerous.

"Now here's where the party is," came a deep voice from behind Lana.

Lana whirled around and instantly smiled when she saw Xavier Lattimore. She had seen his picture numerous times in the *Washington Post,* and at various social events, but she had never met him. He was a legend in DC. He had come to the District in his twenties with a few thousand dollars and started a company that cleaned rich people's homes and then another business and another business until he was one of the people whose homes needed to be clean. He had dark brown skin, intense brown eyes, and a thick mustache that was neatly trimmed. His suit was impeccable and Lana caught a glimpse of a watch that probably cost more than two months of her mortgage payments.

"Mr. Lattimore," Bruce greeted, with a nod.

"She's a beauty, isn't she?" Xavier said in greeting, his gaze drawn to the Hope Diamond across the room. "I held her in my hands once. One of the privileges of being rich and having introduced the museum's curator to his wife ten years ago."

Lana and Bruce accommodatingly laughed while Justin clenched his jaw and placed his hands in his pockets.

Xavier turned to them with a smile and said, "Bruce, introduce me to your beautiful date."

"Xavier Lattimore, meet Lana Hargrove," Bruce said with a smile.

Xavier smiled at her and brought her hand to his lips for a gallant kiss. It shouldn't have impressed her, but it did. She glanced at Justin to make certain that he saw the display of proper manners, but Justin only watched Xavier.

"I'm glad you could make it. Are you enjoying yourself?"

"Absolutely," Lana said.

Bruce glanced reluctantly at Justin, but he was too well-bred to ignore him. "And this is Justin Larkin."

"Mr. Larkin," Xavier said as he shook Justin's hand. Lana noticed a strange gleam in his eyes as he studied Justin closely. "You look familiar."

"I guess I have one of those faces," Justin said flatly.

There was an awkward silence as Bruce cleared his throat, Xavier smiled in response, and Lana tried not to knee Justin in the groin again.

"No, I think I have seen you before," Xavier pressed. "In Paris."

Lana noticed Justin suddenly became still, then abruptly smiled. He took Lana's glass from her hand and drained the remaining champagne. Lana's mouth dropped open in speechless outrage while Bruce sputtered in disbelief. Xavier seemed amused.

Justin handed the champagne glass back to Lana, then said, "I was in Paris."

"Recently?" Xavier asked.

"Very recently."

"On business?"

"You could say that."

There was a strange smile on Xavier's face as he asked, "And what exactly do you do, Mr. Larkin?"

"I work for myself."

Lana didn't know what was going on, but there was a strange undercurrent in the air as the two men stared at each other like two prizefighters. Justin's expression hardened the longer he was forced to talk with Xavier, but Xavier's polite smile never faded.

"I've never been to Paris," Lana said brightly, hoping to interrupt the strange interaction between the two men. "I've always wanted to go."

"Your father never took you?" Xavier asked, turning to face her.

Lana swallowed her gasp of shock and frantically

glanced at Justin, who slightly shook his head at her, as if to tell her not to respond. She didn't know why, but she felt more comfortable knowing that he sensed the strange undercurrents coming from Xavier, too.

"Hargrove . . . You are Frank Hargrove's daughter, right?" Xavier asked, with a pleasant expression. "Frank and I grew up together in Oakland."

"He's my father," she finally responded.

"How is your father?" Xavier asked.

Lana smiled brightly and avoided the question as she said, "I rarely meet anyone from my father's childhood. Do you miss Oakland?"

"Lana, where is your father? I've never heard you mention him," Bruce said, oblivious to her discomfort.

"He's fine," Justin said to Xavier, moving closer to Lana. "I've spoken to him more recently than Lana."

Justin placed a hand above Lana's elbow and said, with more charm than she had thought he possessed, "Lana, you're low on champagne. We should rectify that situation."

Bruce suddenly found his voice and took her other hand. "Yes, we should. Thank you for noticing, Justin."

Justin stared at Bruce for a moment and Lana thought—hoped—that he would meet the challenge that Bruce silently offered. Then Justin abruptly smiled and released her arm. "Have fun."

Lana glanced at Justin, silently thanking him for backing down and for coming to her rescue. He simply stared at her. She turned to Xavier, who smiled at her again.

Xavier kissed the back of her hand once more, then said, "Lana, call me for an appointment. We can have lunch and discuss your father, what he was like as a child. I bet he hasn't told you all the trouble he got into."

Lana smiled and nodded, then discreetly tugged Bruce's arm to lead him out of the room. He finally led her toward the lobby, where the guests talked and laughed and didn't have strange, stilted discussions about fathers and Paris. She glanced over her shoulder to find Xavier watching her with a strange expression on his face. Justin was nowhere to be seen.

CHAPTER FIVE

"Did you have fun tonight?"

Lana screamed at the sound of the deep voice and whirled around to find Justin sitting in the dark leather armchair in the corner of her bedroom. She placed a hand over her wildly beating heart and sagged against the dresser where she had been in the process of taking off her earrings before he knocked twenty years off her life. She glared at Justin, who looked entirely too comfortable lounging in her chair, and her heart began to erratically pound for a different reason.

"You scared me. How did you get in here?" she demanded angrily.

"You, of all people, should know that simple locks don't work," he said, with a nonchalant shrug. "You need a better security system, especially with all of the paintings you own."

"They're all fakes, so don't waste your time trying

to steal any." Justin actually smiled and she almost smiled back before she remembered what time it was and where she was. She tried again, "Apparently, I didn't get my point across, so I'll ask a different way. What the hell are you doing in my home at one o'clock in the morning?"

"Making certain that you got home safe and sound," he said, as if it were entirely his right to break into her town house and wait in her bedroom.

She rolled her eyes in exasperation. "When are you going to accept that it's not your duty to look after me? I've been doing just fine on my own. I don't need you or my father to watch out for me."

"I couldn't agree with you more, but I spoke to Frank last night and he made me promise that no harm would come to you. And I never make a promise that I don't keep."

"You spoke to my father?" she asked, trying not to sound as interested as she was.

"Yes."

She hated herself for asking, but she said begrudgingly, "Is he . . . How is he?"

"He's fine, Lana," Justin replied in a gentle tone that didn't quite fit him but somehow seemed perfect. He urged softly, "Ask me about him. I'll tell you anything you want to know."

"You have to stop following me," she said, quickly changing the subject before she asked more questions about her father. "People are becoming suspicious. Bruce is becoming suspicious. What if Bruce had come home with me? How would I explain you waiting in my bedroom?"

She suddenly remembered the pile of picked-over lingerie on her bed that she had debated wearing that evening. He followed her distracted gaze to the bed and she thought she detected a tightening in his body when he saw the various pieces of lace and silk. He looked at her and one corner of his mouth lifted in a smirk.

"I wasn't worried," he said simply.

She narrowed her eyes and walked across the room, grateful that he sat so she could tower over him. "And why not?"

His gaze dropped to her cleavage and she casually crossed her arms over her chest. All night men had looked at and spoken to her cleavage—if she was being honest, she would admit that was the purpose of the dress. But having Justin stare at her breasts meant something entirely different, she was beginning to realize. Most times, she used her looks to get what she wanted, but tonight she liked her body for another reason. Because Justin Larkin liked it.

His gaze finally lifted to meet hers and he said, "Because Bruce may not be the sharpest knife in the drawer, but he's smart enough to know when he's in over his head, and he's probably realized by now that he's in over his head with you."

"And what is that supposed to mean?"

He smiled once more, that smirk that made her hate herself for feeling weak because of it. "You're a lot of woman, Lana."

"I don't know if you consider that a compliment in that pea-sized brain of yours, but it's not."

"How do you think your precious Bruce would react if he knew you lured a man into an alley to knee him in the groin?" he asked pointedly. "I bet he paid kids in school to beat up other kids for him because he didn't want to dirty his hands."

She refused to laugh when she pictured that scenario all too easily. "I know the idea is foreign to you, but Bruce is a gentleman."

"Is that what they call it these days?" Justin asked, feigning amazement. "I thought he was just a wimp."

She shook her head in disbelief, then walked across the room to the dresser. "Since I had such a wonderful evening and I don't want to ruin it with the police crawling all over my place, leave now before I call them."

"You won't call the cops."

"Why are you so sure?" she asked, amused by his confidence.

"Because then I wouldn't be around to relieve your boredom. When I saw you at the party, you looked like you had been hit by a tranquilizer dart."

"That is not true," she lied.

"Those people—Bruce in particular—bore you. Admit it. I don't know why you want to be around them so bad."

She tried to control the fury that raced through her body as she glared at the man. She didn't know what angered her more, the fact that he was right or that he was observant enough to pick up on it.

"You don't know anything about me, Justin, so stop acting like you do."

"I know a lot about you," he said calmly, his hot gaze raking over her.

She was momentarily frozen by the intensity in his gaze, then mentally shook herself. She was acting as if she was attracted to her stalker.

She cleared her throat and said gruffly, "And how do you know anything about me, since you just intruded on my life yesterday?" He silently stared at her in response and she said, with a snort of disbelief, "Oh, let me guess. My father. My father, who I haven't seen in twenty years, told you all about me, right? I can just imagine what he told you. Just so we're clear, I haven't worn a ponytail or played with Barbie dolls in a long time."

"You're wrong about your father," Justin said, shrugging. "He knows a lot more about you than you think."

"I doubt that."

"He's not a bad person, Lana."

"He's wanted in several countries," she said patiently, as if explaining to a seven-year-old child how to tie his shoelaces. "We can officially declare him a bad person."

"Life isn't so black and white."

She rolled her eyes in exasperation. "Spoken like a

true thief. My father has taught you well. The next thing you'll say is that there is no such thing as ownership, which means it's morally acceptable for you to steal from people's homes and businesses. Forget that simple theory that great art should belong to the public, that it should not be locked away in some private collector's room so he can get off every day for twenty minutes knowing that he has something that everyone else should be able to see, too."

He abruptly stood, looking impatient. "I'm not here to debate your father or the moral ethics of thievery with you. I just came to tell you to stay away from Xavier Lattimore."

"What are you talking about?"

His suddenly sober expression made her stop smiling. "Stay away from Xavier Lattimore."

"Why?"

All the teasing and promised seduction disappeared as he said, "He's dangerous, Lana."

"How do you know him?"

He turned to the window, where he distractedly touched the sheer beige curtains.

"I don't know him," he finally responded. "But your father does. Your father doesn't trust him."

"Xavier Lattimore is one of the most respected men in this town. I trust him."

"Just stay away from him, Lana," he said, finally facing her. A strange quiet fell in the room as he stared at her. He whispered, almost as if he were confused, "You are so beautiful."

Lana had been called beautiful before. Bruce had complimented her that evening at her front door, but this was the first time she felt her insides melt into a ball of sensitive nerve endings over that one simple statement.

As if he had suddenly been touched with an electric prod, Justin turned and stalked to the door. "For once, just listen to me. Keep away from Lattimore."

She grabbed his arm, surprising herself. He stopped and stared at her hand on his arm but refused to meet her gaze. She didn't know where the need to talk to him came from, but it was there.

"Justin, no one is going to hurt me," she said sincerely. "If you really want to help my father, make him turn himself in to the police. He can't run forever."

He looked at her then. He reached up and caressed her right cheek. She froze, scared that any movement would make him stop touching her. His hand was large and calloused and sparked tiny nerve endings throughout her body that were nowhere near her face. His other hand moved to the other side of her face and one of his thumbs gently ran across her lower lip. She inhaled sharply when his hot gaze landed on her mouth.

"I know so much about you," he said softly. "I know that you're a scared little girl underneath all of that bravado. I know that you sometimes wish that you could be nine years old again, riding in the car with your father. And I know that you want me to kiss you right now. You may even want me to make love to you, even though you would rather take ten cold showers than admit it."

His words were a rumbling whisper that rolled through her body, affecting her more than any kiss or touch ever had before. For one breathless moment, he stared at her mouth and she thought it would end, that he would walk out and leave her alone again. And she didn't want him to. A woman who craved her solitude and independence didn't want this one man with a badly scarred face to leave her.

Then he put an end to her misery and insecure thoughts and kissed her. Not just a kiss, but a fusing of his mouth to hers, making her a part of him. His hands rested on her waist lightly, but the heat from his hands sealed her to him. The rest of her body was focused on his mouth and the erotic things he was doing with his tongue. His tongue swept through her mouth, ran across her lips, devoured her. His breathing became heavy, or maybe it was hers that filled the room, but suddenly she felt like there was nothing but Justin and Lana.

Heat spiraled through her body and settled in regions she had forgotten or had ignored. It was as if she had finally awakened from a long sleep and every nerve in her body was suddenly tingling with life. She ran her hands down his arms, outlining the muscles and the hardness that was so addictive. He was so hot. Everything about him was hot. And then he pressed against her and she realized that everything about him was hard, too.

Lana was tired of playing hard to get, tired of acting like nothing affected her. Justin Larkin affected her. She wrapped her arms around his neck and tried to inhale him, tried to make him a part of her, as her tongue snaked along his, enjoying the slick feel of him in her mouth. Then Justin stiffened. It was as if he had gone from being a man on the verge of total loss of control to a man made of stone. Lana opened her eyes and she realized suddenly that her hands rested on his face. On his scars. His hands were not gentle as he grabbed her hands and moved them from his face, then abruptly released them. His expression was hard as he glared at her.

She opened her mouth in speechless confusion as she stared at him. She thought he would mention the kiss, mention his scars, mention her wandering hands.

Instead, he turned and walked out of the bedroom. Not another word was spoken, not another look sent in her direction. He just left. Lana almost wished that he had screamed at her. Anger she could handle. The blank look in his eyes she could not.

CHAPTER SIX

Lana glanced impatiently at her watch, then down the empty tracks as she stood in the middle of the crowded metro platform. The client meeting had run longer than she planned, and she now was going to be late for dinner with Pauline and a few of their mutual friends, who would no doubt pepper her with questions about Bruce. Lana almost didn't want to go. She was annoyed and tired and, more important, irritated with herself for allowing Justin Larkin to kiss her. And most important, she was annoyed that he had been the first to walk away. Of course, she wouldn't have walked away from him at that moment for all the money in the world, but it still annoyed her that she hadn't thought of it first. It had been two days since the kiss. Two days since the man had disappeared after sending her world into a tailspin.

It wasn't like her to let a man affect her. But no matter how many times she told herself that, she still had to deal with the fact that she thought about Justin almost every minute of every day. It was like she was back in junior high school, obsessed with some boy who barely knew her name. She was a highly disciplined person. She had to be after being raised by Harriet Hargrove, and it made Lana angrier that she couldn't stop the thoughts of Justin or the memories of that kiss.

"Excuse me," came a deep male voice behind her. She jumped, startled, then laughed in apology when the man standing next to her on the platform smiled in apology. "I didn't mean to scare you. Do you have the time?"

"Seven-oh-seven," she answered.

The man nodded in gratitude, then turned from her. She silently berated herself for acting like a scared child just because a man had spoken to her in the metro station. She blamed Justin Larkin, because even while she thought about that kiss, she thought about his warning, too. It just seemed too fantastic. Lana Hargrove did not worry about being kidnapped or used as a pawn in a game with a man like Xavier Lattimore. She worried about paying her bills on time, making certain her clients were happy, and who was going to be her date for the evening.

She looked up when she heard the train whistle as the train moved slowly down the tracks toward the platform. The mass of people on the platform moved as one group toward the train, in anticipation of its arrival. Lana somehow wound up being in the front of the mass of people. Her joy at being the first one on the train when it stopped turned into panic when she realized that she was still moving, the crowd was still moving her, to the edge of the platform, toward the oncoming train.

She screamed in protest when it dawned on her that she was being pushed. One moment Lana was on the platform, and the next she was hanging weightless in the air, flailing her arms, screaming as she stared directly into the train's headlights. Suddenly Lana felt a band of steel wrap around her waist and she was being pulled backward. She fell to the platform with a thud, her elbow slamming into the concrete. She grunted as a heavy weight fell on top of her.

She opened her eyes, amazed, and stared directly into Justin's eyes. His hands framed her face, looking as scared as she felt.

"Lady, are you all right?" a man asked, concerned.

Lana looked past Justin to see that a small crowd of people had formed around them. Even the train was stopped on the platform as the conductor jumped from the train. Justin stood and the crowd slowly backed from him, their once-concerned gazes now drawn to his face. Without a word, Justin grabbed her arms and practically hauled her to her feet. Lana was grateful that he kept one hand on her arm; whether to hold her up or to reassure her she wasn't certain.

"She's fine," Justin announced, and no one dared to contradict him, not even Lana.

"Someone pushed her," a woman announced as she cradled a baby to her chest. The woman looked terrified as she stared from Lana to Justin.

"Did you see who pushed her?" Justin asked gruffly.

The woman shrank behind a man who stood next to her, looking confused, as he held the hand of a small boy. Lana placed a hand on Justin's shoulder and he glanced at her. Then she noticed why everyone was scared of him, not because of the scars but because his eyes were wild and angry.

Lana was surprised that she sounded so calm as she asked the woman, "Did you see who pushed me?"

"No," the woman answered quietly, then glanced at Justin.

"Let's go. You're not safe here," Justin said abruptly, grabbing her arm.

"You can't leave," the conductor said, sounding confused and panicked. "We have to wait for the metro police—"

Justin ignored the conductor and led Lana toward the exit. Lana decided, for the first time, not to argue with the man.

"Now do you believe me?" Justin asked, staring at her, concerned, as he half-dragged and half-carried her down the sidewalk away from the metro. The sun was just fading and evening was rapidly approaching. Justin loved the night, the lack of light, the almost numbing effect on his conscience, but the creeping shadows suddenly seemed sinister and he wished for a few more hours of sunlight until he could get Lana somewhere safe.

He cursed to himself when he saw the shock still apparent on her face. He should have known better. He shouldn't have allowed his temper to control him. He never should have left her. He should have taken her insults and suspicion, and his raging lust whenever he caught sight of her, but remained by her side. Because he couldn't control his emotions, Lana Hargrove had almost been killed. Justin cursed to himself again, then glanced at her.

"Say something," he demanded, wanting to shake her so she would insult him or hit him or something. Not just obediently walk beside him.

He stopped at his truck and opened the passenger door. Her blank expression turned to one of disgust as she peered into the cab of the truck. He had been following her, without wanting to be seen, so he had driven his old, reliable truck. A vehicle he knew that Lana wouldn't spend any energy looking at or at the driver inside. Justin rolled his eyes and motioned for her to climb inside the truck. She didn't move.

"The art theft business isn't treating you well?" she asked, staring at him.

"Get in, Lana," he said impatiently while darting glances around the street. No one seemed to be paying much attention to them, besides every man on the street who eyed Lana and her matching short flowing skirt and top with thin straps with interest. Justin groaned in disbelief. Trying to blend in with this woman was going to be very difficult.

"I'm not getting in that," she said, shaking her head.

"I apologize that I forgot to bring the Bentley, but I gave the driver the night off," he snapped sarcastically.

"I don't—"

Justin prayed for patience with spoiled brats; then he said calmly, "I won't tell anyone that you rode in my truck. Your reputation is safe with me."

She hesitated, then held down her skirt as she slowly and awkwardly climbed into the truck. Justin rolled his eyes as it took her about as long as his eighty-year-old grandmother to actually sit on the bench. Still, he couldn't help but notice that Lana's long legs and the expanse of thighs visible as she sat in the truck looked nothing like his grandmother's legs.

He slammed the door, then ran around the truck to climb behind the wheel. He started the engine, then gunned the motor and screeched into traffic, frowning at the blaring horns that followed his entrance into street traffic.

"Do you always drive like this? Or did you specifically want to drive this spring in the seat into my leg?" Lana asked, sounding annoyed.

"Someone followed you into the metro. They may still be following you. I don't want to take any chances."

"Who are *they*?" she demanded.

"I don't know."

"Where are we going?"

"We're going to your town house to grab some of your belongings and then we're going to a safe place to wait for your father."

"Excuse me?"

Justin sighed tiredly at the outraged tone in her voice. He darted a glance at her across the truck cabin and he muttered, "It'll only be a few days."

"I can't place my life on hold for a few days," she said, shaking her head. "I have work and . . . and dates. I have a date tonight, in fact."

"And I'm sure the poor guy will be heartbroken that you can't make it," he muttered dryly.

Lana Hargrove was gorgeous, but as far as he was concerned, her future date should be thanking Justin for having saved him from a night of sheer hell. Even if she could kiss a man into sheer bliss. Because he thought of the kiss that had been one of the stupidest things he had done in his life, he gripped the steering wheel tighter. He had been thinking about that kiss in her bedroom for two days, berating himself for taking what she offered. Until she threw a glass of cold water in his face. She had hesitated. She had touched his face and he had sensed her hesitation. He had pulled away first before she could. But still he thought about the feel of her tongue in his mouth, the feel of her lips on his, the force with which she had accepted his kiss, his touch. It was driving him crazy. As soon as this case was over, he vowed to dust off the ole black book and find a woman who wouldn't mind his scars, just long enough for a few sessions of carnal and intense sex.

She glared at him and said coldly, "I'm sure he will be."

"The poor bastard," he muttered under his breath.

"What did you say?" she asked suspiciously.

"Nothing," he said, then glanced in the rearview mirror again. "Actually, Lana, you're going to have to do without the Gucci and Versace. We can't go back to your town house. Someone is following us."

"What?" Panic filled her voice as she turned to stare out the back truck window.

"The Ford Taurus three cars back," he said through clenched teeth. "Hold on. I'm going to try and lose him."

Whatever she was on the verge of saying was cut off with a shriek as Justin executed a sharp U-turn in the middle of the street and she slammed against the door with a scream. More car horns blared. Justin cursed as the Ford Taurus executed a similar maneuver that provoked more blaring car horns and shouted curses.

Justin pressed on the accelerator and ran through a red light, causing Lana to scream again. He almost smiled. He was in an actual car chase. In six years in the detective business, he had never been involved in one. It was as cool in person as it looked in the movies.

"You're going to get us killed!" she snapped angrily while holding on to the door handle. Judging from her horrified expression, she obviously didn't feel the same excitement about the chase as he did.

"No, I won't." He made a sharp left turn in the middle of the street again and sped across three lanes of traffic to merge onto the freeway that would take them across the Potomac and into Virginia.

Justin sighed in relief when the Ford Taurus got trapped by three lanes of cars and lost in a haze of headlights. Lana sighed in relief, then leaned against the seat.

"I meet you and four days later my life is a complete mess," she said, then moaned in distress. "And I broke a nail."

Justin rolled his eyes in exasperation and disbelief. "Considering you were almost killed, one broken nail should be the least of your worries."

"You're right, Justin. My biggest worry is whether you're a crazy person or not. And then there is my second biggest worry, where the hell you're taking me."

"Everything will be fine, Lana," he said.

"Of course it will," she said dryly, then snapped angrily, "I can't just disappear . . . And I don't know you."

"It's funny you weren't saying that last night when we were kissing in your bedroom."

He silently winced when he felt the anger roll off

her in waves. He had thought maybe they could reach the cabin, be civil, and get through all of this without any mention of the kiss that had completely rocked his world, but he should have known that was a fantasy. Especially since every second when he wasn't arguing with her he was replaying that kiss—in slow motion, fast motion, reverse—over and over again in his head.

Her only response was a cold, "Stop this contraption right now."

Justin took several deep breaths. He said as patiently as he could, "Lana, we have a long drive ahead of us. Let's agree not to talk during it."

"You're kidnapping me." When he didn't respond, she reached into her small handbag and pulled out a sleek silver cell phone.

"Kidnapping? What are you talking about? . . . Who are you calling?"

"The police. That's who you call when you're being kidnapped."

Justin nodded in understanding, then grabbed the phone and threw it out the window of the moving truck. Her mouth hung open in disbelief and shock as she stared out the window after it.

"You just— My phone—! Do you know how much that phone cost?"

"Consider yourself kidnapped," he muttered, then switched on the radio. He turned up the volume, just in case she even thought about talking. Fortunately, she didn't. That didn't stop the memories of the kiss, though, and he couldn't turn the radio up loud enough to drown out those memories.

"I'm being kidnapped," Lana said in a flat tone to the clerk behind the counter at the gas station.

Justin forced a laugh as the clerk peered at him from behind thick eyeglasses. Against his better judgment but out of necessity, Justin had stopped for gas at a remote gas station off the highway en route to southern Virginia. His only choices had been to leave Lana in the truck, which he suspected she would hot-wire, leaving him stranded in the middle of nowhere, or take her inside the gas station and pray that no one was there except some bored clerk. Of course, Justin realized that taking Lana, dressed as she was, into any gas station would wake up any clerk. No man could sleep after seeing a woman like her, dressed in a skirt short enough to be illegal and a tight top with spaghetti straps that constantly slipped from her shoulders.

"Excuse me?" murmured the bewildered clerk as he glanced from Lana to Justin. His watery gaze focused on Justin's scars.

Justin forced another smile that made the clerk recoil in fear. Justin inwardly cursed; then he simply slapped several bills on the counter.

"Fill-up and the bottled water," he said, ignoring Lana.

"Do you understand me?" Lana said coldly as the clerk stared at her blankly. "I am being kidnapped, taken against my will, by this Neanderthal. He threw my cell phone out the window. I need you to call the police for me since I'm not able to do so. Do you understand me, Gomer Pyle?"

Justin smiled when the clerk's expression grew stony. No sympathy to be had here.

Justin wrapped an arm around her waist and squeezed tight enough to make her jab him in the gut. Hard. He nuzzled the hair that framed her face, which was surprisingly soft. He ignored the sharp pain in his gut as her elbow dug deeper. She opened her mouth to no doubt curse him to hell, but Justin pressed his mouth against hers before she could. Unfortunately— or fortunately—for him, her mouth was open at the time, and he slipped his tongue inside. For a brief second time stood still as he tasted Lana. He decided not to push his luck and pulled back before she bit it off.

It was a brief kiss that didn't last more than a second, but that taste of her momentarily stunned him. This kiss had been more potent, more addictive, than the last, even that brief taste. She stared at him, speechless, her eyes wide with disbelief and . . . His euphoria ended as he saw the disgust, too. The same look he had seen two nights ago when he had pulled away. Maybe with her eyes closed she could stand to kiss him, but the disgust obviously returned when she opened her eyes and saw who she had been kissing.

Justin suddenly remembered the clerk, who now gaped at both of them. This was probably the most excitement he'd seen in years.

"We're just having an argument," Justin told the clerk, trying to act like a charming person. "My girlfriend likes to play this game. The 'Help, I'm being kidnapped by a scary man' game. I told her that one day it would lead to trouble."

The clerk didn't respond but stared from Justin to Lana. Justin nodded in gratitude, then grabbed Lana's arm and dragged her from the gas station. She suddenly sprang to life and yanked her arm from his grip.

"If you ever kiss me again without my permission, you will regret it," she said through clenched teeth.

"Then don't ever give me a reason to," he retorted as he snatched the gas hose from the truck.

She leaned against the truck and glared at him, crossing her arms over her chest. Her expression abruptly changed, reminding Justin of all the X-rated pictures he had seen in magazines when he was a teenager. She sauntered toward him, ignoring the gas pump between them, and leaned close to him. It was a complete transformation that would have shocked him if he hadn't been watching her for the last two weeks.

She whispered in a husky voice, "If I really wanted you to, you would let me go."

He swallowed the sudden lump in his throat and

ignored his body, which responded to her sweet perfume scent like a horny junior high school boy. Instantly hard.

"You think so?" he asked, pretending boredom.

"I know so. I can get a man to do whatever I want."

"I'm not your typical man, sweetheart."

"Yes, you are," she whispered as she trailed a hand down his arm, which rested against the truck. Her gaze momentarily dropped to his pants, and a smug smile played on her lips as she murmured, "I can tell by how you look at me. I can tell by how you kissed me just now. And, most of all, I can tell because you're hard right now. Remember you just pressed against me?"

"You're nice to look at, but I have a job to do, and as tempting as you make it sound, sleeping with you is not a part of it." The disdain in his voice was apparent and totally fake, but Lana obviously didn't think so.

Her eyes narrowed and she took several steps back from him. Even though Justin knew he had no chance in hell with her, if possible, even that slim chance diminished even more.

"Where are you taking me?" she asked in a flat tone as she crossed her arms over her chest.

"Somewhere safe. And once we get there, I'll answer all of your questions."

She clenched her jaw, then turned and sat in the truck, slamming the door. Justin rolled his eyes, then concentrated on the gas pump, hoping that if Frank Hargrove came, it would be very soon. Justin didn't think that he and Lana should be left alone in a remote cabin in the woods for long. Either they would end up making love or they would kill each other.

CHAPTER SEVEN

"I have to use the bathroom," Lana announced.

She noticed Justin's surprised glance in her direction, but she refused to look at him. She had been holding it for the last two hours, but she had refused to break the silence that had formed between them since they left the gas station. But Lana was also a pragmatic. The only person suffering in the silence was her. Men never had to use the bathroom on road trips, so there was no telling how long it would be before Justin stopped.

"We only have an hour to go before we reach our destination. I don't think—"

"And I'm hungry," she interrupted him. He tried to protest, but she said, "I haven't eaten since lunch. I was planning on going to dinner tonight with friends, but a certain large man threw me into a certain dirty truck and I was unable to make it. So I'm hungry."

"So there was no date tonight?" he said, with a triumphant smile in her direction.

She ignored that and said simply, "Either I use the bathroom at some restaurant or gas station or I do it on this seat . . . although that may actually improve the smell of this thing."

Justin was silent for a moment as he kept his eyes on the road; then he said, "Fine, but I'm not going to stop you from running this time, Lana. I'm trying to help you. If you can't see that, then if you run, I'm not going to stop you."

Lana actually felt shamed by the hapless look on his face. She rarely felt shame. She rarely felt anything lately. Besides Bruce, who inspired her intense ambivalence, Justin had been the only person to arouse any emotions in her in a long time. She had been thinking a lot during the long ride. And she realized that since her grandmother had died four years ago, Justin Larkin was the first person she had cared enough about to get angry with, to laugh with, and to listen to. It was a frightening realization. And she didn't know what to do about it.

A few minutes later, Justin steered the truck into the dirt parking lot of a brightly lit diner that shone like a lighthouse off the dark highway. There were a few battered pickups and sport-utility vehicles in the parking lot, but besides that there was not a person to be seen. The small fifties-style diner with a sloped roof looked like the set of a creepy movie that began with a young black couple walking into it, never to be seen again.

Lana glanced at Justin to find him looking at the diner with apprehension as he shut off the motor.

His obvious nervousness made her stand away from the truck. She had no idea where she was and she had no idea who had pushed her in the metro. She did know that Justin Larkin knew her father and had saved her life. Right now, her options were limited. She had no choice but to stick with Justin, but he didn't need to know that. Lana ignored his calls for her to wait and she walked across the parking lot, cursing as her heels sank into the soft dirt ground. She stumbled into the diner and was met by tacky bright red booths and a jukebox gargling a country song in the corner of the small room.

Lana swallowed the lump in her throat when she realized that she was also met with hostile stares from four very dirty-looking men wearing overalls, who hovered in one booth near the window, and one woman, who wore a powder blue waitress uniform and looked like she could handle the men with one hand tied behind her back. Lana didn't know who to be more frightened of, the men or the woman.

Justin walked into the diner behind her and she tried not to sigh in relief. She didn't like depending on anyone, especially not a man who could so easily reject her advances, but in this situation she decided she could look to Justin for support and protection. She glanced at him and her uneasiness must have shown, because he winked at her—or maybe he blinked—then he walked to one of the tacky red booths in the corner of the restaurant, far from the men.

Lana hurried to the bathroom, and for the first time since she turned twenty-one years old, she did not put an extra twist in her hips because she knew that men watched her. It was the quickest trip to the bathroom that she had ever taken, mostly because she was scared the waitress would come to find her. She took care of the urgent business, washed her hands, and then only brushed her hair and put on a touch of lip gloss and mascara before she hurried back to the table, forgoing the usual full makeup touch-up.

She hurried across the restaurant and slid into the booth across the table from Justin.

"Our friendly waitress has informed us that we have two choices on the menu tonight—a hamburger or a cheeseburger," he told her.

"Cheeseburger," Lana said eagerly, resisting the urge to lick her lips. She saw the surprise register on his face and she snapped, "What?"

"I don't know. . . . I guess I thought you'd be a vegetarian or you'd want a leaf of lettuce and a tomato."

She looked at him in surprise.

"Why?"

He snorted in disbelief, then motioned to her. She shook her head, confused. "Look at you," he said, as if that were all the explanation she needed. "You look like the type of woman who would always complain about being full and your figure and boring stuff like that."

"I love salads and sushi, but I also love cheeseburgers. What other sexist stereotypes do you have about me?" she asked, annoyed.

"Come on, Lana. A woman like you eats salad—hold the croutons."

"Just order me the damn cheeseburger."

"And she curses, too," he murmured, then motioned to the waitress for two cheeseburgers. She nodded, then disappeared behind a swinging door.

"Don't tell me she's the cook, too," Lana whispered while shuddering in disgust and momentarily forgetting to glare at him. Justin shook his head in amusement, and she said, "If you had seen that bathroom, you would be concerned about our chef, too."

"I've eaten in worse places than this," he said, shrugging, unconcerned.

Lana hated herself for asking it, but she had to. "With my father?"

"No," he said, then studied her.

She met his gaze and tried not to look away first, but it was hard not to when she kept thinking about the kiss and how one swipe of his tongue had made her body tremble. It was embarrassing that this man could have that effect on her. She had held on to the notion that no man would ever control her, but she had a feeling that if Justin put some energy into it, he could make her do whatever the hell he wanted and there wouldn't be anything she could do about it.

"Where did you meet him?" she asked, surrendering whatever apathy she had managed to convey about Frank Hargrove since she kneed Justin in the groin.

"Venice."

"Italy?" she asked, surprised.

"California," he corrected, grinning. She found herself smiling in return. He had an easy grin to return. Then she remembered that she didn't trust him, let alone like him, and she instantly stopped smiling. "Your father doesn't live the glamorous life of a cat burglar that some Hollywood writers put on the movie screen. He's just an ordinary guy."

"I'm about to pull out the violin and start playing a tune."

"You're angry with him."

"I wonder why?" she said, feigning surprise. "Could it be because he left me when I was nine years old? Could it be because I haven't heard from him since then? And could it be that every time I do hear of him it's because there's been a recent art theft in the area—and the police and FBI want to know if I've seen or heard from him? Of course, even they know my father has forgotten my existence, because not even the cops have bothered me in years."

"He's not a bad guy, Lana. He did what he thought was best," Justin said quietly.

"I can't believe that you're defending him."

"Aside from the almost-being-killed part, maybe it's good that you and Frank have to talk to each other, clear the air."

"And I suppose you have a perfect relationship with your father." She expected a smart retort in return or the tale of Justin's perfect childhood, which included family barbecues and potato sack races. Instead, he stared at the table.

"No, I wouldn't say that."

An awkward silence fell between them and Lana couldn't help but feel it was her fault for making Justin think about something he obviously didn't want to think about.

He said quietly, "My father was there every night when I was a kid. Now I call him about once a month and on birthdays and holidays."

"You two aren't close?"

"That's an understatement," he said, with a dry laugh. He actually smiled as he said, "My mom lives in Maryland. She fixes me dinner every Sunday night. I think she'd actually like you."

"Really?" Lana asked, not examining why the thought of Justin's mother liking her made her feel good inside.

"She likes women who don't take shit from anyone. Women like her. It's the reason she and my dad finally got divorced. All the kids were out of the house and my mom had had enough. The day after my younger brother left for college, my mom moved out and asked for a divorce."

"Were you upset?"

"Hell, no. My brothers and I were in awe that she

lasted that long. My younger brother lives in Atlanta and he says that now Dad is working on driving away his new wife."

"My mother died when I was ten," she whispered, staring at her hands.

"I know," he said.

"I don't remember much about her," she admitted, even though she rarely admitted that fact to herself. It seemed like the ultimate betrayal—a daughter who could not remember her own mother. "I was ten years old when she died. I should remember something."

"Her death was probably very traumatic for you. Our minds forget sometimes in order to protect us," Justin said quietly.

"But she's my mother," Lana protested, shaking her head. "I remember Frank. I remember him taking me to get ice cream, to the park, to museums, to baseball games. If my grandmother hadn't had a picture of my mother, I probably wouldn't even remember what she looked like."

His large hand closed over hers and Lana felt comforted. With the touch of his hand, she felt for just that moment that the weight of the world didn't squarely rest on her shoulders. "Your mother loved you very much."

She groaned in frustration. "I know she did, Grandma Harri told me. But things like her favorite color, or if she liked roses or orchids, or if she liked black-and-white movies . . . Stuff that makes her *her,* I can't remember. I had her for ten years, I should remember some details about her. If I don't remember her, who will?"

"Frank. Frank remembers her. He still mourns for her, every day."

At the mention of her father, Lana pulled her hand from Justin's grip. Because her hand suddenly felt cold, she wiped it on her skirt and avoided Justin's gaze. No man's touch had ever comforted her like his had. She had never allowed a man to comfort her, like she allowed Justin.

Justin continued, apparently oblivious to her reaction, "Don't be so hard on yourself, Lana. You were young when she died. You can't blame yourself for not remembering."

"I don't blame myself," she said stiffly. "I blame him."

"Who? Frank?" he said, surprise and confusion crossing his face.

"He took my mother away from me—"

"Your mother was hit by a car—"

"He took her away from me by leaving," she said, her voice louder than she intended. She cleared her throat and hissed through clenched teeth, "After her death, Frank removed all the pictures of her in the house and refused to talk about her. Two months later, he took me to my grandmother's house and left. He left me there, Justin. He was the only one who knew my mother, the only one who could remember her, remember me with her, and when he left, he took all of that with him. He didn't leave any pictures of her or mementos or anything to let me know her. No phone calls on her birthday—or on mine, for that matter. Just silence, as if she had never existed, as if I had never existed. Do you know what that's like? Growing up, without a clue about who your mother is . . ." An uncontrollable sob cut off the rest of her tirade and tears filled her eyes. She quickly looked down at the table and prayed that Justin didn't speak or touch her or she would break down in the middle of the diner.

It was as if Justin's concerned expression and dark eyes were the key that finally released all the emotions she had been holding in for the last twenty years. Her grandmother had been a tough woman. Harriet Hargrove didn't cry, she rarely laughed and she believed that hard work and getting up early in the morning were the secret to a long life. Lana had loved Harriet, and had known that Harriet loved her, but the older woman didn't believe in displaying emotions—happiness, love or sadness. And it was the sadness that had hurt Lana the most that she could never talk about with her grandmother.

Lana took several deep breaths, willing away the tears, then forced herself to meet Justin's gaze. He held her gaze, his expression direct and . . . Lana could only describe it as tenderness. She had seen calculated lust on men's faces, anger and, a few times, longing, but never such tenderness.

She immediately tried to lighten the moment and

blurted out, "I can't believe I'm talking to you about this."

"You need to talk about it," he said simply, not allowing her to escape the heavy feelings in the air between them.

"Why? It's all in the past." Lana squared her shoulders and said matter-of-factly, "I now realize that Frank leaving me with Grandma Harri was the best thing he could have done for me. She taught me that I'm stronger and smarter than any man could ever be, and that I could do anything I wanted, with or without a man. She taught me that I don't need a man to succeed in life, but to also be smart enough to know when to control one to help me."

A small smile played across his lips and Lana balled her hands into fists in her lap because she was reminded of their kiss in front of the store clerk. Justin had given her that same look right before he kissed her, right before he rocked her world. She should have been repulsed by him—by his arrogance and rudeness, even by his scars, since she once had dumped a man who owned a Fortune 500 company because his ears had been too big—but that small smile made her thighs involuntarily tighten.

"Your Grandma Harri sounds like quite a woman," he finally said.

Lana smiled at the memory of her grandmother and was a little surprised by the pang of loss she allowed herself to feel.

"She was. Her husband left her when she was eight months pregnant with Frank. She had no job skills or work experience or money, but she could cook. She got jobs assisting in the kitchens of some of the wealthiest families in San Francisco, she watched and learned until she was running their kitchens. She saved her money and eventually opened her own restaurant in Oakland that was a raging success until she closed it a few years before she died. I promoted the closing event. All of her former employers came, the mayors from San Francisco and Oakland came, a few state senators and city council members . . . It was a huge success, standing room only."

"You admire her," Justin said.

"Of course I do. After Frank's father deserted her, she was in the worst possible position a woman could be in at that time—alone, with a baby and no money, but she pulled herself out of it. She never depended on another man again, and she taught me to do the same."

Justin shook his head with a wry smile. "You've certainly taken her lessons to heart."

"Why do I get the feeling that's not a compliment?" she asked, amused. "But then again, it's not surprising. Men tend to be very sensitive upon learning they're nothing but accessories."

Amusement glinted in Justin's eyes as he said, "I bet most men would be willing to give one or both of their testicles just for the chance to be one of your accessories."

Lana couldn't resist grinning as she said, with a feigned casual shrug, "I wouldn't have much use for them then, now would I?"

Justin stared at her, shocked for a moment, then he roared with laughter, disturbing the stillness of the diner.

And it suddenly occurred to Lana how much she liked to make this man laugh. It was a new feeling for her. Being around him inspired all new feelings for her, and she didn't like it.

"Here you go," the waitress said gruffly, setting down one plate with two cheeseburgers on it in the middle of the table.

Lana stared at the cheeseburgers, which looked like they had been stolen from a real hamburger restaurant five days ago, frozen, and then thawed out just for her and Justin.

"Do we, at least, get our own plates?" Lana asked, staring at the waitress.

The waitress pointed to the four men in the booth, who continued to watch Lana and Justin too closely.

"They have the last clean ones. If you want to ask for them, feel free," the waitress said. She slapped the bill on the table, then turned and walked away.

Justin stared at the cheeseburgers, as if he weren't sure whether to eat one or shoot it. Lana grabbed hers and took a big bite. Justin watched her carefully, as if whether he chose to eat his depended on whether she suddenly dropped dead in the next few seconds.

"Not so bad," she said, with a shrug. She added

through a mouthful of beef and stale bread, "You were saying about my father."

"I met your father a few months ago," he said. "We got along. He needed assistance on a certain job and I needed work."

"A black version of Butch Cassidy and the Sundance Kid, no doubt. But how does this all lead to me?"

Justin lowered his voice as he said, "A few weeks ago, we got a phone call from a man in Cairo. He told us that the African-American Smithsonian was arranging an art deal with a museum in Cairo for a loan of Nefertiti's obelisk."

"What is that?"

"It's an ancient Egyptian artifact recently found near Alexandria. It's a miniature of the obelisk that Nefertiti planned to build at her tomb. There are positive markings on it that indicate it belonged to her and that it was once buried with her."

"Where is she buried? In one of those pyramids?"

"No one knows where she's buried. It's one of the great mysteries of ancient Egypt," Justin said. "As you can guess, that miniobelisk is worth a lot of money. There are a lot of private collectors out there who will bargain their firstborn child for anything from ancient Egypt, not to mention anything related to Nefertiti."

"And you and my father were going to steal it to sell to the highest bidder?" she guessed, not bothering to hide the disgust in her voice.

He ignored her question and said, "We got information on the shipping plan and the security procedures for the obelisk at the warehouse in Paris, a stopover before DC. The plan was to . . . to observe the obelisk before it left Paris—"

"In other words, you were going to steal it in Paris."

"But something went wrong. In the warehouse, Frank and I got separated. By the time I got to the room where the obelisk was supposed to be, it was gone. So was Frank. I went back to our prearranged meeting place and he called me. He said that the obelisk was not there when he reached the room and that he was being set up.

"I didn't believe him at first, not until he asked me where I was. I told him that I was at the meeting place and he told me to run as fast I could. For some reason, I didn't question him; I just ran. I wasn't more than a block away when the police swarmed the entire area. Frank told me that it wasn't safe for him or for you. He gave me directions to find you and the directions to this safe location. He wanted me to take you there as soon as possible and he planned to follow us a few days later."

"Have you heard from him since Paris?"

"When I landed in DC, he told me where to find you. He wanted me to follow you for a few days to make certain that no one was following you. I wasn't supposed to have contact with you until he had spoken to you first."

"Did you call him and tell him what happened at the metro?"

He looked bashfully at the burger that he hadn't touched and murmured, "I don't know how to reach him. He's called me every time."

"So he doesn't even know we're on our way to this supposedly safe location?" she asked, shocked.

"And I didn't want to tell you this because you'll overreact, but my cell phone . . . the phone that Frank uses to reach me, I lost it in the metro." He hesitated, then stared at her, waiting expectantly.

Lana debated on whether or not to explode. On an emptier stomach, she probably would have. Instead, she finished the last morsel of her cheeseburger and reached for his.

"You're not upset?" he prodded.

"What's done is done," she said, shrugging.

"Remember I threw your cell phone out the window?" he asked. "Aren't you going to mention that?"

"No," she said simply.

"That's not the Lana Hargrove I know."

She laughed, surprising him and herself; then she said, "You should note this for future reference. Break bad news to me while I'm eating. But I reserve the right to yell at you later."

Justin shook his head. "I'll note that. I'm going to check my messages at the hotel, maybe Frank called there when he couldn't reach me on my cell phone, and then we should get going before *Hee Haw* over there build up enough courage to talk to you instead of just staring and licking their lips."

She nodded, concentrating on the second cheeseburger, which tasted almost as good as the first one. She knew he watched her as he stood up from the table and she almost wanted to wink at him, but then he would get the impression that she was beginning to like him. She ignored him instead.

"I was beginning to worry about you," Clarence greeted him on the other end of the telephone.

Justin glanced around the corner of the restaurant wall to make certain that Lana couldn't hear. Their booth was across the restaurant and there was no way she could hear Clarence on the other end of the telephone and, even more important, she was in the middle of her second cheeseburger and Justin doubted she would hear an explosion outside the restaurant. She had not been joking about the eating thing.

"I'm touched, Clarence. Truly," Justin said into the telephone.

"Only because I can't find your password to our emergency account. I need both of our passwords in case I ever want to use it."

"That's enough of a reason to keep me around in case you get any ideas," Justin said, grinning.

Clarence grumbled but then demanded, "Where are you? I don't recognize the area code on the caller ID."

"I'm in southern Virginia on my way to Frank's cabin . . . with Lana Hargrove."

There was a moment of silence; then his cousin screamed again. "Lana Hargrove is with you?"

Justin silently cursed, then said, "It's a long story

that I can't get into because she's waiting for me."

"I heard on the news that a woman was pushed in front of a train on the metro, but she was saved at the last moment by a Good Samaritan. Tell me that was not Lana Hargrove."

"It was, and then someone followed us after we left the metro. I couldn't take her back to her apartment or to the hotel."

"Justin, I won't say it—"

"Then don't."

"You have to pull out. This is getting too dangerous."

"What am I supposed to do now, Clarence? People are trying to kill Lana, who is completely innocent in all of this. I have to see this through to the end." Justin didn't add that he had had his first real conversation with Lana, no insults, no screaming, no snarling, and it had felt good. It had felt comfortable. There was no way he was abandoning this woman now. Things had been touch-and-go before they stopped at the diner, despite the kisses, but now no one was coming near her if he had anything to say about it. Justin was beginning to think he actually liked her, besides wanting to make love to her. For the next twenty-four hours.

He heard Clarence's heavy sigh over the telephone, then silence before Clarence said, "Don't make me worry. My ulcer is bad."

"I'll call when I can."

"Do better than that," Clarence said, sounding worried. "If these people are willing to push an innocent woman in front of a train, there's no telling what they're capable of."

Justin hung up the telephone and gave himself several moments to stop being a private detective and return to being Justin Larkin.

He walked back around the corner and stopped in his tracks when he saw the four hillbillies in the accompanying overalls standing around Lana. Justin's shock gave way to anger and outrage and he stormed across the diner, prepared to take on as many rednecks as he had to. Then Justin realized that Lana was smiling and the rednecks were laughing.

"Hi, Justin," one of the men said, grinning at him.

Lana smiled at Justin and said, "These men were telling me all about the local sights. There's a waterfall that bubbles when it falls into the pond, and they call it Satan's Cauldron."

"That's nice," Justin said, reaching for his wallet. "But we have to hit the road."

"We have the bill, Justin," one of the other men said with a bashful grin in Lana's direction.

"This is what we need more of in America," Lana said, smiling. "Men like you. Gallant, chivalrous, and handsome as sin."

Justin tried not to choke on her obvious flirting, but apparently *Hee Haw* ate it up, because they all laughed.

"Thank you, Lana." One of the men turned to Justin and his expression turned murderous as he said, "You hurt her and you'll have to answer to us."

Justin tried not to snort in disbelief—that would have masked his small flash of fear because he could tell the man was serious—and instead grabbed Lana's arm, resisting the urge to drag her out of the diner.

"Bye, boys," she sighed, waving. The four men waved in unison while Justin nodded and gritted his teeth.

"That was fun," Lana said cheerfully.

Justin rolled his eyes and tried not to imagine a Lana who used her powers for bad.

CHAPTER EIGHT

"We're lost, aren't we?" Lana asked matter-of-factly.

Justin clenched his jaw and decided to ignore Lana for the moment because the truth was, he was lost. They hadn't passed another car in the last hour and the road had become more narrow and overrun with large trees the farther from the diner the two drove. And then the sheets of rain had started. He blamed Lana. If she hadn't smiled at him in the diner, if she hadn't made him think that she was more than a spoiled brat with expensive shoes, if she hadn't given him that look after he kissed her in front of the store clerk, he wouldn't have been distracted while he drove.

"We're not lost," he said through clenched teeth.

"I recognize that bridge. We've passed it two different times in the last hour."

He squinted through the rain and darkness at the bridge to the side that the truck headlights illuminated in the distance. He squeezed the steering wheel because he recognized the bridge, too.

"We're not lost," he repeated, then added uncertainly, "We're just . . . We're a little turned around."

"Is that what they call 'lost' now? Turned around?"

Her voice was surprisingly calm, which did not bode well. She had been silent since they left the diner, and he had felt the tension building like an approaching storm. And he had a feeling that it was now about to be unleashed. And even worse, he began experiencing "aura" symptoms. Those hints that his body was on the verge of betraying him with a migraine that would render him weak and useless. The blind spots had started twenty minutes ago. He cursed the weakness. He had never been weak before the fire, but now he was. The doctors couldn't tell him why he suddenly suffered from migraines after the fire, but he did. And it was too damn late to do anything about it.

A spasm of pain shot through his head and he momentarily lost control of the steering wheel. The truck swerved abruptly and he yanked the steering wheel back toward the road. Lana screeched in horror, then glared at him.

"What is wrong with you?" she demanded angrily. "Not only are you kidnapping me, but you're trying to kill me. . . ." Her voice trailed off and she actually sounded concerned as she asked, "Justin, are you all right?"

"I'm fine," he snapped even as he blinked to clear his blurred vision. He silently cursed when the road became one black and gray blob in front of him. The rain, the darkness, and Lana sitting in obvious concerned silence was too much. He cursed out loud this time.

She moved across the seat and touched his arm. Her voice was soft as she asked, "Justin, what's wrong?"

"My head . . . My medicine . . ." His voice trailed off as he pulled to the side of the road, the truck ambling off-road slightly as he jerked to a stop. He closed his eyes and leaned his head against the window. He was so tired, and his head blared with pain. People often confused migraines with common headaches, but migraines were much worse. Debilitating. Embarrassing. Justin wanted to curl into a ball, but not from the blinding, jabbing pain—that need would come later—but because Lana was seeing him at his worst. He closed his eyes, unable to open them against the pain any longer. Besides, he probably couldn't see much anyway. Not when his entire body was trembling and he felt nauseous and weak—like Superman on kryptonite.

He heard the passenger door open and he prayed that she would leave him alone to die in shame and misery. Then his door was opened and the cool air and stinging rain were almost a relief. He felt her hands pull on his arm as she tried to make him stand away from the car.

"Come on, Justin; work with me," she said, straining under his weight. "I'm going to drive."

"No—"

"Yes." She sounded guilty as she confessed, "I saw a cabin through the woods about twenty miles back."

Justin actually laughed. Through the pain and embarrassment he laughed because he didn't think any man could outwit Lana Hargrove. Justin didn't know what possessed him, but standing in the rain with her practically collapsing under his weight, he pressed a hard kiss against her lips. She felt so damn good. That was his last thought before the world went black.

It had been a long time since Lana had been worried for anyone besides herself. Her grandmother had been a wonderful woman. She had taught Lana to be self-reliant, to never depend on a man for anything, and to use every weapon at hand—mainly her brain and looks—to take advantage. Harriet Hargrove had never taught Lana, however, how to care for someone else, how to completely give her heart over. And Lana didn't know if that was what Justin inspired in her, but she was pacing the small cabin like an expectant mother waiting for any sign that he would wake up soon.

She hadn't even cared about her wet clothes or aching muscles as she half-carried him into the cabin after she had driven them through the woods, probably destroying the underside of the truck, and hustled him into the small one-room cabin. Then Lana had retrieved firewood from the porch, and after a lot of cursing and remembering every episode of *Little House on the Prairie* that she could, she actually started one. She had stripped Justin to his briefs, only ogling his well-defined chest and legs for a few seconds, before she laid him on the sofa in the center of the room, closest to the fire, and covered him with a blanket.

That had been two hours ago. Justin had fallen into a deep sleep, the exhaustion washing off of him in waves. If his chest hadn't moved up and down regularly, Lana would have been scared that he was dead. And she would have had no one to blame but herself. She had seen the cabin when he said it should have been "right here," she had seen the slump in his shoulders the longer he drove, but she had wanted to prove a point—a point she couldn't remember anymore. She only knew that she was more scared than she had been in a long time. Even facing the train was nothing compared to this horrible worry lodged in her stomach.

And the worst thing was she couldn't do anything. She couldn't leave the cabin to find a doctor because she didn't want to leave Justin alone. Neither one of them had a phone, and a quick search of the cabin revealed none. And she had no idea where they were. If Lana didn't know better, she would think that she was close to tears.

She ignored her soaking wet and probably destroyed designer skirt and knelt next to Justin to wipe the sweat streaming down his face with a cloth she had found in the bathroom. With his eyes closed, Lana stole the moment to examine his scars, which she hadn't thought much about until that moment. She touched the brown hardened skin and traced the shape of the mass of jangled tissue from the edge of his naturally arched eyebrow past the corner of his left eye, skirting close to his nose and ending at his ear and at the corner of his mouth, which remained untouched. The pain that he must have gone through brought suspicious moisture to her eyes that she recognized as tears.

She leaned close to him to kiss his face just as his eyes fluttered open.

"Where am I?" He sounded disoriented and slightly panicked as he tried to push himself off the sofa.

Lana placed her hands on his shoulders and she knew he was weak because he easily fell back.

"You're at the cabin," she whispered, wiping the cloth down his face, far from the scars.

He focused on her, but she didn't think he knew who she was. He reached for her, but his hand remained in the air for a moment, close to her cheek but not touching it. She took his hand and rested it against her face, a surprisingly tender move for a woman who despised any sign of tenderness.

"Kiss me," he said in a throaty voice, as if he had the right.

Lana blamed it on the strange feelings of worry

and tenderness coursing through her, or she could have blamed it on her guilt because she was partially responsible for the state that Justin was in, but she kissed him. His mouth opened under hers and she tasted the distinctive salty smoothness of him that set her blood on fire. His mouth against hers became more insistent, his tongue pressing harder into her mouth. She pulled back before he hurt himself, before he hurt her.

A small smile played across his perfect lips. His eyes slid closed as he murmured, "Caroline."

Lana stared down at him, devastated, but he had already fallen back asleep and Lana felt a new emotion—jealousy. Whoever this Caroline was had a claim on a man who could kiss Lana into a state of euphoria, even while sick as a dog.

Justin woke up feeling like a herd of four-wheelers had used his chest for pavement. His chest hurt, his head hurt, every muscle in his body ached, and he had a foul taste in his mouth. At least, the migraine had passed, and he was thankful for that. He squinted when he realized that sunlight was pouring into the room. He forced himself to get up, but the world momentarily spun, so he sat on the sofa for a moment, his hands on his knees.

He glanced around the small, neat cabin—the kitchen area, one neatly made bed, and a fireplace. It wasn't much, but it was clean and he could see the touches that told him it belonged to Frank. There were the model sailboats that Frank loved to build, on a shelf in one corner of the room. And, of course, there were the distinctive framed paintings on the wall that seemed out of place in a cabin. He wondered if he had time to search the cabin for some unrecovered pieces. . . . Then the whole night came rushing back. Lana. His migraines. He raked a hand over the coarse morning bristles on his face. He needed a shave, a shower, and preferably to never see Lana again.

As if in direct contradiction to his prayer, Lana walked through the open door where the majority of sunshine was coming in to offend his eyesight. Even in yesterday's wrinkled clothes, the woman was gorgeous. Her perfect hair was no longer perfect but sexier than if she had spent hours in a salon, and she still wore her towering heels. Of course, he instantly began to visually scan the cabin for his clothes, which were missing, he realized as he soon as he saw her, because him being nude around Lana was not a good idea. He bunched the blanket around his waist when she noticed him awake.

Whatever carefree moment she had been having disappeared and concern crossed her face as she walked toward him. It was the last thing a grown man wanted from a woman. Pity.

"How are you feeling?" she asked softly.

"Great," he muttered, avoiding her eyes. "Where are my clothes?"

She hesitated for a moment and he wondered if she

was seeing the scars on his back and chest. His face was one thing, but his back was a whole new world of distaste. She apparently overcame her shock, because she pointed to his clothes hanging off the chairs near the fireplace.

"They were wet. I laid them out to dry."

"Great." He cringed as he said that word again. There was nothing "great" about waking up in a cabin wearing his underwear and having a woman such as Lana Hargrove look at him like he was too weak to put on his own damn pants. Then he gulped because he realized she had probably taken off his pants last night.

He stood, refusing to give in to the wave of dizziness that shot through him, and he grabbed his pants. He turned his back to Lana and pulled on his pants and shirt. Feeling at least more like a man—or maybe a very tall fourteen-year-old—he dropped the blanket and turned to Lana. She still looked at him with that expression of pity that had his jaw clenching in anger.

Justin inwardly cursed again, then said gruffly, "Look, Lana, about last night, I . . ." His voice trailed off because he didn't know exactly how to finish the sentence. He had no idea what to say the morning after when a woman had seen him debilitated and whimpering like a child.

"I found some packaged toothbrushes, toothpaste, clean razors, and soap in the bathroom. I think Frank has been here recently. We have food, too. I used all the hot water this morning, but a cold shower is better than nothing, right?"

Justin stared at her, speechless for a moment; then he asked suspiciously, "Why are you being so nice to me?"

She didn't look at him as she responded, "Take a shower, Justin. You're stinking up the cabin."

He frowned, then lifted one arm and sniffed. He quickly turned to the bathroom, because she was right. And because he was relieved he wouldn't have to talk about it.

CHAPTER NINE

"You have to hold the pole like this," Justin said, adjusting her hold on the fishing pole.

Lana gritted her teeth but barely restrained the urge to tell him exactly where he could shove the pole. They sat on the dock that jutted into the wide, gleaming lake behind the cabin. Fishing. Lana Hargrove was sitting in her Gucci outfit, fishing. Her pink Via Spiga heels were sitting on the dock next to her. She didn't belong there and neither did her heels.

But she forced a smile when Justin glanced at her. Her smile slowly disappeared when she saw him laughing. She shoved him in the shoulder and he grunted in protest as he juggled the fishing pole in his hands to keep it from falling into the lake. When Lana continued to glare at him, he smiled at her. God help her. The man was beautiful.

"Why are you laughing at me?" she asked.

"I was trying to see how far I could push you before

you snapped. Next I was going to suggest that you show the fish your bra and see if that helps us catch one."

She narrowed her eyes at him, then laughed, against her better judgment. She threw up her hands in defeat. "I'm a city girl, Justin."

"And I'm a city guy." He laughed when she turned to him with an amazed gasp. "I don't know what the hell I'm doing here. We don't even have the right bait on these hooks."

"You said the raisins from the raisin bran . . ." Her voice trailed off when she pulled the fishing pole from the water and stared at the shriveled raisin at the end of the line that Justin had told her she could use for bait to catch fish for dinner.

"Yeah, I couldn't believe you fell for that one," Justin said smugly. "Hell, Lana, I don't even know if there are fish in this lake."

Lana glared at him, but his too-proud smile made her laugh. She shoved him again, but he didn't budge.

"Why?" she asked in between laughs.

His smile faded as he said, "Because you're being nice to me and it's not like you. You're scaring me, Lana. Stop it."

Lana heard the discomfort hidden behind his sarcastic response. This was about last night. He felt ashamed. She debated touching him like she wanted to, but she had a feeling that he wouldn't like that. Justin did not like to be touched. He advertised it like a neon sign. Usually she considered men like him a challenge to see how fast she could wrap them around her finger. But he was different. He made her different. She hadn't thought about work or the fact that she was missing it in at least thirty minutes.

"You're right; I am being too nice," she decided.

"And you never agree with me."

"You're right."

"Lana," he said in a warning tone.

"I don't know what to do," she said, feigning helplessness as she got to her feet.

"Just stop it—" Justin's words were cut off by a shout as she pushed him off the dock and into the lake. He splashed to the surface, sputtering and waving his arms. He was laughing. Lana laughed, too. For making her worry, he deserved being pushed into the lake and a lot more than that.

"I deserved that," he said, nodding as he ran a wet hand down his dripping wet face.

She tried to sound annoyed as she said, "I sat on this dirty dock for you. I think I have a splinter in my ass."

"I can help you take it out." She thought he was serious for a moment and she almost about-faced, before he abruptly laughed, then swam toward the dock. He pulled himself onto the platform and Lana's amusement instantly disappeared as the water sluiced off the clothes that stuck to his body like a second skin. The man was too perfect to be real. Her entire body stilled and she couldn't have looked away, even if she had wanted to. Defined pectoral muscles, a six-pack, and strong, long legs. She sucked in her breath.

He smiled, then walked toward her, advancing like a predator in the jungle. Lana was frozen by that smile. He put two wet hands on her shoulders and the cold-ness of the water penetrated through her clothes to her skin, shocking her out of her daze.

"You wouldn't," she whispered when she saw the wicked gleam in his eyes.

"Of course I wouldn't," he said just as he pushed her off the dock and she went flying in the air toward the water. But she had a death grip on his arm and pulled him with her. Water flooded her mouth as she went un-der with a scream.

In the mass of bubbles, she saw Justin underwater next to her. She would have laughed if she could when she saw him stick out his tongue at her. He grabbed her arm and they both kicked to the surface. His laughter rang in her ears as he held his arms around her to keep her afloat.

"Are you all right?" Justin asked while wiping long strands of wet hair from her face.

Lana nodded, then laughed, longer and louder than she had laughed in a long time, maybe ever. She wrapped her arms around his neck and said, "I'm ac-tually having fun and without a *Cosmopolitan* or a sushi roll in sight."

"Who would have thunk it?" he asked dryly.

Lana's retort fell out of her mouth and into the water

when she realized how close she was to him. Her gaze unwillingly dropped to his mouth as their bodies rocked together with the soft sway of the water. She felt Justin's muscles bunch under her hands and she realized that she wasn't the only one being affected by their nearness. Desire ripped across his face. Whatever laughter had been between them instantly vanished. Everything ceased to exist except the feel of his body under her hands, the feel of him around her, sheltering her.

She leaned toward him, needing to taste his mouth at least one more time; then she would be able to stick to her strict no-Justin diet. But he abruptly moved underwater and out of her grip. He swam toward the dock without another glance in her direction. It was the third time he had walked away from her, and Lana vowed there would not be a fourth. She wanted Justin Larkin, and Lana usually got what she wanted.

Justin darted a glance across the cabin at Lana, who stood in the kitchen slowly slicing carrots as if the perfect slice would mean the cure to cancer. Mostly she ignored him. Justin told himself it was best if they did ignore each other. No more kissing, no more touching, and no more close contact in water. He shook his head in disbelief, because no man could ignore Lana Hargrove. It was impossible.

Even after a cold shower—not by choice but because Lana had used all the water when she showered after they returned from the lake—he still thought about their kiss in the convenience store, the feel of her in his arms in the water, and the look of pure joy in her eyes that had almost made him forget why he was at the cabin with her.

But Justin Baxter accepted no woman's pity, and as coldhearted as Lana pretended to be, she felt sorry for him. It was the only explanation for her sudden change in attitude, for the almost kiss in the water, for everything. It was a matter of pride, but Justin was a Baxter after all and a Baxter had to have his damn pride.

"That happens to me sometimes," he said, breaking the heavy silence in the cabin that had fallen since they had returned from the lake and their separate showers.

She didn't look up from the carrots as she murmured, "What?"

"The migraines, Lana." She looked at him then and Justin wished he had never brought up this subject. He didn't owe her anything. She didn't owe him anything. But then he found himself explaining quietly, "Since the fire, sometimes when I push myself too hard for too long . . . I get weak and the migraines start. I hate it."

"I'd hate it, too," she said simply.

Justin almost smiled at her. Instead of lying to him and telling him it was all right, she was being honest with him. If he wasn't planning to turn her father in to the proper authorities, he almost thought he could have liked this woman.

"And thanks," he added begrudgingly. "For helping me last night."

She shrugged simply and turned back to the carrots. "You're the only one who knows where the hell we are. If something happened to you, I'd die up here alone."

"I knew there was a reason you were being nice to me," he said, grinning.

She picked up the plate of carrots and carried it across the cabin and sat at the table across from him. He smiled at the perfect arrangement of carrot slices in a perfect circle on the plate. She smiled proudly, then motioned for him to take a carrot slice, as if it were actually something besides a vegetable.

She asked nonchalantly, "So what's the plan now? We sit here and wait for my father to show up?"

"That's the plan," he said, his suspicion returning at her lack of anger.

"What about lunch and dinner? These carrots will only hold me for so long."

"You could cook."

She looked horrified as she said, "I don't cook, Justin."

"I'll make something," he said, with a slight smile.

"I have a manicure and pedicure appointment tomorrow morning, but I don't think it will be a problem to reschedule," she said with a content sigh. "Don't you love carrots? What a perfect vegetable it is, but I think it should be a fruit. Something as good as a carrot shouldn't be considered a vegetable—"

He asked suspiciously, "Why are you being so co-operative suddenly?"

"What choice do I have? In case you haven't noticed, the truck isn't going anywhere."

Justin hadn't noticed, but the truck was parked haphazardly in front of the cabin with two flat wheels and wires dangling underneath. It looked as if it had been dragged across a forest, and then Justin saw the direction of broken trees and brush that Lana had obviously driven across in making her trail to the cabin even though a dirt driveway sat no more than fifteen feet on the other side. He inwardly groaned. He loved that truck. He had driven from Atlanta to DC in that truck six years ago.

"You really expect Frank to come here looking for us?" she asked doubtfully.

"Yes," Justin said, still shocked by the condition of the truck.

"I don't want you to be disappointed, but he's not known for being where he's supposed to be when he's supposed to be," she said, as if warning him.

"He'll be here," he said firmly.

"And if he's not here by tomorrow, we hitchhike back to DC or, at least, some place where we can find clothes, hot water, sushi, and telephones. Deal?"

Justin nodded in agreement and she smiled proudly. He suddenly felt like he had been taken in a strange con that only another con man could figure out. Since he wasn't a con man, he didn't think he would ever have a clue about what had just happened.

"What?" she asked, batting her eyelashes innocently.

"This is too easy. You're being almost accommodating. What are you not telling me?"

"Has anyone ever told you that you're a suspicious man?" He continued to stare at her, waiting for her explanation. She sighed, then said, "My father isn't coming, Justin. You've been had. My bet is that he has the obelisk and he's somewhere in the South Pacific right now, hoping that you'll stay up here long enough for him to get away and find a fence and for people to find you and think that you stole it. He'll collect the money and you'll go to jail. It's Rule Number Two—make them look one way and then go the other."

"Rule Number Two?" he asked uncertainly.

"When I was a kid, my father taught me the Five Rules of Being an Art Thief—"

"You knew what he did?"

She actually smiled as she shook her head. "I thought it was a fun game that he made up. I didn't know they were the rules of his trade."

"When did you find out the truth?" Justin asked curiously.

The amusement faded from her expression as she said dully, "I was twelve years old. I came home after school one day and I saw a big, black car in front of my grandmother's house. I walked inside the house and saw my grandmother talking to two white men in dark suits."

"FBI," he guessed, his jaw clenched in sympathy for the little girl who had discovered the truth about her father in such a heartless way.

"FBI, Interpol, LAPD . . . My grandmother and I have gotten visits from all of them over the years," she dismissed. "I don't know which agency these men were with, but as soon as I walked in the door, my grandmother told me to go to my room. Normally, I did everything she said, without question. But she looked . . . She looked scared and that made me scared. I hid in the hallway and I listened to them. They were asking her questions about Frank. They wanted to know where he was, if she had heard from him . . . They threatened her. They said she was harboring a wanted man, a thief, and that once a thief, always a thief."

"I'm sorry," Justin said sincerely, needing to touch her and caress away the pain in her eyes that she probably didn't know was there. He resisted because the need was so strong.

"It's not your fault," Lana said, with a slight smile.

Justin returned her smile because he couldn't help it, then said, "I didn't think I'd ever hear those words from you. Aren't we, men, responsible for every bad thing in the world?"

"Not every bad thing, just most of them," she said simply, but then she smiled at him. He realized it was insane—this need he had to make her smile, to take away her pain. Especially her. Lana had made it clear that she didn't need anything from him or any other man, but Justin wanted to convince her that she needed him. She needed him to make her laugh.

"What are the other four rules?"

She smiled as if she had the secret to the mystery of the pyramids, which he realized Frank had probably stolen and given to her when she was a child.

"Now if I told you, Justin, I would have to kill you," she answered with a wink.

"You still aren't taking any of this seriously," he said, amazed. "You were almost killed last night—"

"I'm still not certain that the metro incident wasn't an accident that we blew out of proportion."

He sputtered in disbelief, then said, "The look on your face last night told a different story."

She shrugged, then tossed a carrot slice in her mouth. She chewed thoughtfully for a moment, then said, "You know, you're smarter than you look."

Justin didn't want to switch subjects until he realized that she had just complimented him—sort of. "Is that supposed to be a compliment?"

"When I first met you, I wouldn't have been surprised if your knuckles dragged on the ground. I thought you were a rude, ignorant jerk. But you're not ignorant," she said matter-of-factly.

He noticed the omission of any correction of her other impressions. "I guess you can thank Clark University for that."

"You're a college graduate?"

Justin laughed dryly and drained the glass of water in front of him. "You don't have to sound so surprised."

"You're a college graduate?" she repeated, sounding more doubtful.

He rolled his eyes and set down the glass. He had made it a general rule to never mention his banking days in Atlanta. It was an old part of his life that he didn't like to think about. Except he wanted to brag. To Lana.

"I was vice president of one of the largest banks in Georgia before I threw it all in and became the man you see before you today."

"You were a banker?"

"I was one of *the* bankers. My dad had my career planned out for me since he began reciting math problems to me while I was still in my mother's womb."

She laughed. "What happened? How did you become one of society's usual suspects?"

"When I was seven years old, my parents sent me to my Uncle Dwayne's for the summer."

"Was he an art thief, too?"

Justin nearly choked on the truth he had been on the verge of telling her. He wiped at the small beads of sweat on his forehead. He shouldn't have told her this much. He should have just stayed outside, pretended to fish some more. Except he realized that he liked talking to Lana. He liked having her talk to him.

"He was a private detective," Justin said when he

realized that Lana continued to stare at him, obviously expecting further explanation. "He lived by his own rules."

"And that's what you want? To live by your own rules?"

"I thought so, but it's a lot harder than it looks," he muttered. "I thought leaving Atlanta would be the answer to all my problems; I thought that I would suddenly be happy, as if the only things wrong in my life had been the bank and my father. After the fire, I realized that I still wasn't living life on my terms. It was a sad realization. I had destroyed my relationship with my father, completely turned my life around, and I still lived according to everyone else's rules. And then one day, I heard about your father."

Lana's expression became wary and Justin told himself to shut up, but he needed her to understand.

"Don't romanticize him, Justin," she said, shaking her head. "Don't romanticize what you two do. You're stealing."

"Frank Hargrove and my uncle live life on their own terms. And that's what I've always wanted to do."

Lana studied him for a moment, then bit into another carrot slice. "How did it happen?"

Justin didn't have to ask her what she meant, because he already knew. "I wish that I had an exciting story to tell, where I rush into a burning building to save a pregnant woman and her Seeing Eye dog, but it's nothing like that," he said dryly. She didn't laugh and he suddenly felt very nervous. He had talked about the fire twice with a hospital-appointed therapist, but when the therapist had become too bored with the fire and moved on to his dysfunctional relationship with his father, Justin had never gone back. "I fell asleep and I left a pot burning on the stove."

"It was an accident."

"An accident," he repeated the word, and it sounded strange in his mouth. It seemed like such a small word to explain how much his life had changed.

"Who's Caroline?" she asked flatly. "You said her name last night."

Justin inwardly cursed. He could just imagine what Clarence would say to this bit of information. Not that the two men ever talked about Caroline or the fact that Clarence was now married to her.

"My ex-wife."

Lana obviously had not been expecting that answer, because she flinched, then stared at her carrots. She didn't take one but just moved them around the plate.

"How long were you two married?" she asked.

"Two years."

She finally looked at him. "You still love her?"

"No."

"Was she . . . The fire . . . ?"

"She wasn't hurt. We were still married at the time, but, thankfully, Caroline was out with her current husband while I was being burned alive," he muttered. When he saw the sympathy creep into Lana's eyes again, he rolled his eyes and said suspiciously, "Now that you know my sad tale, you're not going to start being nice to me again, are you?"

"No," she answered quietly, with a slight smile.

"Then why are you looking at me like that?"

"Like what?"

"I don't know," he said, shrugging. "Like I'm a Longfellow or Shortfellow or whatever those types of men are named."

"Because you have the most amazing mouth I've ever seen, and every time I look at it, I think about how it feels and how I would do almost anything to feel it again."

Justin was shocked into silence while Lana went back to her damn carrots. He coughed over his shock; then the anger and a different type of weakness flooded his body. He could almost pretend that a woman such as Lana would want him, if he didn't have to live with himself after this night was over.

"Stop it," he said through clenched teeth.

"Stop what?"

Justin stared at her speechlessly and gripped the table so that he wouldn't throw it over and drag her to the bed in the corner. "Lana, don't play with me."

"I'm not playing with you," she said in a sultry voice, then leaned across the table, and his gaze was instantly drawn to the soft pillow her breasts presented. He felt like a pervert, but he also couldn't drag his gaze from the brown skin, from the small mole at the top of her right breast.

Justin stared at her for a moment, then he stood. "I know you're bored because your usual followers aren't around to worship you, but I'm not going to provide your entertainment," he said through clenched teeth.

Her expression hardened and Justin wondered if he had seen the last of the nice and flirting Lana.

She said coolly, "I don't know who that insult is directed at more, you or me, but I'll stick up for both of us. Whether I want to sleep with you has nothing to do with pity or boredom. I sleep with a man because I want to. Obviously, I made a mistake about you."

The two stared at each other for a moment; then Justin averted his gaze and muttered, "I'm going on a walk."

He walked out of the cabin and headed toward the darkness of the trees. Far from Lana. Far from the pity and comfort that she offered but wouldn't admit.

The man was a raving lunatic, that was all Lana could think about as she paced the length of the cabin in her bare feet. Lana could admit that she had a healthy dose of self-esteem—maybe more than her share—but even she was starting to feel doubts. The next time she needed her ego trampled on, she would talk to Bruce about marriage and he would no doubt mention again how Lana was the perfect wife because she didn't care if her husband slept around on her or not.

Lana groaned in frustration, then walked onto the porch and sat on the stair so the evening air could cool off her raging temper. She was so annoyed with the men in her life. More annoyed than usual. Bruce and his ridiculous almost-marriage proposal. Her father because he was her father. And Justin. Justin had looked at her like she went around having pity sex with every man she met. Why? Because she wore short skirts? She had never had pity sex in her life! In fact, she had never had much sex in her life. And she had never propositioned a man the way she just had propositioned Justin. She allowed men to think whatever they wanted when she flirted with them, but Lana Hargrove was not as experienced as people assumed she was.

As far as she was concerned, she didn't need to sleep with men. When she did that, she lost whatever hold she once had had on them. Except Justin. She had no power over him, and she didn't want power over him. She wanted him to come to her willingly. To want her as much as she wanted him.

It was that Caroline woman, Lana decided. Justin was obviously still hung up on his ex-wife. Lana already had a picture of the woman in her mind, and she automatically hated her. She pictured a woman who always wore a respectable outfit, one of the soccer moms whom Lana sometimes had to stand behind in line the few times she dared to venture into a grocery store.

She tensed when she heard leaves crunching underfoot as Justin approached the cabin. She ignored him and continued to stare into the darkness of the trees. She really wished her stomach didn't flutter like she was back in junior high school every time he came near. She just had to catch a glimpse of him and her stomach went rolling like she was on a wild ride and her breasts felt as if a thousand butterflies had kissed them.

She shook her head when she thought how nice she had been to him. It hadn't been because he had been sick. It hadn't even been because he was the only person for her to talk to as they sat in the middle of nowhere for the last two days. It was because she liked him. The first man she liked—not lusted after or used for some reason—since probably Mickey Dalloway in tenth grade.

"I'm sorry," he said, stopping in front of her. She continued to ignore him. "When I'm wrong, I say I'm wrong. I shouldn't have reacted like that. It has nothing to do with you."

"Frankly, Justin, I don't care. If you could leave me alone, I'm trying to commune with nature." He actually burst into laughter until she glared at him. "What? You're suspicious of my motives in communing with nature, too?"

Justin tried to hide his smile but failed miserably

as he sat next to her on the porch stair. Lana rolled her eyes, pretending irritation and trying to ignore the riot of sensations that he ignited in her body with his nearness.

"I like you, Lana, a lot more than I thought I would."

"Is that supposed to make me feel better?" she snapped, glaring at him.

"After the fire and the divorce, there have been women," he explained haltingly. "But not anyone who I care about or who cares about me. And I want to keep it that way for a while. I'm still trying to sort out a lot of things—"

"Save us both this talk, Justin."

"Lana, come on," he urged, nudging her with his shoulder as if to torture her more, since explosions rocked her body from the touch. She was in hell right now. For the first time, she felt the lust and uncontrollable desire that men always claimed to feel for her, and there was nothing she could do about it. She silently apologized to each and every one of her past victims.

"I care about you," he said quietly. "And I care about your father. I don't want anything to happen that would jeopardize that."

"You're so responsible," she muttered dryly, then stood. "You promised to make me something to eat. I'm starving."

"One can of chili coming right up," he said, jumping to his feet, obviously eager to change the subject.

He looked at her and said once more, "I'm sorry. I just don't think it's a good idea for anything to happen between us."

She watched him walk into the cabin and then she smiled, because whether Justin knew it or not, he had just issued her a direct challenge. And if there was one thing Lana Hargrove could not do, it was ignore a challenge.

CHAPTER TEN

Justin stared at the twinkling stars in the night sky from the front porch of the cabin the next night, surprised by how quickly the day had passed. He and Lana had talked and eaten, and he had even coaxed her into sitting by the lake again and pretending to fish just for the hell of it. He had realized that Lana was more spoiled than he had ever imagined and that she was more generous and kind than he could ever imagine. It wasn't until that moment that Justin realized that the past two days had been the best of his adult life. And the most torturous.

Lana apparently had forgotten about last night. She treated him like a friend or, worse, like a big brother. Except that the more she treated him like a big brother, the more he wanted her in a very unbrotherly way. This morning when he had awakened on the lumpy sofa, he had looked over at her on the bed and had instantly become hard when he saw the sheet twined around her body leaving more honey-smooth skin exposed than covered. He had almost seen one full breast before she turned onto her stomach. Things had gone downhill—or maybe more appropriately up—since then. Like when they fixed lunch together and every time he turned, there she was. In his way, standing next to him, looking at him with those brown eyes. It was driving him insane. He had finally escaped to the porch, hoping she would go to sleep before he had to return to the cabin so he wouldn't have to witness the before-bed stretching she did last night that would have rivaled any G-string diva performing in a strip club.

Justin was almost buying the fantasy that he was in the mountains sharing a cabin with a friend, except he kept having to remind himself that this was all a mirage. There was no Justin Larkin, professional art thief. Justin had told her the truth about his childhood, about Caroline, about himself, but he had lied by omission about the most important thing. He wasn't really her father's friend and he wasn't really a thief. A small part of him thought that telling her the truth would make her actually like him more because then she wouldn't categorize him as a thief like her father, but the larger and more sensible part of him knew that if there was anything that Lana hated more than stealing, it was lying. She would hate him forever, and for some reason Justin Baxter, who normally didn't give a damn what anyone thought of him, didn't want this woman to hate him.

Lana walked from the cabin and sat next to him on the steps. He defensively shifted farther away from her, but she didn't seem to notice as she stared at the trees.

"I could get used to this," she said companionably. "Pave the driveway, put in an air-conditioning system and a better showerhead, redecorate in there, and add another level . . . this could be a nice place."

Justin couldn't resist laughing. "All of that would take away the whole point of the rustic retreat."

"Rustic is highly overrated," she informed him. "What would it hurt to put in wall-to-wall carpeting? The bears and trees wouldn't notice."

He shook his head with a smile until he began to notice the flare of her cheekbone, the smoothness of her skin, and her long eyelashes. He lost the ability to smile then and the ability to breathe.

She stretched her arms overhead and his gaze was drawn to her breasts that strained against the shirt. His hands ached to touch them, to touch her brown skin bathed in the white-blue glow of the moon.

"I think all this fresh air is making my lungs hurt." Then she asked dreamily, "What do you miss the most about civilization?"

"Cell phones," he muttered, because if he had one he would have called Frank and told him to watch his own daughter instead of shoving this torture on him. "What about you?"

"Massages," she murmured, then slowly stretched and began to rub her neck. "My neck is so sore. I sit in front of a computer for most of the day at home and I never feel this sore. It must be all this fresh air and exercise."

He stared at the length of her neck as her head fell back under her own hands. His mouth suddenly went dry when she moaned deep in her throat. It was the type of moan that a woman made for a man. He instantly became hard, although he didn't think he had stopped being hard since watching her eat the canned peaches for dessert with juice that she kept dribbling on her fingers and licking off with her skilled pink tongue.

He could no longer resist. He touched her. Just her cheek with his thumb, but then his thumb moved down to her neck and lower to the line between her breasts. Her eyes opened and she froze, staring at him.

"What are you doing, Justin?" she whispered.

He moved closer to her on the stair, encasing her against the railing. The salty sweetness of her skin beckoned to him, but he barely restrained the urge and moved his hand to her hair, which had dried naturally in the air from yesterday and was now a soft cloud of brown warmth.

"Touching you," he responded softly.

"I told you not to do that without my permission."

"You told me not to kiss you without your permission," he corrected her softly, moving his mouth only inches from hers.

"What about the caring-about-me part?" she asked

carefully, but he felt the tremble of her body as his hand gently ran from her cheek to her neck and the soft skin above her breasts. "You weren't going to touch me because you care about me, remember?"

Justin smiled when he realized what the day had been about. Lana proving that she could get him to do whatever she wanted. And now he saw the wariness in her expression when she realized that her plan had worked. She had succeeded and it was too late for Justin to control himself. He had spent too long wanting her, being close enough to her to touch her.

"You've been trying to seduce me all day, haven't you?" he murmured, then licked her neck like he would have an ice-cream cone.

Her skin was hot and soft under his tongue and he felt, more than heard, her moan. He didn't know that the taste of her would make him half-insane, but it did. He barely managed to keep his one hand gentle as he continued to rub the soft skin above the neckline of her shirt.

"Justin—"

"It worked," he whispered, before he placed another open-mouth kiss on her neck. "I'm seduced."

She sounded breathless as she whispered hesitantly, "Maybe you were right and we shouldn't—"

"You want to know when you first had me?" he whispered, his mouth moving to her ear to lick the shell. There was that intriguing moan from her again. His other hand moved lower to rest on her knee, and whether she knew it or not, her legs opened slightly, offering him access. "I had been resisting just barely all day, until the peaches. Seeing you lick things . . . it's too much for a mere man to resist."

"I don't know what you're talking about," she lied badly.

"Remember, I'm smarter than I look, Lana," he said, then cupped one beautiful breast with his hand.

He nearly lost control at that moment. Some men would have said her breasts were too big or maybe too little, but she was just right for him. She flowed out of his hand and made him think of hard loving and soft loving and everything in between. It had been too long for him. Since he had met Frank and had researched his life and found Lana, Justin had not touched another woman. It had never occurred to him until that moment that he had been waiting for Lana. No other woman would do when he had dreams about the woman in his arms. Dreams, he was beginning to realize, that did not fit the reality.

Her head was thrown back and her eyes closed and he placed another kiss on her neck. Justin traced her thick bottom lip with his thumb and was satisfied when her eyes opened and desire danced in their depths.

His voice was low as he asked, "Why'd you do it, Lana? Just to prove that you could?"

"I already told you. I want you," she said, then ran one hand down his face. The scar-free side, he noted. Her other hand rubbed his arm, squeezed his bicep, which involuntarily flexed as a result.

"Why?" he pressed.

She shocked him by placing a hand on his hardness and rubbing one long, slow stroke up and down it through his pants. "Do you have to ask?" she whispered, holding his gaze.

Her gaze was too direct, too intense. It made him think about the truth, who he really was and who she thought he was. He stared at her breasts instead. Then he murmured, "You had your chance to get away, Lana. Just remember when you're crying for mercy that you caused this."

"I'll remember," she said, sounding more excited than scared.

Lana wouldn't have left the porch at that moment unless dynamite dislodged her, but at the look that suddenly crossed Justin's face, she had the urge to run. He looked like he was walking the fine line between control and sheer, dangerous recklessness. She had finally pushed him to the edge. And it was exhilarating and scary all at once. But life was nothing without fear, and while she would be scared of finally trusting a man enough to give him her heart, she would never fear that Justin would hurt her physically.

She abruptly pushed from him and stood to her feet to reestablish her equilibrium and to look down on him. If she forgot that she was supposed to be the one in control, then she would definitely lose her heart, and that couldn't happen. After her pep talk, she turned to him again, intent upon making him see her as the sexpot she pretended to be, except whatever remark she was going to say died on her lips. There would be no pretending with Justin.

If anything his expression became more unreadable and his gaze darker as he moved toward her. She hadn't realized she took a step back until she bumped against the porch railing.

Justin lifted one eyebrow in question and he stopped. She forced herself to hold her ground as Justin watched her. She felt a confusing series of trembles quiver through her body as the scent of the soap he had washed with floated around her and caused strange sparks of intense emotion throughout her body.

"You aren't scared of me, are you?" he asked, concerned.

"Never," she said, sounding much braver than she felt.

She *was* scared of him. Scared of how he made her feel. Weak and under his power. She had kissed many men, she had even made love to some, although a lot fewer than most people would think, but none had made her feel like Justin did. Just by standing next to her, looking at her, he could make her do anything he asked. And that would mean she would lose her pride, and losing her pride was something Lana Hargrove would never tolerate.

"Having second thoughts?" he asked, for some reason still not kissing her, still not taking her in his arms. Her hands balled into fists, because she refused to make the first move, especially since she was shaking so much. Shaking from something that was supposed to be as insignificant and unimportant as sex, or at least that's what everyone wanted people to believe. Except she knew that there would be nothing insignificant and unimportant about sex with this man.

"Don't worry about me. Nothing will happen that I don't want to happen," she responded, in a voice that shook slightly from emotion.

The concerned expression on his face didn't leave as he caressed her cheek. Almost like a lover, not a one-night stand, would have done.

"We don't have to do this, Lana."

"You don't want me?" she asked uncertainly.

He laughed for some unknown reason; then his amusement disappeared as his intense gaze traveled over her face and rested on her mouth. She forgot about pride and anything else not related to his mouth. She licked her lips in anticipation. His hands settled on her shoulders, then ran down her arms to entwine his fingers with hers. He moved even closer to her, until his body and the hard feel of him through his pants pressed her against the railing. She sighed at the contact.

She thought he would kiss her, but he didn't. Instead, he moved as if in slow motion, raising her shirt only a few inches. His right hand released hers and moved slowly under her shirt to gently touch her stomach, as if he expected her to stop him. When she only sighed again, his answering grin caused a wave of heat to wash over her. His hand traveled over her smooth skin, the hardness of his palm making her feel surprisingly delicate. His hand traveled up and up and then under her shirt until he covered one satin-swathed breast and squeezed. Hard.

Cool air circled around her bared stomach, but it did little to penetrate the heat that he caused in her body by his touch. The warmth that made her breath come out in shortened gasps began to swirl around her body as he massaged one breast, then the other in a slow rhythm as if he and Lana had all the time in the world. His other hand continued to imprison hers at her side as he lowered his mouth to the crook of her neck, the rough feel of his cheek scraping along her shoulder with delicious aftereffects. She wrapped her free hand around his neck, running her fingers through the silki-ness of his hair.

She sighed his name as he kissed the nipple of one breast through the lace. He hadn't even kissed her yet and already she wanted to scream his name and shat-ter the stillness of the night. She squirmed against his body and the porch railing as she felt his hand move to the zipper at the back of her skirt. He momentarily paused as if waiting for her to protest. When she said nothing, he pulled it down, creating a soft song in the still night to combine with the crickets' chirping and other rustling sounds of the forest.

Her eyes slid closed and she rested her forehead against his chest as his hand reached underneath her skirt and inside her cotton, not-very-sexy underwear. One part of her mind noticed the way his tongue ran over her neck and the soft kisses that followed the length and she wondered if she would have a mark there the next day, but her entire body was focused on the lazy way he trailed his fingers through her feminine curls and then lower and lower until she bucked against his hand. She threw back her head at the searing hot riot of sensations he released with one circular movement of his hand. He slowly moved one finger inside of her and it felt invasive and welcoming all at once. She shifted and then it felt nothing but delicious and she hummed in delight. He met her shocked gaze and the slow smile he gave her made her clutch his shoulders and bite her bottom lip to keep from screaming for more.

"You feel so good, Lana." His voice sounded deep and strained as his lips tickled against her skin, his moist breath on her neck driving her a little crazier as it mixed with her damp sweat. He turned his head until his lips hovered over hers, close enough for her to feel their heat. "You're so wet. I shouldn't have done this here. I should have waited—"

"Don't stop," she gasped, the only words she was capable of forming as she heard the hesitation in his voice.

"Not now, baby."

"Don't stop," she repeated, more as a frantic plea than an order, as she squeezed his hand that still imprisoned hers. "Please don't stop."

Then he began to kiss her. His tongue moved in her mouth, soft and hard, demanding and giving. There were too many emotions centered in different parts of her body. She thought she was being torn apart. He could have given lessons in kissing. He could have given lessons in making her feel cherished. Lana dug her nails into his shoulder and continued to squeeze his hand still in hers.

She couldn't control the movement of her hips as his finger worked faster, now joined by a second one, driving her closer and closer to the point of no return. Just when she knew she would explode, he stopped. His hands left her body. She grunted in protest until she realized that he was trying to speak.

"Inside," he finally managed in between pants of breath.

Lana nodded and walked inside the cabin. He followed close behind, slamming the door and locking them inside.

CHAPTER ELEVEN

Her body still hummed with need and desire and the promised fulfillment as Justin led her toward the bed. He was everywhere as he hovered over her and she sank into the softness of the bed. She wanted him everywhere. She wanted to taste him everywhere. She thought he would pounce on her, but instead he softly moved strands of hair from her face. Though the lights in the cabin were dimmed, she saw the tenderness on his face, and she bit her bottom lip to prevent the tears and her own feelings of tenderness. No man—not even the numerous ones who had proclaimed their love to her, who had showered her with gifts—had ever looked at her like that, as if she was only his and he would fight to the death to make certain it would always be that way.

"Can we take this a little slow at first?" she said hesitantly. "Just because I . . . I . . ."

"You're running the show," he told her in a low,

husky voice that seemed deeper and richer than she had ever heard it before. "I'm just a willing participant."

She laughed and it felt strange to laugh when her body was as tense as a spring, but with him it also felt right.

"I think we're both stars of this show," she said, smiling.

He grinned and she had to touch his mouth to see if it was real. He kissed the fingers she placed on his mouth; then he said, "Let's take turns running the show then."

He slowly lay on top of her, and she saw his smile right before he pressed his mouth against hers. At first, their kisses were hesitant, uncertain, as if they hadn't just almost kissed each other to orgasms on the porch. Then gradually the awkwardness faded and their kisses became more urgent, more passionate, deeper. As if in a dream, her hands moved around his neck and she pulled him closer. She wanted to feel every inch of him against her; every cell of his she wanted to connect with hers. And it was like everything was right and perfect and she didn't need to worry about doing anything wrong because nothing would be wrong with Justin.

His hands moved to caress her face and his powerful legs rested alongside her body, drawing her into his full protective cocoon. Through her skirt, she felt the hard length of him, the muscles in his legs. His hands gently tugged strands of her hair as he broke their kiss and just looked at her. He placed a soft kiss on first one eyelid, then the other.

Then it happened. He hadn't kissed her like in her bedroom; he hadn't touched her like on the porch only a few minutes ago. And her clothes were still on. He was just gentle, and no man had ever been gentle with her, and that was enough. The waves started in the far corners of her body, then intensified and crashed into one spot that made her wrap her legs around him and scream his name at the top of her lungs.

When the last ember faded into a pleasant glow, Lana felt the sweat on her forehead, between her breasts, and the intense embarrassment as Justin continued to watch her.

"Maybe we should go a little slower," he teased in a voice as smooth as a syrup.

Lana actually laughed again, and he kissed her again. His tongue slipped inside her mouth and she felt as if they had done it a thousand times. He unbuttoned his shirt and she stared hungrily at the T-shirt he wore underneath it. As he pulled that over his head, she openly eyed the bulge in his pants. She licked her lips and didn't feel the slightest shame when he caught her staring at him. Nor embarrassment. He grinned and continued to undress and she realized that she had missed this the most, not being able to watch a man do the small things, like pull his T-shirt off by the back of the collar, that a woman didn't do.

He climbed into bed again and lay next to her. He touched her back and she stretched like a hedonistic animal. He traced one finger down her spine and she moved into his touch, lying on the bed next to him. She stared at his beautiful eyes, then couldn't resist touching his face, careful not to touch or even look at the scarred side because she didn't want him to stop and she knew the reminder of his scars might make him stop. She never wanted him to stop.

She stared at his muscled chest. He always seemed so big, but he was leaner than she had thought. And definitely more chiseled than she had imagined. And he had more scars from the fire on his chest and back, and for the first time she realized that he probably should have died in that fire. She traced the outline of his pectoral muscle and felt the hardened, scarred skin. She wanted to kiss it, but instead she touched his flat stomach, which caused him to hiss and suck in his stomach. She removed her hand before it went even lower like it wanted to.

"You're beautiful, Justin," she whispered.

"And you're nice," he murmured in return, patiently watching her examine him, except she saw his muscles bunch in his arms. He apparently wasn't that patient. "Is it my turn yet?"

She smiled and shook her head. He sighed in relief and murmured, "Good."

She swung one leg over to straddle him, her skirt riding up her thighs to her waist, then kissed him on the mouth. It wasn't a simple kiss. It was a kiss she had saved all of her life for the one man who made her feel as Justin did. She swept her tongue through his mouth, twirling with his tongue like two ropes in a rodeo. Her hands swept over his body, feeling the hard muscle, digging into the firmness of his skin.

Justin responded by running his fingers through her hair and down her body to cup her behind through her underwear to press her against his groin. Her thin clothes were the only barrier between them and she had a feeling he was waiting for a sign from her on when they should be removed. She couldn't think about clothes at a moment like this, though. Her body flowed with the response of his and she reflexively began to ground against him. She dragged her tongue along his neck, his beautiful brown neck, then placed an open-mouth kiss on his hard chest, twirling her tongue around his tiny nipples, which made him flinch with each swipe of her tongue.

His eyes reflected black in the darkness as he guided her head so he could have her mouth again and then he rolled her onto her back. He rested his arms on either side of her face and gasped for air as he stared at her. She matched his raging breaths as she tried to control her own body's response.

It was another explosive kiss, another spark that started the fire within her that only Justin knew about. He growled deep in his throat, then began a sensual attack that left her shivering and sweating at the same time in the bed. She didn't know how or when he got rid of their clothes, but one second she felt like her skirt and blouse were in the way of feeling his skin and the next second all she felt was bare skin against bare skin.

Justin nipped her bottom lip, then he dragged his tongue across her lower lip to soothe and placate. He hovered above her once more and she met his gaze. Lana wanted to ask him what he saw, but he abruptly leaned off the bed and reached for his pants on the floor. She smiled in relief when she saw the small square package he pulled out of a pocket.

Before she could remember how to form words to ask him if he needed help, she felt him nudging at her entrance. She gasped when he abruptly surged into her, enough to make her scream in surprise.

He instantly stopped moving and looked at her, concerned. Under the moonlight, sweat glistened on his forehead, chest, and arms from the strain, but he waited and loomed over her.

"What is it, darlin'?" he asked, concerned.

Lana almost told him to get off her because he was too big, but then he moved slightly and she lost her breath at the sinful pleasure that washed over her. He felt so good. He felt thick and powerful and all hers. Justin smiled in male satisfaction, then slowly began to move. His body tensed as his pace quickened and Lana groaned from the magical feel of him.

She had never felt this out of control, so she dug her fingernails into Justin's shoulders to anchor herself. The pace continued and Lana thought she could stay that way forever while the feelings grew and grew until it became unbearable and she exploded with a scream. Justin followed her with his own groan, then he lay on top of her, breathing hard, warming her with his weight.

He touched her cheek, in reverence.

Lana sent him a weak smile, since she didn't think she had the energy to do more. He smoothed a hand over her hair, then dragged one hand around her waist and held her hand with his other one. She didn't know how active she would be, but she was willing to make another attempt. But when she looked at him, his eyes were closed and her hand was safely encased in his.

CHAPTER TWELVE

Moonlight filtered through the open windows into the room, elongating the shadows. Justin felt the moment she woke up. She had been lying on his chest, but she shifted, moving off of him. He felt the loss, but he did nothing. It was probably for the best that she was already distancing herself from him.

The woman had rocked his world with her sincere and almost hesitant responses, and if she thought that she could roll over and go to sleep, she had another think coming. Justin needed answers and he needed them now, because her responses and her tightness, her wetness—which made him sweat just thinking about how velvety she felt—had meant something important.

"What just happened here, Lana?" he asked quietly.

"For a man who knows how to make it happen

pretty easily, you should know," she said flippantly, but she kept her back to him.

Since the indirect approach wasn't going to work, he asked flatly, "How many men have you been with?"

She turned to him, her annoyance obvious in her expression. "How am I supposed to answer that question, Justin? If I give you a high number, your fragile male ego will be bruised—"

He smiled, then placed his index finger on her mouth. She instantly stopped talking and stared at him in surprise.

"Don't worry about my fragile male ego; just tell me the truth."

He removed his finger and she said defiantly, "Well, if you count college and my time in DC and then there were my free-spirit years, and the time I spent in Europe with Pauline . . . one."

He tried to hide his shock. He really did, but he was lying naked in a bed next to a woman who had just made him believe in pots of gold at the ends of rainbows, leprechauns, and every other magical thing that was out there.

He cleared his throat and said hesitantly, "You've only been with . . . had sex . . . any type of sex . . . with one man?"

"Yes," she said, her chin stubbornly set.

"But your . . . You move . . . I . . ." Justin's voice trailed off when he noticed how her eyes narrowed.

He ignored her protests and pulled her into his arms. She eventually snuggled against his chest, but he could feel the tension in her shoulders. He rubbed one shoulder for a moment, trying to control his emotions. She was not what he expected.

Although he hadn't been thinking much when she had been squirming under his hands and mouth, a small part of him had used her obvious experience as an excuse for making love to her while she still thought he was Justin Larkin. He had thought she was experienced enough to protect her heart. That had been idiotic thinking, because their lovemaking had been anything but safe. And he had been wrong about her, wrong about himself. This had become infinitely more complicated than he had ever imagined. Justin had loved Caroline, obviously not enough for her or himself, but he had. But kissing her had been nothing like this. For the first time, he knew what he had been searching for when he left Atlanta. And he was going to lose it the moment Lana knew the truth.

"Thanks, Justin. I never felt self-conscious about my lack of sexual experience until this moment. You're such a confidence-builder," she said dryly, breaking the silence that extended between them.

He kissed her forehead to assuage the doubt he heard under the sarcasm. He asked quietly, "Why me? Why now?"

"What else am I supposed to do in the middle of the Enchanted Forest?" she asked, with a casual shrug.

"Serious time, Lana. Why me? Why now?"

"I don't know," she said, sounding as confused as he felt.

He shook his head. "I don't understand."

"I have high standards. I refuse to hop into bed with just any man who asks me, and believe me, there have been numerous men, countless men; the number of men could form a line from this cabin back to civilization—"

"I get the picture," he said, with a frown.

"Good," she murmured, then snuggled deeper into his arms. One of her hands began to run distractedly across his chest and he felt the stirrings of lust and something else he didn't want to name bring life to his body, which, moments before he had thought would need a coma-induced sleep to rejuvenate itself.

He abruptly smiled and said, "So I meet Lana Hargrove's impeccable high standards?"

"Believe me, it surprised me, too," she muttered, then pressed a kiss on his nipple. He was surprised by the strength of the shudder that wracked his body. He never had known how sensitive his nipples were.

"Is it my turn yet?" he asked, pretending impatience, but he could spend the rest of his life having to "suffer" through her turns.

"OK," she said begrudgingly, but her eyes twinkled as she stared at him.

All the reasons that Justin should have jumped out of the bed—like his job, Frank, the agency—disappeared and it was just the two of them. For right now, he didn't want to think about any of that; he just wanted to make love to her again.

He nipped her lips, first the top one, then the bottom. She clung to his lips a moment longer, then slowly released his bottom lip, and Justin almost lost whatever control he had left.

Justin momentarily pulled from her and saw the passion in her eyes, the desire for him. He swallowed the sudden lump in his throat.

"Lana—"

She kissed him again before he could speak. Justin had been married, he had even been in love, but he had never known such acceptance from anyone as he felt in Lana's kiss.

She framed his face and said quietly, "You only get one turn a night, Justin, so make the most of it."

Justin didn't know whether to kiss her or check her temperature because she had implied there would be other nights. So, instead, he pushed the sheet from her shoulders and stared at her breasts. For the first time that night, she didn't try to hide from his gaze, but she stuck out her chest. Justin bent his head and gently kissed her nipple. He would never grow tired of the gasp that drew from her. Each and every time he did it. His other hand went to her other breast and delicately plucked her nipple, drawing more short gasps that made him harder than any other woman ever had.

Lana audibly sighed and pressed his head and co-incidentally his mouth closer. Justin took one full breast into his mouth, then pulled away slowly, torturously, until the brown globe popped from his mouth, glistening with his kiss. He traced the length of her neck as she shuddered in response, pure enjoyment and anticipation on her face. And in that moment Justin almost felt like a full man again.

And Justin could no longer lie to her. He had to tell her the truth, about himself, about the agency, about why he was following her. Justin suddenly knew how his wife had felt when she blurted out to him in the hospital after the fire that she was in love with someone else. She hadn't done it to hurt him; she had done it because she loved Justin even then and she couldn't stand the secrets between them anymore.

"Lana—"

She screamed as the door suddenly flew open. Justin threw her behind him on the bed and faced the dark shape that stumbled into the cabin. Justin's outrage turned into confusion as he watched a man stagger for a few feet, his face covered by a dark hood; then the man collapsed. There was no other sound as the heap lay in the middle of the floor.

"Justin," Lana whispered, peering around his shoulder as she clutched the sheet between her breasts.

Justin jumped from the bed, dragging the blanket around his waist. He carefully crossed the room, then knelt next to the still man. He slowly recognized the dark green coat the man wore and instantly turned the man over on his side. There was the familiar peanut-brown-colored face of Frank Hargrove. Justin heard Lana's gasp of shock and disbelief as Frank's eyes fluttered open for a moment.

Frank's familiar smile crossed his face, along with a spasm of pain. "I always did know how to make an entrance," Frank muttered; then he fell unconscious again.

That was when Justin saw the blood.

Lana crossed her arms over her chest as she stood near the window and watched her father lying on the sofa. He had been stabbed in the right thigh and had lost a lot of blood. Justin had cleaned the wound and bandaged it in the morning light; then he had taken Frank's car, which had been haphazardly parked a few yards from the front door with the engine still running, and tried to find a doctor in the nonexistent town that was apparently a few miles away. Lana had been left alone with Frank Hargrove, and she had nothing to say to him. Fortunately for them both, Frank was sleeping, completely oblivious to the world, which was probably best, considering the pain he would be in otherwise.

Lana studied her father's familiar face. He looked exactly the same. There were a few more lines around his eyes and his once-black curls were now liberally littered with silver, but he was still her father. Still tall and lean, still with a smart retort and a quick smile. Even near death he had been acting as if he were on stage at a comedy show. Lana didn't know what she expected. Maybe she expected him to look as different as he had acted for the last twenty years, because the father she had known when she was a child would never have left her.

Frank groaned in his sleep and Lana had to prevent herself from going to him. And it upset her that she actually cared. She told herself that she shouldn't care about a man who had abandoned her.

"Hi, Peanut."

Lana whirled around at the sound of her father's voice. He sounded tired and old and amused. For some reason, it was the amused part that made her angry.

"Justin went to find a doctor," she said stiffly.

Frank didn't appear to care about his pain or about Justin. Instead, he watched her closely and his trademark cavalier grin completely disappeared.

"You're wearing it," he said softly. Her hand instantly went to the sapphire pendant that hung around her neck. "Do you remember when you gave that to me? The night I left you at your grandmother's house?"

"No," she lied defensively.

He studied her for a moment as if he knew she was lying; then he asked, "They didn't hurt you, did they?"

"No. And who are they? I've spent the last two days hiding from the bogey monster."

Frank hesitated, then abruptly grinned, as if she hadn't just asked him a question. "I'm so proud of you, Peanut. Your grandma would have been proud, too. You accomplished everything that she wanted for you."

"I know."

Frank laughed in a short snort that ended in a grunt of pain as he shifted on the sofa. "Are you going to hate me forever?"

"I was planning on it," she retorted, then walked toward the refrigerator and yanked it open.

"What can I do?" he said, with a shrug of surrender. "You have my mouth and your mother's intelligence. I'm no match for you."

Lana rolled her eyes in annoyance and was preparing to tell him exactly what he could do, which included leaving the cabin even if he had to crawl out the door, when Justin walked into the cabin. Even though Lana was still shocked and angry at her father's appearance, at his acting as if the two ran across each other every day, she couldn't help but feel the slight dip in her stomach at the sight of Justin.

With just his mere presence, she could remember every emotion he had evoked in her the previous night, every kiss, every touch. And in the cabin, under her father's watchful gaze, she felt a little embarrassed. Even though Frank had rarely been around to play the role of father, she still felt as if she had been caught with her hand in the cookie jar. Frank had been unconscious when Lana and Justin showered and changed into their clothes, but Lana still wondered if Frank had heard or seen anything.

Justin glanced at Lana, then quickly walked across the room and sat on the sofa. Lana's welcome died on her mouth at Justin's strangely neutral greeting. He had only been gone a couple of hours, but she had expected at least some acknowledgment that the two had spent a few hours wrapped in each other's bodies.

"I got some antibiotics and painkillers from the local veterinarian. The only doctor in this area is sixty miles away," he said as he handed Frank different bottles of pills.

"A vet gave you painkillers to use on a person?" Lana asked, surprised. She realized how stupid her question was when both Justin and Frank sent her identical glances. She had momentarily forgotten in her orgasm-induced haze that Justin and Frank didn't ask for or wait to receive anything; they took whatever they could.

"Lana, get Frank a glass of water," Justin ordered as he unscrewed the bottles.

Lana narrowed her eyes and crossed her arms over her chest, refusing to move. Frank looked at her, amusement dancing in his eyes. He nudged Justin, who was still trying to open the bottle.

"Either you have to get me the glass of water or I have to hop over there on one leg, but my Peanut isn't going anywhere," Frank told Justin.

Justin glanced at Lana and for a moment she thought he would take her father's side, that he would make her get the water for a man she had vowed not to ever give anything, not even her sympathy. Then Justin stood and walked across the room. He filled a glass with water from the faucet, the running water the only sound in the tense cabin. He returned to Frank's side and handed the glass to him.

Frank broke the silence, "As soon as I've had enough rest, we have to get back to DC."

Justin nodded and said, "You and I can leave tonight."

Lana noticed that Justin didn't include her in the traveling show. She tried not to feel insulted, but the longer Justin kept his back to her, refusing to look at her, the more insulted she became. Of course, she could be insulted or just plain hurt; she wasn't certain which.

Frank apparently noticed that Justin had left out Lana, too, because he glanced at her, then said to Justin, "Lana has to come with us."

"No," Justin said at the same time that Lana snapped, "No."

Justin glanced at her but then quickly looked back at her father. Lana narrowed her eyes at Justin's broad back. It wasn't her sudden insecurity. Justin could not meet her gaze.

Frank ignored Lana momentarily and said to Justin, "We need to get into Lattimore's house to look for the obelisk."

"I'll do it alone," Justin said while shaking his head.

"It's a two-man job, Bubba," Frank said with a soft smile of regret; then he glanced at Lana and added, "Or, in this case, it's a one-woman, one-man job."

"If you think I'm going to break the law for you or for him, those painkillers must be working really fast," Lana said simply as she sat in the chair at the kitchen table.

She crossed one leg over the other, slowly, making certain that her skirt rode sufficiently high, while she watched Justin closely for a reaction. His only reaction was to turn his back to her to take the glass her father had drained to the sink. It was as if he didn't notice her anymore. Her legs that had caused traffic jams. Lana frowned, then uncrossed her legs and tried to pull her skirt down.

Oblivious to her performance, Frank said, "Justin and I need you, Lana."

"No, we don't," Justin snapped, whirling around to Frank.

Lana was surprised and annoyed by the anger on Justin's face. He couldn't wait to be rid of her. Typical man. She wouldn't make that mistake again— confusing lust and desire with concern.

"Yes, we do," Frank said, with a tired sigh. "Lattimore lives in a fortress, Justin. One man cannot do it alone. In fact, two men couldn't do it. But one woman, who knows someone invited to a private party being held at the aforementioned fortress two days from now, could easily get into the house—"

"What are you talking about, Frank?" Justin asked irritably.

"Lana's boyfriend, Bruce Longfellow," he answered simply, staring at Lana.

Lana shouldn't have been surprised that Frank knew about Bruce, but she was. She could have taught seminars on the art of making a man jealous, but the brief flash of jealousy in Justin's eyes also surprised her. He didn't have anything to be jealous about—any thoughts of Bruce had been ruined after the first kiss in her town house, but Justin didn't need to know that. If he cared.

Lana pushed aside her thoughts of Justin and asked her father, "How do you know about Bruce?"

"He's a hard guy to miss," Frank said, with a hint of distaste. "You talk to him for five minutes and you know that he's a Longfellow and that it means something. What it means, he can't tell you, but he can tell you it means something."

"You've spoken to Bruce?" Lana asked angrily, narrowing her eyes.

"Only for a few minutes," Frank said defensively. Lana glared at Justin when he made a strange cough that sounded suspiciously like laughter.

Lana turned back to her father, who was trying hard to look innocent, except his twinkling eyes made that an impossibility. She warned through clenched teeth, "I swear, old man, if you stole anything from Bruce, I'll—"

"I didn't take anything from Longfellow," he quickly interrupted, but his averted gaze made Lana vow to discreetly make certain that Bruce's belongings were accounted for. Frank quickly changed the subject, "Anyways, he's our ticket into Lattimore's party."

She shook her head. "No."

"I agree. Longfellow needs to stay far, far away from Lana," Justin said quickly.

"It's the only way. I've studied the floor plans to Lattimore's house backward and forward. There are no vulnerabilities, no discreet points of entry. We need his help to break into it so we can get the obelisk before Grimes finds me and disables my other leg."

"Grimes," Justin said, instantly alert. "Seth Grimes? What does he have to do with any of this?"

"Who is Seth Grimes? Wait. I don't care about the Days of our Cat Burglar Lives. The answer is still no," Lana said simply.

"Why are you so certain that the obelisk is in Lattimore's home?" Justin asked, pointedly ignoring Lana's glare.

"I saw it," Frank answered. "I saw one of Lattimore's goons transfer it into his fortress late last night, the same night that I got stabbed. One of them caught me from behind. Somehow I got away and I drove straight here."

"You should have gone to the hospital first. You've lost a lot of blood."

"I wanted to reach you," Frank said, an urgent tone in his voice. "You have to get the obelisk before he takes it somewhere else, sells it, or destroys it."

"Why would he do that?" Lana demanded.

"To destroy me," Frank said simply. "I was contracted to acquire the obelisk by Seth Grimes—"

"There's that name again," she said, with a sigh of exasperation. "Who is he?"

"You don't want to know, but when you make a contract with Seth Grimes, if you fail, he doesn't take you to court to pay him back."

"Why are you doing business with a man like that, Frank?" Justin demanded angrily.

"Because I knew Lattimore wanted the obelisk, too, and I wanted to get it before he could. The only person who could bankroll that operation is Grimes." Frank didn't look as carefree and unconcerned as he sounded, and Lana realized that Seth Grimes was as serious as Justin looked.

"The obelisk could already be gone," Justin said, shrugging. "Just because you saw it being taken to Lattimore's house last night doesn't mean it will still be there during this party."

Lana noticed a strange light gleaming in Frank's eyes as he smiled. "It's still there because Lattimore wants me to try and get it. It was his plan all along, Justin. I thought that he wanted to frame me for the theft and get me in deep with Grimes, but there's more to it than that. He wants to be the one to catch me. I have to get the obelisk; Lattimore has it and Lattimore knows that I know he has it. We have to get it back before Grimes loses patience."

Lana decided that she was done being ignored and she got to her feet. Both men looked at her as if surprised she was still there.

"You two are insane," she said, matter-of-factly. "I'm going home now."

She should have made that announcement a long time ago, because Justin was suddenly across the cabin, standing in between her and the door and actually looking at her.

"You're still in danger, Lana," he said in a tight voice that didn't sound anything like the gentle tone he had used when he whispered her name while they were in bed.

"If Lattimore has gone through all of this trouble to get me, you're not safe," Frank agreed.

"I can't believe that we're standing here accusing Xavier Lattimore of . . . I'm not sure what we're accusing him of, but it doesn't sound good," she snapped, annoyed. "You two are the thieves, not Xavier Lattimore. I'm going home."

"You're not going anywhere," Justin said, suddenly angry. "You promised to stay here unless Frank didn't show up. He's here."

"I lied," she retorted. "You two do that often enough to know how it works."

Justin's eyes narrowed and he said, "I have the keys to the only operating vehicle. Unless you want to hitchhike the ten miles to town, you're going to stick around until we figure out this mess."

"You can't tell me what to do," Lana said, her anger making her face hot.

"He just did," Frank cheerfully chirped from his position on the sofa.

Justin glared at Frank and muttered, "You're not

helping." Justin turned to Lana and said gently, "Lana, your father was stabbed. Don't you want to help him? Help me?"

Lana felt her resolve crumble a little, just because Justin had turned on the charm, just because he acknowledged her. Just because she loved him. She almost staggered at the self-revelation. She loved Justin Larkin, a cat burglar, a criminal, a man who could sleep with her one night and ignore her the next day. Her back grew ramrod-straight. He was just like her father. He only wanted her when it suited his purposes. Last night he had been horny. Today he was not. It was that simple to him. She had been the foolish one to fall in love.

"No," she said through clenched teeth.

"Lana." Her father's voice was surprisingly calm and sober and she looked at him, surprised. "Xavier Lattimore is the man who killed your mother."

Silence filled the cabin as Lana and her father started at each other. For the first time in several days, Lana even forgot about Justin. Her father's eyes shone with unshed tears and an anger so fierce that Lana took an involuntary step away from him. She had never been scared of her father, but a part of her was now. As if Frank understood his emotions were too powerful, his expression melted into a blank mask.

Lana could only react in a way that wouldn't hurt her. She laughed. Her disbelieving laughter resounded through the cabin. "You expect me to believe that

Xavier Lattimore, one of the most powerful men in Washington, DC, killed my mother?"

For once, Frank didn't smile or have a flippant comeback prepared. Instead, he stared at her with that blank expression and that uncharacteristic reaction alone made Lana's laughter fade.

"You seriously believe that Lattimore killed Mom," she whispered, surprised.

"I was a thief—and a lot worse, but I went legitimate. It was hard, and just when I thought I couldn't stand another day of honest labor, which includes honest money and being honest-poor, I met Bea. She made it easy. Not because she nagged or asked or threatened to leave me if I did, but because I wanted to be a better man, an honest man for her and for our children. When Lattimore took her away from me, I went back to that life, except now I don't steal for the money or the thrill." Frank's expression hardened as he finished quietly, "Now, I do it to make Lattimore pay for what he's done. Every painting I steal, every jewel, every damn vase . . . It all belongs to Lattimore in some way. Whether he owns the art, does business with the owner, owns the building where the art is housed, or employs the person who owns it, it all connects to him. Over the last twenty years, I've cost him millions of dollars and it's starting to take a toll. People are starting to question him, question his business instincts, question giving him their money. Rich people don't like losing things, and it's now clear that when you deal with Lattimore, you could lose a lot. I can't prove he killed her, but I know he's responsible for it."

Lana shook her head, almost feeling sorry for her father. "Mom died when she ran into the street and a car hit her. It was an accident—"

Frank shook his head and said firmly, "Lattimore was in Los Angeles that day, Lana. She was running from him, or maybe he pushed her, I'm not sure how it happened. I just know that he's responsible."

Lana's response died on her lips at the fire in Frank's eyes. He was telling the truth. She glanced at Justin to see if he had known, but he looked as surprised as she felt.

"Why?" Lana asked, confused. "How would Lattimore even know her?"

"Lattimore and I grew up together."

"And you both knew Mom from Oakland?"

Frank visibly hesitated, then said, "Lattimore knew your mother from DC. Lattimore had been trying to get me to work with him again, but I had always refused . . . He flew me out to DC one day and I met Bea."

"He knew her first?" Lana pressed.

Frank groaned in frustration and said impatiently, "All of that is not important. You just need to know that Lattimore was obsessed with your mother. Since we were kids in Oakland, he had always gotten everything he wanted—either through force and intimidation or through money—but he couldn't have your mother, and that drove him insane. He sent her letters, he called so much that we had to change our phone number several times, he would show up at her job unannounced. Bea and I thought he would eventually realize that he could never have her, but I should have known. That man doesn't ever give up. He must have confronted Bea . . . He must have paid someone to drive—"

"You're lying," she interrupted, grateful that her voice didn't crack.

"No, I'm not."

Her whole life, when she had accused her father of lying, he had always laughed and admitted it. He didn't do that this time.

Lana didn't know what to do except walk out of the cabin and ignore Frank calling her name.

"That did not go how I planned," Frank muttered while running his hands over his forehead as if to rub away the thoughts and memories.

Justin shook his head in disbelief, then glanced out the window for Lana. She was nowhere to be seen. He wanted to go after her, make certain that she was fine, hold her. He didn't move precisely because there was such a gnawing need for him to do so. Last night had been better than his best fantasy, but it had all been make-believe.

"Should I go after her?" he asked uncertainly.

"She needs time to cool off," Frank said, shaking his head. "I tried to think of a million different ways to tell her the truth where the scene wouldn't end with her stomping out the door. I guess I still didn't get it right."

"That's a lot to handle," Justin finally said, falling into the seat that Lana had occupied.

"I know."

"Why didn't you ever tell her about Lattimore?"

"I don't know," Frank said tiredly. "I guess I didn't want her to turn into me, to have this burning and consuming hatred for one person like I did. Then when all this happened and I saw him talking to her at the reception the other night—"

"You were there?" Justin asked, surprised because he had specifically looked for the older man.

Frank ignored his question and said, "You don't know him like I do. You don't know what he's capable of. Xavier and I grew up together. He taught me how to pick pockets—"

"Are you saying that Lattimore was a thug?"

Frank actually had the energy to look insulted as he said, "That would mean I'm a thug, which I'm not, so Lattimore wasn't, either. He just had a special set of skills that helps a gentleman in the hard life we live."

"Sorry," Justin said, trying not to laugh even though there was absolutely nothing funny about anything that had happened since Lana had stepped into his arms last night.

"I left that life a long time before Lana was born. I wanted to have a job that wouldn't make me ashamed, where I could look my mother in the eye and tell her the truth when she asked where I got my money. I became a trashman. It wasn't glamorous or particularly clean, but I didn't mind. For the first time in my life, I didn't have to run around a corner or jump behind a tree because the cops were driving by.

"Lattimore couldn't stand the fact that I didn't need him anymore. He tried to get me to help him out on different jobs, but I always refused. I don't think he cared that I was a trashman; he just didn't like that I was doing something that he couldn't do—live an honest life. Then he moved to DC and went legitimate, only as a front for his own illegal activities."

"And this justifies you going to Grimes?" Justin demanded, angry with Frank for being so stupid. He had thought Frank was careless in his own safety at times but had never thought the man was stupid. "A man like Grimes would chew up and spit out Lattimore and you . . . and me, for that matter."

"I'm not worried about Grimes. Lattimore is the major force behind the black-market trade in DC, Justin. The man is ruthless."

"And you're obsessed."

Frank appeared to wince from pain, but Justin had a feeling the pain wasn't physical. "I had something more important, more beautiful, and more valuable than either Lattimore or I could ever dream of. He wanted it, but he couldn't take it from me no matter what he did."

"What was it?"

Frank smiled for a moment before he answered, "Beatrice, my wife."

"I'm sorry, Frank," Justin said quietly, feeling sympathy for a man whom he should be investigating and watching, not feeling sympathy for.

"Me, too," Frank said, with a shrug that Justin suddenly realized was not as casual as Frank tried to make it appear.

Justin knew that he shouldn't have cared about Frank's motivations, because a thief was a thief and a commission for Justin's agency was a commission, but he did care. And if he could nail a bigger criminal such as Xavier Lattimore, that would be the true reward, not throwing a man like Frank Hargrove in jail. Frank would wither away in prison . . . or he would have himself elected jail warden within a few months.

"I don't want her in Lattimore's house with me," Justin said flatly. "She's an amateur and she'll freeze, even if we could get her to do it. She's a liability."

"Lana is the only one who can get you in the house," Frank said, sounding almost proud as he smiled. "We'll find a discreet location—a door or a window for her to leave unlocked—and once she unlocks it, her part is over and she returns to the party. No one will ever know that she was involved."

"She's not going to help us."

"Underneath all of that bravado, my Peanut has a strong sense of family and loyalty. She and her mom . . . You should have seen them together, Justin.

Lana will do it, not because of you and definitely not because of me, but because she'll want to make the man who took her mother pay."

"You're that certain?" Justin asked doubtfully.

"I'd stake my life on it," Frank said simply, then added with a laugh, "I'm doing exactly that."

Justin shook his head and ran a hand down his face. This was not the turn the assignment was supposed to take. He couldn't catch Frank in the act of stealing the obelisk if Justin himself was stealing it. Then again, Justin hadn't expected anyone to steal the obelisk. He hadn't expected Xavier Lattimore to be involved, either, or Frank to reveal deep family secrets that came straight out of a soap opera. And most of all, Justin didn't expect to fall in love. And Justin cursed because he realized it was true. He was in love with Lana Hargrove. And she didn't even know his real name.

Frank interrupted his thoughts, saying with deceptive casualness, "I notice that the bed is unmade and both sides look slept on."

Justin's thoughts turned to the bed and Lana, and he had to mentally shake himself. Not the kind of thoughts to be thinking with her father in the same room. He forced a smile as Frank continued to watch him.

"Do you want something to eat?" Justin asked abruptly. "You shouldn't have taken that pill on an empty stomach."

"You know, I've watched her over the years,"

Frank confessed quietly, obviously not sidetracked by the offer of food. "She never knew, and I'll never tell her, but every once in a while I'd check in or have a friend check in for me, make certain that she was doing well. She always was. My mother did a better job than I ever could have done without Bea. She's a good kid, a strong woman."

"Yes, she is," Justin said quietly.

Frank's expression turned surprisingly hard as he said through clenched teeth, "I may not show it, and I know she sure as hell doesn't think so, but make no mistake, Bubba, I love my daughter."

"I never doubted that," he said sincerely.

"If you're using her or—"

Justin straightened, feeling surprisingly hurt that Frank trusted him with everything in his life except Lana. "I'm not trying to hurt Lana, Frank. And let's be real: I couldn't hurt her if I tried."

Frank didn't smile but instead said soberly, "Don't be fooled. Lana is not as tough as she pretends to be."

Justin snorted in disbelief and shook his head. "Don't you think it's a little late to play the role of concerned father?" he asked.

Frank's eyes grew dark with anger, and Justin thought that he had done the impossible. He had gotten a genuine emotion from Frank Hargrove. The moment passed quickly, because Frank abruptly grinned.

"Don't get serious on me, Bubba. We have a long way to go."

Justin glared at the older man for a second, cursing his knowing laugh because Frank's warning was too late; Justin realized that he was already serious. Very serious.

CHAPTER THIRTEEN

Justin found her sitting at the end of the dock, her legs dangling over the edge, her stiletto heels on the planks next to her. He paused for a moment because she looked so deserted and lonely and he hated seeing her that way. He didn't want to think of her as anything but invulnerable and strong. She had held him when he needed it, she had watched over him, and he had no clue how to make her feel better. And for the first time in a long while, he wanted to try to be there for someone else. Being around the Hargroves didn't leave a lot of time for self-pity.

Justin stuffed his hands into his pants pockets, then walked onto the dock. She didn't acknowledge him or look at him as he sat next to her on the dock. For a moment, he just stared at the lake as it glistened in the moonlight.

"If you think we're going to have a heart-to-heart about my sordid family history, then you should just go back inside and trade more war stories with my father," she informed him in a cold tone.

"You don't have to push me away every time something happens that shows you're human just like the rest of us."

Lana turned to glare at him and he almost wished that he hadn't come out here to talk to her, until he saw the pain underneath the anger.

"You think that just because we slept together you now can tell me what to do?"

Justin sighed deeply, because he was beginning to wonder if he was like poor Bruce and just not man enough to handle Lana. He slowly got to his feet and Lana watched him with anger still gleaming in her eyes.

"I know what you're doing, Lana, because I've done it ever since the fire."

"And just what am I doing?" she asked sarcastically.

He only kept the irritation out of his voice through patience and the fragile love he was beginning to feel for this woman. "You're trying to push me away. I did the same thing after the fire because I didn't want anyone to know how lonely and scared I was."

"I'm not scared of anything," she snapped, her face a blank mask.

"Yes, you are. You haven't seen your father in twenty years. He hurt you, and the fact that he could hurt you that much scares you. And when you get scared, you get angry and then you start the man-woman thing, how men are so much weaker than women. And maybe you're right and we men are horrible, vile, and dumb creatures. But when you let yourself forget that you think this is a competition between us . . . Forget it. Frank is asleep; I'm going back to the cabin to get something to eat."

He turned to leave and he thought she wouldn't stop him, but then she said his name very quietly. Justin turned to face her, but she only looked at him. He waited for her to say his name again, and when she only stared at him he sighed and sat down next to her. She turned to stare at the water again and he followed her gaze.

"What would you do if your father suddenly appeared at your front door?" she asked abruptly.

He hid his surprise at her question. "Invite him in, I guess," he said, then grimaced. "Actually, I wouldn't get the chance. He would walk in, as if he owned the place." He shrugged. "But he'd never visit me."

"Why?"

"You don't visit your disappointments."

"I bet he doesn't think that, Justin," she said softly.

"That's what my mother says, but when I look at him, all I see is disappointment. He wanted me to go farther in the banking world than he did. And I could have. And that's what really burns him. That I could have and I didn't."

"It sounds to me like he loves you."

Justin stared at her, surprised. He shook his head, on the verge of protesting, when a vague memory crossed his mind. He had been in the hospital drifting in and out of consciousness and all he could remember was his father, sitting by his bedside. Whether it was day or night, no matter the hour, his father had sat in that hard chair next to Justin's bed. Sometimes he had been reading, but most of the time he had just stared at Justin. Once, Justin thought that Robert Baxter had been crying. But as soon as the doctors said that Justin would make it, his father returned to Atlanta. Not one word, not one kiss or hug. Had his being there meant something?

Lana broke into his thoughts. "Do you believe Frank? Do you believe that Lattimore killed my mother?"

He shook his head to clear his thoughts and said, "I believe him."

"You shouldn't. He's a liar."

"He doesn't lie," he said, then added dryly, "unless he has to."

"Of course," she responded, rolling her eyes.

She stared out across the lake.

"That bastard," she said, suddenly furious.

"Who?"

"Both of them," she snapped, then raked her hands through her hair. Lana's expression suddenly turned thoughtful as she mused, "It's always the men, isn't it?"

"What do you mean?"

"It started with my grandfather leaving Grandma Harri, and then Lattimore and my mother, and now me. Everything I've worked for in the last few years is on the verge of being destroyed. Grandma Harri was wrong; she thought we, women, were above the antics of men, but their antics have been controlling our lives for three generations."

"No one controls you, Lana. Remember? It's one of your most annoying qualities," he teased. She didn't answer him, but continued to stare at the dark, gentle waves at her feet. He gently nudged her arm. She looked at him and Justin's chest filled with a strange emotion at the tears in her eyes. Her tears were ripping him apart. "Darlin', if this is too much for you, just say the word. You can stay here in the cabin until this all blows over, or I can send you to Maryland to stay with my mother, or if you're a glutton for punishment, I can send you to Atlanta with my dad and brothers. Anything you want."

Lana stared at him for a moment and appeared on the verge of saying something, then sighed and said quietly, "He wouldn't lie about her. It's probably why he won't talk about her because she's the one thing he can't lie about."

"I don't think he would," Justin said quietly, then wrapped his arms around her.

She resisted for a moment, then begrudgingly laid her head on his shoulder.

"I want him to pay," she said fiercely. "Lattimore has to pay."

"You'll get your life back, Lana. I promise."

"Are your promises worth anything?" she asked, looking at him.

"Yes," he said simply. "I know that you don't want to hear this, but you have to listen to your father."

"I don't want to hear anything that he has to say."

"Lana—"

"You can believe that he's the Boy Wonder, but I know the truth about him."

Justin placed a hand on her face and she actually stopped talking. It almost made him feel powerful that he could make her be quiet with one touch, but he also liked when she talked back. He loved that sharp tongue of hers.

"Talk to him, for me," he said quietly.

She studied his face and for the first time Justin didn't try to hide his scars, maybe because she was the only person he felt could truly accept them.

She leaned back and said simply, "You're cute, but you're not that cute."

Justin laughed and shook his head. When she smiled, he knew that she would talk to Frank. Justin was beginning to understand Lana; he was beginning to understand that she always did the exact opposite of what she wanted people to believe she would do.

It seemed as natural as breathing for Justin to lean over and kiss her. He meant for it to be a kiss of friendship and comfort, but he should have known that the taste of her lips would drive any thoughts of friendship out of his mind. The moment he tasted her softness, the moment he inhaled her, he forgot about being comforting and only thought about how it had felt being inside of her, loving her, having the freedom to touch her.

Her mouth opened under his and Justin tasted her fully, his hands moving to cup her face to make certain that she didn't move. She made a small sound in the back of her throat and Justin growled into her mouth and moved closer, pressing his body against her soft one, his hardness against her softness. Her hands clutched his shoulders, drawing him closer, her tongue and lips growing more insistent with each drugging kiss. She gently bit his bottom lip and Justin could have taken her right there, on the dock, with her father no doubt watching them from the cabin window.

His hands traveled to her behind and he squeezed like he had done last night. She moaned into his mouth. It took a disturbing few moments before Justin realized that she was pushing him away. Her hands balled into fists in his chest. Justin quickly released her before she kneed him again and before he lost all control.

She looked at him for a long moment, her eyes wide with desire and confusion, and then she walked away from him. And Justin watched her leave.

Lana sat across from her father at the kitchen table and covertly watched him, as he spoke on his slim cellular phone in French.

Frank had been on the phone since she returned to the cabin. Justin had returned a few minutes after her and immediately sat on the bed and began poring over blueprints that had been in Frank's car, ignoring her. After that mind-blowing kiss on the dock, Lana decided it was better to concentrate on her father than to attempt to figure out Justin at the moment. He had come out to the dock and made her laugh, he had made her believe in herself when she had thought that maybe her grandmother had been wrong about that too—that Lana couldn't do it on her own. Justin made her believe she could. And, if possible, she had fallen more in love with him at that moment. Not to mention the serious kiss he had laid on her before she had been able to prepare herself. Instead, she had clung to him like she actually needed him, wanted him. Lana could admit that she wanted Justin, more than she had ever wanted anything else in her life, but she didn't like thinking that she needed him.

But Justin was another headache for another day and right now Lana needed to deal with her father, who spoke fluent French, as if he had been born and raised in the country. She could only handle one confusing man at a time.

Frank ended the call with a jaunty *"Au revoir,"* then faced Lana with a grave expression. "You're not going to like this."

"You speak French?" she asked instead, not wanting to hear more life-altering news.

"A little," Frank said, with a shrug.

"It sounded like a lot just now."

"You'd be surprised how much saying 'umm' can get you by in a lot of languages," he said with a wink, then he sobered and said, "Lana, I was trying to tell you some bad news."

"What now?"

Frank exchanged glances with Justin, who had finally looked up from the blueprints. Frank finally looked at her again as he pushed his cell phone across the table. "Maybe you should call Pauline."

Lana refused to show her surprise that he knew Pauline's name. "Why?"

"The man I was speaking to on the phone just now, he's a friend in DC," Frank began hesitantly. "He keeps an eye on things for me from time to time."

"What things?" Lana asked, snorting in disbelief.

"You," he replied simply.

"Of course," she said, throwing up her hands in surrender. She didn't believe half the things that came from her father's mouth and the other half she didn't want to believe.

Frank continued, unfazed by her obvious disbelief, "He said that . . . your town house, your office . . ."

Lana's eyes grew wide as she leaned forward in the chair. "What about my town house and office?" she asked, hearing the borderline panic in her own voice.

"There's been a fire," he said simply.

"A fire," Lana repeated, then glanced at Justin. He tensed, as if prepared to jump off the bed and put out a fire in the cabin.

"It's all . . . It's gone, Lana," Frank said quietly.

"Gone?" Lana whispered, not comprehending the simple word. "How can it be gone?"

Frank spat out the one word, "Lattimore."

"I can't believe . . ." Her voice trailed off as she thought of all her client files, her paperwork, her pictures with satisfied clients—one-of-a-kind things that could never be replaced.

"Lattimore is dangerous, Peanut. He tried to have you killed in the metro and now your town house. There are too many coincidences, Lana. You have to believe me now. The man is evil and he won't stop until he's wiped us both out."

Lana turned to Justin, who intently watched her as if waiting for a sign. She didn't know what sign. She didn't know anything anymore. Her entire life had been turned upside down and the only thing that made any sense was Justin.

Justin's voice was harsh and deep as he asked Frank, "How did it happen?"

"The official explanation is that it was an accident—a gas leak—but my friend knows people in the fire department and the unofficial word is that it was arson."

Lana repeated in a hoarse whisper, "Arson."

"Frank, if you're lying about this, so help me God, I will hand you over to Grimes myself," Justin said through clenched teeth.

Frank pushed his phone across the table to her. "Call Pauline. Ask her. She's the one listed on your emergency contact forms. They would have contacted her."

Lana didn't ask him how he knew who was listed on her emergency contact forms. Nothing surprised her about her father anymore. Only because Frank obviously didn't believe that she would do it, Lana picked up the telephone and dialed her friend's phone number.

There were several short rings and then Lana heard Pauline's voice. She was surprised by how familiar but foreign Pauline's voice seemed at that moment.

"Pauline, it's Lana," she said quietly into the receiver.

"Lana! Thank God." Pauline shrieked into the telephone. "I've been worried sick about you. You've given me two new wrinkle lines. After the town house and—"

"What town house?"

"Your town house. There was a fire, something about a gas leak. The police called me and I thought . . . I thought you were dead, Lana, and then they couldn't find a body and I didn't know what to think," Pauline said, sounding close to tears. "Where are you? Are you all right?"

"I'm fine," Lana said, feeling her father's gaze on her.

"Where are you?"

"I'm safe," Lana said, not certain why she didn't tell Pauline the truth. She glanced at Justin, who had a strange expression on his face. He averted his gaze. "I'll call you later, Pauline."

"Lana, what is going on—"

"Don't worry about me, Pauli. I'll be fine." Lana pressed the disconnect button on Pauline's frantic questions, then carefully set the telephone on the table. She stared at her father, and for once he didn't smirk at her. He looked sympathetic.

"I'm sorry, Peanut," he said quietly.

"Don't call me that," she muttered, then took several deep breaths. "This won't be over until Lattimore is behind bars, will it?"

"No, it won't. He wants to destroy me and he knows that by destroying you, he'll destroy me."

"Too bad he didn't ask you about it. You could have told him that I don't register on the Frank Hargrove Meter of Importance."

Frank visibly hesitated, then said, "Lana, we can't do any of this without you."

She hated herself for saying it, but then she muttered, "What do I have to do?"

Lana didn't like the glances that her father and Justin exchanged, almost as if they had known she would say exactly that.

CHAPTER FOURTEEN

"You don't look like a flower deliveryman," Justin said, as he tried not to laugh at Lana in the androgynous blue overalls with the ACE FLOWERS patch above her right breast. Even in the overalls, she made his blood throb.

Lana narrowed her eyes at him, then straightened her matching blue baseball cap in the side view mirror of the used black van that Frank had rented. She tucked errant strands of hair behind her ears, then pursed her lips together.

"I'm not a flower deliveryman," she finally said, turning to him. "I'm a flower delivery woman. And a very good one, I bet. In fact, I bet that I'm the employee of the month at Ace Flowers."

Justin laughed and Lana grinned at him in return. It was the first smile she had given him since they had arrived in DC that morning. Lana had gotten a hotel suite for the three of them while Justin and Frank had rented a nondescript van and several overalls for the fictitious Ace Flowers. Justin had been surprised that Lana had readily agreed to check out Lattimore's mansion. In fact, he almost suspected that she was enjoying herself as much as he was.

"From a public relations guru, to kidnap victim, to Ace Flowers employee of the month all in one week," he noted with a laugh.

She grabbed several boxes of flowers and stared at the large white mansion at the end of the curved driveway in the hills above Georgetown. Xavier Lattimore's mansion. Besides Ace Flowers, there were other delivery people and gardeners milling around the front lawn. Obviously there was going to be a huge event. In other words, it was the perfect opportunity for them to slip inside the mansion and do reconnaissance.

"Are we really going to do this?" she asked uncertainly.

Justin smiled in amusement and asked, "Are you actually scared, Lana?"

"I keep telling you that I'm not scared of anything," she said, straightening her shoulders.

"And I keep forgetting that when I see those flashes of fear cross your face," he said lightly. She glared at him, then quickly looked away when he winked at her. He lifted the heavy bags of mulch and dirt, then said seriously, "Ten minutes. No more, no less. We pretend to be the florists, we set the flowers down as soon as we can, and then we look for any vulnerable and hidden points of entry."

"We've been over this, Justin; I know what I'm doing."

He continued as if she had never spoken, "Don't make eye contact with anyone, but don't avoid eye contact, either. We want to blend in, not stand out. We're tired, underpaid delivery people and we want to do our jobs as soon as possible—"

"Should I also think about that louse of an ex-husband and my three hungry kids at home as motivation for this character?"

Justin rolled his eyes as she giggled. He actually cracked a smile, but only because he couldn't withhold it any longer.

"Are you two done motivating and stretching back there?" Frank called from inside the van, where he sat in front of the monitors and enough surveillance equipment to make the FBI jealous. Justin had noticed that Frank had been strangely tense since he pulled behind the ornate gates of Lattimore's property.

"We're going," Justin muttered, then added, "This is Lana's first time and I want to make certain that she's—"

"I'm ready," Lana snapped.

"Remember to keep the cameras in your frames pointed at whatever you see. We need a better layout of the mansion," Frank said, no sign of a smirk or laugh or joke anywhere in his voice.

Justin nodded, then slammed the van doors. He turned to Lana and she glared at him, as if daring him to ask her again if she knew what she was doing. He decided to test fate, because he asked carefully, "Are you sure—"

"I'm sure," she said, then rolled her eyes and started toward the mansion. Justin had no choice but to follow her.

Justin stared at the imposing height of the mansion the closer they approached. He picked out three security cameras at various vantage points on the mansion, all directed toward the entrance and driveway. He wouldn't have been surprised if there were other cameras hidden somewhere, too. Then he noticed that all activity had stopped. Every man in the front yard was watching Lana walk toward the mansion, their eyes on her hips and her behind.

"Could you try to walk a little less . . . a little less like you?" he said, in a low voice, as they walked in the front door.

"What do you mean?" she asked blankly.

"You didn't notice what just happened?"

"Of course I did," she said simply.

"The object is to blend in, remember, Lana?"

"Lana Hargrove can't blend in anywhere," she said, with a helpless shrug. She stopped in the middle of the foyer and stared at the ceiling that was high enough to house the Smithsonian Natural History Museum.

Justin noticed that her gaze zeroed in on the paintings in the foyer. He was no art expert, but even he recognized the famous paintings.

"Gorgeous," she whispered in awe, moving as if to touch the portrait of an old white man.

"I didn't know you were into that stuff, too," Justin said, surprised.

"Of course I am. This is an early American portrait of Thomas Jefferson, Justin. See the fatigue the artist manages to convey with a few brushstrokes? It's beautiful."

"Sure," he muttered, shrugging.

"May I help you?" came a deep female voice behind them.

Justin and Lana whirled around to see a woman dressed all in black. She didn't wear a maid's uniform, but she looked like the stereotype of every elderly maid in the movies. Thin, tall, and frowning at the dirt that clung to their boots.

"Where should we put these?" Justin asked, motioning to the flowers.

"In the ballroom down the hall." The woman stared for a moment longer at Lana, then turned and disappeared behind the door where she had come from.

Justin grabbed Lana's hand and dragged her toward the ballroom. They walked into the large room, which was partially arranged for the dinner with several round tables covered with white linen tablecloths throughout the room. There were already enough flowers in the room to start a small rain forest, but Justin dropped his load in a corner of the room and Lana followed suit.

"I'll meet you at the van in ten minutes," she told him, and turned to leave.

Justin laughed in disbelief, then grabbed her arm, stopping her from leaving. "We're not separating."

"Of course we are. This is a big house. We can cover more ground separately."

"Lana, you're in the lion's den. This is exactly where Lattimore wants you. I'm not leaving you."

"We have eight minutes," she said, then turned and quickly ran up the stairs.

Justin cursed to himself but quickly circled the bottom floor. He couldn't find anything that satisfied his requirements for a good point of entry. Then he peered through the open doors of the library. Inside, a small door was open that led to a closet. He investigated further and found a skylight in the closet. A skylight that could be cut open. He smiled to himself. The ballroom was far enough from the library that no one would notice or hear his entrance if the doors were closed. Satisfied, he returned to the foyer and became worried and pissed when Lana was not there.

He peered around the corner, and when he saw no one coming he catapulted over the banister and ran up the stairs. If anything, there was more opulence on display upstairs. Plush Oriental rugs, exquisite tapestries on the wall, and more paintings in the type of ornate gilded frames Justin had only seen in museums. He crept down the carpeted hallway. Then he heard the deep voices. Close. One voice belonged to Xavier Lattimore. Justin glanced around the wide hallway for a hiding place. He tried one door, but it was locked. He tried not to panic. He had been in tight situations before, but Lana was somewhere upstairs and Justin was on the verge of seriously panicking.

A door behind him abruptly flew open, and before he could scream or protest, someone grabbed his shoulders and dragged him into a dark room; then the door closed.

"It's me," Lana whispered, her hands still on his shoulders.

"What the hell are you doing in here?" he snapped, annoyed.

"Hiding," she said, as if it should have been perfectly obvious, which it was.

The cramped confines of the closet made him suddenly aware of how close the two were, of how her breasts were pressed against his chest, her warm breath on his mouth. As if she suddenly sensed the change in his mood, her hands fell from his shoulders.

Justin cursed inwardly and tried to move away, but she grabbed him when the voices stopped directly in front of the door. The two instantly became still.

". . . I want him found," Xavier said, sounding up-set. "He's one man. This is my city. He should al-ready be rotting in jail."

"He's more resourceful than you give him credit for," came the reply from a deep, calm voice.

"He's not that resourceful or his blood wouldn't be in my study right now, would it?"

"A small security breach."

Xavier's voice dropped to a deadly whisper as he said, "There'd better not be any security breaches—small or otherwise—tomorrow night. I want the night to go off without a hitch."

"Yes, sir."

The voices faded and Justin released the breath he didn't know he held. He turned to Lana and found her staring at his mouth. Whatever he was about to say about the danger, about Lattimore and Frank, was lost. This was the least optimal position he could find himself in and all he wanted to do was kiss her. His hand went to her jaw and he caressed the soft skin.

"Hiding in a closet in an out-of-season blue wasn't on the list of activities for me today," she said, her voice soft.

"Neither was this," Justin growled before he slammed his mouth into hers. It was hard and wet. He jammed his leg in between hers and one of his hands went around her waist while the other hand plunged into her hair, dislodging the ponytail and the baseball cap. Her tongue rammed into his mouth and he tried not to groan like he wanted to. She responded. Hot and hard. Her hands on his back, her tongue fighting with his, soothing his.

He abruptly released her when he realized that if he touched her for a moment longer they would be making love in a closet in Xavier Lattimore's house. In front of cameras that her father was watching in the van.

When Lana stared at him, confused, Justin motioned toward the eyeglasses that he wore, which gave Frank a bird's-eye view of everything they did. He didn't think it could happen, but Lana actually looked embarrassed as she quickly grabbed the glasses and cap and moved to the door. He slowly cracked open the door, and seeing the hallway empty, he motioned for her to follow him out of the closet. Justin decided no matter whatever anyone else said, being in the closet was fun.

"You don't have to do this, Lana," Justin said for what seemed like the tenth time in the last ten minutes as he navigated the rental car through the streets of DC.

Lana thought that when she returned to DC, she would breathe a sigh of relief and then immediately call the police, but she did neither. Instead, she had broken into a man's house, almost made love in a stranger's cramped closet, and then gone shopping. After all, she had no clothes and she had been wearing the same outfit for the last three days. After stopping at a hotel, showering, and changing into a tight, short blue Gucci dress, Lana was now on her way to a lunch date with Bruce. Bruce, who suddenly didn't seem as interesting and perfect for her as he had only two days ago.

"Yes, I do," she retorted, refusing to look at Justin.

"Think of it as a character you have to play," Frank said cheerfully from his position in the backseat.

"Thank you for the hustling tips, Frank," Lana said dryly through clenched teeth. "I had forgotten the warm glow I get from our father-daughter chats on How to Bilk As Many People As You Can."

"That's how you tell a good lie, Peanut," Frank said, either ignoring or oblivious to her sarcasm. "You have to believe that it's the truth."

"I like Bruce," she felt the need to say. "Having lunch with him will not be a chore or an opportunity to test my hustling skills."

"But he hasn't invited you to Lattimore's dinner, has he?" Frank pointed out.

"Because I was kidnapped and dragged to a deserted cabin in the middle of nowhere," she said through clenched teeth.

Justin glared at her and she returned his glare.

"Don't worry; I'll get into Lattimore's house tomorrow night," she said, daring either man to contradict her. "Everything will go according to plan."

The two were obviously intelligent enough not to say anything in response.

"Nice weather we're having," Frank said, obviously attempting to change the subject.

"Bruce is not as simple as he seems," Justin said, his voice strangely silent as he stared straight ahead. "Be careful."

Lana snorted in disbelief. "Now you think that Bruce is involved in this? Maybe he's the one who flew to the Paris warehouse and stole the obelisk before you two could? I remember he did leave town a couple of days last week. He did say he was going to New York, but we can't trust anyone."

"Just be careful," Justin muttered, glancing at her.

She rolled her eyes, then stared out the window at the passing buildings. She hated feeling confused. She always knew where she stood where men were involved—on top—but with Justin she wasn't certain.

Justin stopped the car down the block from the restaurant where Lana was supposed to meet Bruce. Lana didn't know why, but she turned to Justin one last time, as if waiting for him to stop her. He stared straight ahead, his jaw clenched in anger.

When she started to move out of the car, he grabbed her arm and said, "We'll be right outside, waiting for you to finish."

"Bruce will give me a ride to Pauline's house."

"Lana—"

"I'll see you later."

Lana snatched her arm from his grip, then stood away from the car, slamming the door. Only then did she allow the fear to invade her body as she

glanced around the street at the numerous people.
Maybe one of them had destroyed her town house or
tried to push her in front of the metro train. She
gripped her purse more tightly and sauntered toward
the restaurant, because no one would make her lose
her swagger.

Justin walked into his house and didn't bother turning
on the lights but fell into his favorite easy chair. He
leaned his head back and closed his eyes in exhaustion. He was tired and he was worried, more worried
than he had ever been about anyone. He had sat in the
rental car for an hour while Lana ate lunch with
Bruce. And then Justin had watched with a clenched
jaw as Lana walked from the restaurant with the man
and climbed into a very expensive and illegally parked
Porsche. Justin had looked around for a cop. There
was never a cop when a man needed one. Then Justin
had taken a surprisingly silent Frank back to the hotel
and made an excuse about going to the store, but
Justin needed to go home, to be by himself for a little
while.

Justin popped open one eye and looked in the
direction of his answering machine. The red light
blinked incessantly. Since no one called him or left
messages besides bill collectors or his cousin, Justin
dialed his cousin's private line at the office.

"Baxter and Baxter Investigations," Clarence said,
sounding preoccupied.

"It's me."

"Justin," Clarence said, sounding relieved. "Where are you?"

"Home."

"Your home?"

"Yes—"

"Justin, this investigation is over," Clarence said, his tone agitated. "Last night, Lana Hargrove's town house was set on fire. Fires, metro accidents . . . you're not ready for that and neither is this agency—"

"I'm seeing this through to the end, Clarence. Fire me," Justin said calmly and quietly.

"Why is this case so important to you, Justin? Is it because of her?"

Justin immediately became still, then said quietly, "What are you talking about?"

"I'm talking about Lana Hargrove and your obsession with her. I've seen her. She's beautiful, Justin, but is she worth all of this? The longer you stay as Justin Larkin, the more explaining we have to do to the authorities—"

"Lana is not a part of this," he said through clenched teeth.

"She's beautiful and obviously charming and I can see how being around her makes you feel better, but she's not worth risking your career," Clarence said, lowering his voice to a quiet whisper. "I know that . . . Caroline—"

"This has nothing to do with Caroline," he interrupted Clarence angrily.

Whatever Clarence had been on the verge of saying, he had decided to leave it alone. Justin heard Clarence take several deep breaths before he said, "Justin, come to the agency. We need to talk."

"It would compromise my cover. I can't."

"But you can go home?"

It was a lame excuse that Justin didn't think Clarence would catch, but he had. Justin knew that sometimes he underestimated his cousin. He had made that mistake once a long time ago, and he was making it again.

"Justin, I just want to talk," Clarence said, sounding calmer.

"There's nothing to talk about. I'm seeing this through until the end."

"The end? What does that mean? Frank is the end, Justin. Do you know where he is?" Clarence asked. "That's all our client wants. Frank Hargrove."

"I'll contact you later." He replaced the phone on the receiver, then forced himself to stand.

He needed to shower. He needed to forget Lana and Frank Hargrove. He laughed at the futility of doing either.

Twenty minutes later, Justin walked out of the bathroom, wrapping a towel around his waist. He stopped in midstride when he saw a man sitting in the corner of his bedroom in one of his chairs. He was camouflaged in the shadows and Justin would have reached for his gun under one of the bed pillows, but he recognized the cologne.

"Frank," Justin said, surprised, as water dripped from his nose to the floor.

"Good evening, Bubba. Nice place you have here," Frank said casually. He slowly got to his feet and walked to the bedroom window. He moved the bedroom curtain aside and glanced at the street.

Justin glanced toward his pillow again. He had never seen Frank hurt anyone, none of the reports said that Frank had ever hurt anyone, but Justin also knew that Frank did not behave predictably. Maybe it was Rule Three or something.

Frank abruptly turned to Justin and held up Justin's familiar .357 Magnum. Justin's heart pounded against his chest. He had wondered, after the fire as he lay in the hospital swathed in bandages and later after months of physical therapy, if he cared about dying, and he had a feeling that before this weekend, he probably would not have cared. Now he did.

"Is this what you keep looking for?" Frank asked.

There was a tense moment of silence as the two stared at each other, measuring one another. Frank abruptly threw the gun on the bed, and Justin released the breath he didn't know he held.

"Did you honestly think I was going to shoot you, Justin?" Frank asked, with a short laugh. "Why would I shoot you? My partner, my colleague, my friend? The only man I've ever trusted besides Xavier Lattimore? But then, I make bad choices, don't I? My wife always told me that I did."

"Frank—"

Frank continued calmly, "I never believed you were a thief. I could tell from your eyes. Your eyes tell me that you couldn't steal a grape in a blackout. It's always the eyes."

"How long have you known?"

"From the first moment you sat next to me in the bar. Call it boredom, but I let you last longer than the rest, the other folks that have posed as friends to catch me. You even found me in Paris, after that first meeting, which impressed me because no other man or woman had gotten that far—finding me when I don't want to be found. And you entertained me; you . . . I don't know; maybe I was lonely. It had been a long time since I was close to anyone." From his pants pocket, Frank pulled Justin's billfold, the one that Justin had placed in the false bottom of his dresser drawer. "Justin Baxter of Baxter and Baxter Investigations. I've seen the other Baxter. I'm not impressed."

Justin hid his own thoughts about "the other Baxter" and instead walked slowly toward his closet.

"You don't mind if I put on some pants, do you?"

Frank shrugged and Justin turned around as if to pull a pair of slacks from his closet but reached into his shoe rack for the small gun he kept hidden for emergencies.

"Looking for this?" Frank asked, holding up the gun, with a smug smile on his face.

"As a matter of fact, I was," Justin said, hiding his frustration.

"I'm used to betrayal. It doesn't anger me that

much," Frank said, tossing that gun on the bed next to the other one. "I just want to know, Justin Baxter of Baxter and Baxter Investigations, what exactly you're getting out of this. Prestige? More business? What, Justin?"

"All of the above."

"Who hired you?"

"The Smithsonian. You've cost the Smithsonian a lot of money over the last few years. They can't take the losses anymore, and they don't want to."

Frank's expression momentarily hardened before he shrugged and said lazily, "The moment they stop doing business with a man like Xavier Lattimore, they won't have to worry about me."

"That's not your decision to make, Frank," Justin said, frustrated.

"I wondered who was behind this sudden vendetta against Frank Hargrove," he murmured. "Who could it be? I wonder who?"

Justin smiled because he half-expected Frank to yell out "Satan" like Dana Carvey in a *Saturday Night Live* skit as the "Church Lady."

"It's not a sudden vendetta. It's been in the works a long time," Justin said. "Your actions have reactions and one of those reactions is me."

"For little old me?" Frank asked, pretending ingratiating humility. Frank abruptly laughed. "And once you had me in DC, what stopped you from turning me in?"

When Justin didn't answer, Frank smiled for a moment, then said, "The possibility of Xavier Lattimore."

"You're small fish compared to him, Frank," Justin said, with a small shrug.

Frank's smirk disappeared and he asked hesitantly, "Does Lana know?"

Justin knew true fear at that moment. Staring down the barrel of a gun was nothing compared to the threat he felt at Lana knowing the truth, knowing that he had lied.

"No," Justin answered, averting his gaze. "Lana doesn't know."

Frank whistled softly, then smiled. "What a tangled web you've managed to weave here, Justin Baxter. You got my daughter to fall in love with exactly the type of man she always vowed to never fall in love with. A man just like dear old Dad. And yet if you tell her that Jason Larkin is a lie, she'll never forgive you. What's a traitor private detective art thief supposed to do?"

Justin clenched his jaw and resisted the urge to pummel Frank. "Lana is not in love with me," he said, hating the almost hopeful note in his voice. He hoped Frank didn't notice. But Frank Hargrove noticed everything. It was what made him a good thief and an even better friend.

"Maybe she doesn't love you, but she does trust you, and my daughter does not trust many people. Not even her own father."

Justin hesitated, then asked blankly, "Are you going to tell her about me?"

"If I told her that you're a private detective hired to send me to jail and to see if she's implicated in any of my less-than-legal activities, she would spit in your face—and probably mine—and call the police. We would never get inside Lattimore's house and I would never get the chance to make certain that that man pays for all he's done." Frank laughed bitterly, then said, "No, Bubba, I'm not telling Lana anything about you."

Anger on Lana's behalf flooded through Justin's body. He told himself to shut up, but he couldn't. He asked stiffly, "Have you ever done anything for your daughter without thinking of yourself first?"

Frank winked and said, "You're the one who's been investigating me all of these months. You tell me."

Justin rolled his eyes, then found a clean pair of slacks from the closet and pulled them on. He tossed the towel on the bed and turned to Frank, feeling a little more on balance now that he wore pants.

"Once Lana gets into Lattimore's house tomorrow night, she's going to let me in and you'll coordinate surveillance from the van. After we get the obelisk, Frank, all bets are off. My objectives are to get the obelisk and bring you in, and that's what I'm going to do."

The two men stared at each other for a moment and Justin actually glanced at the two guns on his bed.

Frank abruptly smiled and said with a shrug, "You can try, Bubba. You can sure try."

Justin watched the older man leave the bedroom. He didn't move until he heard the front door close.

CHAPTER FIFTEEN

"Where have you been?" Pauline demanded while throwing her arms around Lana. "I've been worried sick."

Lana grunted at the impact of all of Pauline's 150 pounds thrown against her frame as she walked into Pauline's condominium. She forced a smile as Pauline pushed her away, then pulled her back for another bone-crushing embrace.

"Are you all right?" Pauline asked, the concern and panic on her face making Lana feel a slight case of guilt. She hadn't known that Pauline would be this worried. Maybe Pauline was the friend that Lana wanted, but Lana had never seen it because she was so busy proving she was independent.

"I'm fine," Lana lied, then closed the front door and led Pauline into the living room. Pauline followed her like a lost puppy dog. "Do you have any food?"

Lana asked abruptly when Pauline continued to stare at her.

"Of course. I have a nice salad in the—"

"Real food, Pauline," Lana said impatiently. "This is definitely a time for real food."

Guilt crossed Pauline's expression before she whispered, "I have a Sara Lee cheesecake in the freezer."

Lana sighed in relief, then grabbed Pauline's hand and led her into the kitchen. She deposited Pauline on a stool, then went to the freezer, where she smiled at the sight of the familiar box.

"How can you eat at a time like this?" Pauline asked, sounding amazed. "And was that Bruce who dropped you off just now?"

Lana took a bite of cheesecake, then rolled her eyes heavenward at the sheer ecstasy of the rich-tasting dessert. She allowed the taste to sink in for a moment; then she realized that Pauline was watching her, looking scared. Lana knew it was because Lana had eaten the forbidden food, instead of because she was acting like a madwoman.

"Where have you been for the past forty-eight hours?" Pauline asked in a careful voice, as if she were talking to a crazy person.

"If I told you, you wouldn't believe me," Lana muttered through a mouthful of cheesecake.

"Try me," Pauline said simply, then stilled Lana's hand, which held another forkful of cheesecake. Lana saw the concern in her friend's eyes and actually set down the fork. "I thought you were dead."

"I'm sorry, Pauline. I should have called you earlier."

"We waited for you at dinner the other night. And when you didn't show up without calling, I knew something was wrong, because that's not you."

"My father is here," Lana confessed in a rush.

Pauline's eyes grew wide with surprise. "I thought he was dead."

"I never told you that," she said, surprised.

"I just assumed it because you never talk about him."

"He's very much alive and he's in trouble. Him being in trouble means that I could be in trouble."

Pauline gasped worriedly. "Lana, what kind of trouble?"

"I'm fine, Pauline; nothing will happen to me. By tomorrow night this will all be over."

"What's happening tomorrow night?"

"Xavier Lattimore's private party at his mansion."

"You're going to Xavier Lattimore's private party? I hear the vice president is going to be there."

Lana rolled her eyes at Pauline's preoccupation with the guest list, then admitted, "I've had a really bad last few days here, Pauli. I was pushed in front of a metro train and at the last minute Justin came from nowhere and then he took me to this cabin because it was the meeting point with my father. And then my father—"

Pauline held up a hand and said, "One confusing thing at a time. First, who is Justin? And, second, why do you say his name like that?"

"Like what?" she asked, going back to the cheese-cake because she didn't want to meet Pauline's direct gaze.

"Like he means something to you." Pauline's gaze grew quizzical as she openly examined Lana's face. "You were in a cabin alone with a man all of this time?"

"What are you implying?"

"I know you, Lana, and an opportunity like that would not go by Lana Hargrove without something happening."

"Thanks for the cheesecake."

"You suddenly don't kiss and tell?" Pauline asked, sounding amused and surprised.

Lana grabbed her purse and said tightly, "I have to go."

Pauline jumped to her feet and asked, concerned, "Where are you going?"

"I'm staying at a hotel with my father and Justin—"

"There's that name again."

Lana ignored Pauline's comment and continued, "Don't worry about me. I can take care of myself."

"I know," Pauline said reluctantly. "But sometimes I worry that you can take care of yourself too well. It's not good to be alone."

"You're the queen of alone. You once told a man you had been dating for six months to get out of your bed at two o'clock in the morning because you wanted to be alone."

Pauline didn't smile as she said, "And that's why I'm getting married now, because everyone has to change."

"Not me," Lana said simply, refusing to think about Justin. She cleared her throat, then continued, "I have some nervous clients to see and deliveries to pick up before I head back to the hotel."

"Lana, don't leave yet."

Lana hugged her only friend, then said with a forced smile, "Everything will be fine. I promise. Then sometime later this week we can have a nice dinner and sit down and I'll answer all of your questions."

Pauline stared at her for a moment, then smiled. "I have a feeling that's all I'm getting from you. You'd make a great spy, Lana."

Lana laughed, then kissed Pauline's cheek and walked out the door. She turned back to look at her friend and realized that Pauline was her friend, whether she had been a friend to her or not.

Lana walked into the hotel suite that she would share with her father and Justin for the next two days. Or what she hoped was only two days. Strangely, a part of her wouldn't have minded spending a longer time with Justin, even though her usual method was to leave a man as quickly as she picked him up, but spending even ten minutes in the same room as her father was asking a lot.

Lana set down, or dropped, the numerous packages in her arms and closed the door and engaged the chain lock as Justin had lectured her, then turned. She gasped when she realized that her father and Justin were both silently sitting in the lounge area. Her father was in a chair at the corner of the room, expectantly grinning as he glanced at Justin. Justin looked angry enough to scare a small child but only to irritate Lana.

"You're in trouble," Frank sang, amused.

"What have I done now?" she asked dully.

"Where have you been?" Justin asked, his voice strangely cold and quiet.

She glared at him and ignored the small jump in her stomach at the sight of him, clean-shaven and in neatly pressed slacks and a crisp white button-down shirt. The man should have been posing for magazines, not giving her lectures.

"I'm going to a party tomorrow night, remember? What did you expect me to wear? The same outfit I've been wearing for the last two days?"

Justin's expression didn't change as he said through clenched teeth, "The plan was for you to go to lunch with Bruce and then for Bruce to return you to the hotel."

Lana narrowed her eyes in anger and she heard her father laugh in delight before he murmured, "You've done it now, Bubba."

Lana ignored her father and crossed the room to poke her finger in Justin's solid chest. "This concept may be foreign to you, Justin, but I have a life, and when I suddenly disappear from that life I have to answer questions and make apologies and give discounts for missed appointments to keep business . . . Discounts. I can't afford to give discounts. I can barely afford the mortgage on my office space, although since that office space was destroyed thanks to you and Frank, I don't have to worry about that anymore."

"You should have stuck to the plan!" Justin yelled, his anger matching her own. "You were supposed to go to lunch with Bruce and return—"

"I know what the plan was, Justin," she retorted. "And I told you that I had to buy something appropriate to wear tomorrow night and that I needed to talk to my clients and friends—"

"You told people where you were staying?" Justin asked, horror and anger crossing his face.

"Of course I didn't," she snapped. "But I have responsibilities, Justin. I can't just disappear for two days and not expect questions."

"We needed two days, Lana. Couldn't your line of men have waited two damn days?" Justin snapped.

Frank interrupted Lana's gasp of outrage and got to his feet, waving his hands in surrender. "Kids, kids, let's take a break. Everyone to his or her respective corner." When Lana and Justin only glared at him, he smiled, then said, "You're going to have security come in here. Bubba, Lana is sorry that she didn't check in, and, Peanut, Justin is sorry that his concern came out as anger. Neither one of you meant it. Now kiss and make up."

Lana snorted in disbelief, then grabbed her shopping bags and stormed into the bedroom that she had claimed as her own. She slammed the doors and threw the packages on the bed. She wanted to kick something, but she glanced at her stilettos and decided that wasn't a good idea.

Lana didn't know who she was more angry with—Justin, because he was proving that he was the typical man who thought a woman's sole purpose in life was to cater to his every whim, or herself, because she was allowing herself to care about his typical male reactions. If any other man had spoken to her the way Justin had, she would have laughed in sheer amusement, then turned around and sauntered out of the hotel room—Lattimore and his goons or not—without a second thought.

She decided that she was definitely more angry with herself. She had always been in control of her emotions, her grandmother had taught her that, and for the first time in her life, her control was failing. One good roll—she had to correct that, one excellent night of unrestrained passion—in the hay and she lost all control of her life. Grandma Harri was probably rolling in her grave.

There was a hard knock on the door and Lana whirled around, prepared to unleash all her confusion in herself on whoever entered.

The knock on the door was harder and the door shook on the hinges. "What?!" Lana screamed towards the door.

Justin stalked into the room, slamming the door behind him. His jaw was clenched in anger and his eyes were dark. If he had been any other man, she would have been planning her exit or her scream. But he was Justin, and because she knew he would never physically hurt her, she felt safe enough to argue with him. If she hadn't been so angry with him, she would have kissed him right then for making her feel so safe.

He sounded too calm as he said, "I'm tired of you walking away from me when we're in the middle of something."

"We aren't in the middle of anything, Justin, especially if it involves you lecturing me," she retorted.

Justin's nostrils flared as he obviously struggled to rein in his temper. "I'm not lecturing you, Lana. I'm doing this for your own good—"

"I cannot believe those words just came out of your mouth," she sputtered in disbelief, planting her hands on her hips. "For my own good? Those are the exact words that every man has said when he's exerted his power over a woman."

Justin rolled his eyes and threw up his hands in disgust. "Can you stop with the feminist crap for two seconds, Lana? Please."

"Feminist crap," she repeated, outraged. "Standing up for myself and not allowing you to yell at me like a two-year-old child is feminist crap?"

Justin cursed and ran his hands down his face in a picture of exasperation. "Not every conversation we have is a battle between the sexes. Sometimes it's just a conversation. Like now. Like you wandering around DC by yourself when you know that someone is trying to hurt you, when you know that Frank and I are back here worrying about you. This is not about you being a woman and me being a man, this is about you being considerate. I'd be just as angry if Frank did this."

Lana's hands balled into fists as Justin equated her with Frank. He had made love to her until tears formed in her eyes, and now he was saying that he cared about her like he cared about Frank.

"I tried to call the room an hour ago, but the line was busy. I left a message with the front desk," she said, through clenched teeth. "I bet if you called down there right now, there would be a message from me."

"Have you heard of cell phones?"

"What a surprise . . . I don't have my father's cell phone number," she said dryly. Justin glared at her, obviously at a loss for a response. Lana smirked in triumph, then turned her back on him and crossed the room to her shopping bags.

She yanked items from the bags, throwing them on the bed and ignoring Justin, as if his overwhelming presence didn't affect her, as if her heart wasn't pounding against her chest loud enough for him to hear. Even angry with him, she still could not control her reaction to him. The way her nipples tightened beneath her shirt, the way her skin tingled, and that feeling that rolled through her stomach.

She felt him move across the room to tower behind her. She didn't turn until she heard his deep voice rumble in shock and anger, "What the hell is this?"

Lana whirled around to see him holding the evening gown she had bought for Lattimore's party. The gown was a bright, neon pink that was probably closer to something a woman would wear in a bedroom than to a party. It was a few scraps of sheer material that drifted to her ankles but revealed more than it covered. Of course, Lana had been thinking about Justin's reaction to the dress and not the party.

"It's a dress, Justin," she answered, annoyed.

"This is not a dress. This is . . ." He was obviously at a loss as he stared at the dress with wide eyes. No words would come out as his mouth flapped open and closed. "This is a nightgown," he finally said in an accusatory tone.

"It's a dress, Justin," she repeated calmly. "A very expensive dress that I'm going to wear to Lattimore's party."

"You're not wearing this to that party," he said. His arms were crossed over his chest, the dress still balled in his right hand and satisfaction on his face as if the matter was settled. "You're not wearing this dress anywhere."

"I'm not?" she asked, amused.

Justin's gaze held hers for a moment before he said, "No."

"For the sake of argument, I'll ask: Why?"

"Because it's too . . . Damnit, Lana, this dress . . ." His voice trailed off and his eyes darkened for a different reason and he moved towards her as if in a trance. His gaze dropped to her mouth and Lana unconsciously licked her lips. She could have sworn he groaned. He finally lifted his gaze to meet hers and, for the first time, she saw the worry. "This is a dress meant for me alone. This is a dress meant for me to peel off, slowly and gently, and then to rub across your skin—across your breasts and down lower and lower, until goose bumps rise on your skin and you tremble and beg me like you do when you're on the verge of shattering in my arms. I've been thinking about that moment. I can't stop thinking about that moment, being inside of you, feeling you clench me, watching you come apart."

She swallowed the sudden lump in her throat and felt the arousal that singed her skin from his deep voice that had turned as warm as the South Pacific. Lana knew she was lost when she had to remind herself that he was being an overprotective, sexist pig.

She opened her mouth to attempt to speak, but Justin placed one finger on her lips. She couldn't have spoken if she tried, not when she was drowning in his dark gaze.

"I was worried, Lana," he whispered, his thumb gently running across her lower lip. "When you didn't show up, I . . . I haven't been that worried about anyone in a long time."

"I'm sorry," she said, quietly. "I should have told you that I was planning to stop at Pauline's house and to run some errands."

Justin nodded, then smiled. "And I shouldn't have yelled at you."

She narrowed her eyes at him and said, "You've gotten me to do something that no other man on the face of this earth has gotten me to do."

"And, hopefully, I can get you to do it again tonight," he said, his hips grinding against hers.

Lana laughed and playfully pushed him in the chest. "I'm not talking about that. I'm talking about . . . You got me to apologize to you."

Justin grinned, then said, "And now you deserve your reward."

Their mouths ground together in a mix of tongue and lips and sheer passion. Justin pulled her against him and she gasped at the feel of his rock-hard muscles, of how rock-hard he was. His hands went from her waist and up her back and down past her waist. Lana's mind whirled in confusion and desire and she tried to move closer to him.

Her mind focused on his tongue as it swirled through her mouth. She loved his tongue; she loved his mouth; she loved everything about him. Lana gasped in protest when he suddenly moved from her, his mouth moving from hers. She noticed the hesitation on his expression.

"What are we doing, Lana?" Justin asked quietly, his hands dropping from her waist.

"I thought we were kissing," she answered, confused.

"We're doing more than that."

Lana forced a smile as she said with a wink, "Isn't that part of the plan?"

His brow furrowed as he studied her. "After the fire and Caroline, there have been women, but I didn't think—I never expected—that I'd find anyone again. I didn't know if I wanted to with this face—"

"Justin, your scars don't—"

"Don't," he interrupted her, with a gentle smile. "You're a nice person, Lana, even though you try to hide it, but you are. And it's one of the things that draws people to you, not because of your looks or your clothes, but because of you. It's what drew me to you even while I was trying to hate you."

"What are you saying, Justin?" she asked, attempting to keep the hope out of her voice.

He shook his head, confused. "I don't know what I'm saying, but I don't want you to think that I'm taking any of this lightly. Not after the gift you gave me last night."

Her face flushed with embarrassment and pleasure and she ducked her head. Lana couldn't remember the last time she had blushed. It had probably been in high school when the boys had begun noticing her developing breasts.

To hide the emotions racing through her body, she grinned and said, "I knew that you men could say and do the right thing when you put your mind to it."

Justin's response was interrupted as she heard her father scream her name from the other side of the closed door and then the sound of breaking furniture.

Lana had started toward the door, fear racing through her body, when Justin grabbed her by the waist and threw her to the floor just as bullets tore through the bedroom doors. She screamed and covered her ears as Justin covered her with his body, his body flinching with each shot that splintered the wood.

CHAPTER SIXTEEN

Justin didn't have time to contemplate what he had admitted to Lana, because he was now cowering in the hotel bedroom for his life. Frank had been right; Justin's concern had come out as anger. He had been pacing the hotel room, imagining every possible scenario that could have delayed Lana from being at the hotel room at the precise time that she was supposed to be there. And when she had walked in looking fresh and beautiful and almost drowning in shopping bags, he had accepted that he was in love with her. In love with Lana Hargrove. That was like asking to be punched in the stomach.

Then bullets had started flying. Fast. Justin ignored the bullets and grabbed Lana's arm and pulled her on the other side of the bed toward the window. Her eyes were wide as she stared at him and covered her head to protect it from the shattering glass and wood that rained through the room.

Justin peered through the window toward the bottom. It was a long way down. A bullet skimmed past his head and shattered glass. Justin felt Lana yank his arm toward the ground.

"Do you have a gun?" she screamed over the loud explosions.

Justin suddenly remembered the gun in his waistband and pulled it out. Justin carried a gun, but he rarely used it. First, Clarence had lectured him on the potential liability that the agency could face with any lethal injuries, and Justin always remembered each and every lecture whenever he thought to pull it out. And, second, if Justin wanted to be forced to kill someone, he would have joined the military or the police. He had become a private detective because he liked being his own boss and he could break the law for a legitimate reason. Not because he ever wanted to shoot someone.

"We have to get out of here," Justin said, stating the obvious, while pointing to the window.

"We're ten stories high," she retorted, then flinched as wood from the dresser near her head exploded in bits and pieces.

Justin placed his arm around her head to protect her from the flying debris and said, "But we're only two floors from the roof."

She stared at him in confusion and then he saw the understanding cross her face, and the fear. Then the window over their heads opened and a figure that blended in with the night blocked the window. Justin slid in front of Lana, placing himself in between her and the intruder, and aimed his gun at the window.

Frank's face came into view in the moonlight. His face with that irritating smirk. Justin heard Lana's sigh of relief at the same time that he muttered a curse and reengaged the safety on the pistol. He peered out the window and noticed that Frank balanced on the thin decorative ledge that circled the hotel.

Frank held out his hand and shouted, "Come on!"

Justin felt Lana hesitate and he suddenly noticed that it was silent. Too silent. He cursed when he heard the sound of magazines being reloaded into semiautomatic guns. He made Lana's decision for her and pushed her toward Frank. Frank grabbed her hand and hauled her out of the window, despite her scream.

"Hold on, Peanut; it's a long way down," Frank said, with a truly amused laugh.

"Oh no, oh no," Lana said softly as she shook her head. "I cannot be out here. I hate heights. I despise heights. Heights and I do not get along. We're pretty high up, aren't we—"

"How can I have a child who is scared of heights?" Frank asked while shaking his head in amazement.

Justin rolled his eyes at the fact that neither one appeared the least concerned that there were people trying to kill them on the other side of the barely-hanging-there door. He climbed out onto the ledge that suddenly seemed too crowded as the three pressed their backs to the building.

"We have to move. Whoever is out there is going

to be coming in soon. Hotel security has probably been notified, but they won't be here fast enough. Can you do it, baby?" Justin said quietly to Lana as Frank scanned the building.

Justin watched her face as the wind whipped her hair around it. Her eyes were glued to the sidewalk below. She clung to the building with an iron grip. Justin knew Lana must have been scared as hell because she didn't even complain about her obviously broken nails.

Justin prayed as he removed one hand from holding on to the building and touched Lana's face. She finally stopped looking at the ground and turned to him. It was the most scared he had ever seen her, and he realized that he didn't like it. He wanted her strong and angry and in love with him.

"Lana, you can do this. Just think, if two idiots like your father and I can do it, then you can, too." She stared at him, fine trembles wracking her body, but she may as well have been a part of the building, because she obviously wasn't moving one muscle.

"I think I can reach the balcony above us," Frank said, oblivious to his daughter's impending mental breakdown. He used the building as leverage and held on long enough to reach for the bottom rung of the balcony. With a grunt, he took a leap of fate and caught the bottom of the balcony railing. With the grace and ease of an acrobat, he flipped his legs over and pulled himself to the top of the balcony.

Frank lay on the balcony floor and held out his hand to Lana. "Come on, Peanut."

Lana briefly glanced at Frank, then stared back at Justin. Tears filled her eyes as she shook her head. "I can't," she whispered, her voice cracking.

"Peanut, we don't have time," Frank said, his voice urgent.

Justin glared at Frank, then said as patiently as he could, considering he balanced on a three-inch-wide concrete ledge that was not meant to hold his weight, let alone him and Lana, "I'm not leaving you, Lana. Both of us can die on this ledge. Or we both can try to get the hell out of here."

"I can't do it—"

"Yes, you can," he interrupted her in a firm voice. "Do you trust me, Lana?"

Confusion crossed her face, but then she slowly nodded.

Justin smiled and whispered, "Then trust me when I tell you that you can do anything. Anything you want, Lana."

She took a few deep breaths; then she nodded and reached for her father's hand. She stepped on Justin's offered thigh as Frank pulled. Her legs dangled over the edge of nothing for a moment before she climbed over the balcony railing. Justin jumped, then pulled himself onto the balcony at the same time that he heard a group of men burst into the hotel bedroom, screaming and shouting threats. Frank and Lana both helped him onto the balcony.

Justin got to his feet and was greeted with the most awesome hug of his life as Lana threw her arms around his neck, holding him tight while her hard, ragged breaths screamed in his ears. He wrapped his arms around her waist and held on to her, his eyes closed, just enjoying the feel of her in his arms. Enjoying having her close and just his for a moment.

"Come on," Frank said, sounding strangely upset.

Justin reluctantly released Lana, and Frank tried to open the window to the hotel room that was directly above theirs. It wouldn't budge and he pulled a slim black case from his inside coat pocket. He pulled out a slender silver rod and inserted it in the window. The lock popped with a small click that sounded deafening in the now-silent night.

Frank tugged open the window of the lit room, then helped Lana into the room. Justin fell in after her. A man stood near a table with a telephone in his hand as a woman sat up in the bed with a sheet held against her obviously bare chest.

"We're just passing through, folks," Frank said as he tugged Lana and Justin toward the hotel door. "We're filming a movie here, one of those big Hollywood movies. Stunt gone wrong. Wait until Spielberg hears about this one."

The man and woman looked at each other, then warily watched Frank, Justin, and Lana run from the room.

Lana didn't know if she would ever be able to forget the sound of the gunfire or the feel of the wind on her face as she clung on to the side of a building. She sat in the backseat of a car that her father had pulled up in after she and Justin had been hiding in a parking garage a few blocks from the hotel. She didn't want to know where her father got the car, and she didn't care. She just wanted to get far away from the hotel, from the men with guns, and from the complete idiot she had made of herself on the hotel ledge. Frank and Justin had acted like the professional thieves they were, while she had completely turned into a pile of nerves as soon as she looked down. Of course, she still broke into a cold sweat at remembering how high up they had been.

Frank turned the car into a residential neighborhood of restored, pre-war homes in southeast DC. He passed a few houses, then turned into an alley where the garages were. He parked the car under one of the carports.

Lana noticed Justin glancing at Frank and Frank muttering under his breath, "If you have any better ideas, just let me know."

"Where are we?" Lana asked, glancing around the dark alley.

Neither man answered her, but instead they stood from the car. Justin opened the door for her, then abruptly turned and walked to the steps that led to a back door. He pulled a ring of keys from his pants pocket and unlocked it. Lana stood from the car, still confused, but followed her father as Justin opened the door and walked into the house, turning on light switches.

She walked through the door that led directly into

the clean and tidy kitchen that was surprisingly modern for the obvious age of the house. She noticed the all-new kitchen appliances and gleaming pots that hung from the rack over the island in the center and the bowl of fresh fruit on a counter. This was the home of someone who took a lot of care with it.

Justin continued down a hallway where he turned on more lights. Lana turned to her father, who headed straight for the refrigerator.

"Whose house is this?" she whispered. "Should we be in here?"

Frank shrugged, then pulled a loaf of bread from the refrigerator. "Do you want a sandwich?"

"Frank, I cannot handle being arrested on top of everything else that's happened tonight. Is it all right that we're in this house? Whose house is this?"

"Mine," Justin said from his position in the door frame of the kitchen. Lana whirled around to see him watching her, a strange expression on his face. "It's my house, Lana."

"It is?" she asked, surprised. "You live in DC?"

He visibly hesitated, then asked dully, "Do you want a tour?"

"Justin—"

Justin interrupted Frank, "The living room has a nice view of the Capitol."

Lana glanced at her father, who was shaking his head in disappointment. She nodded at Justin and he walked down the hallway. Lana followed him and sighed in wonder at the living room at the end of the hallway. There were large windows covered by sheer curtains, and the almost bleak surrounding colors didn't match Justin's personality. She would have expected something thoroughly modern and expensive from Justin.

She smiled when she saw the gaggle of framed photographs on the fireplace mantel. She hadn't expected Justin to have pictures in his home. She didn't know what she had expected of Justin. He had a family, friends, and a history before her, but she thought he would be too private to put it on display. She crossed the room and stared at the pictures. She saw a picture of an older couple, who could only be Justin's parents. Justin looked like his father, but Lana could not see him wearing the three-piece suit with the starched shirt collar that the man wore.

Then Lana's gaze rested on another framed picture. Her heart skipped a beat, then began to pound so hard against her chest that she could barely hear anything over it. She grabbed the frame and studied the picture more closely. Three men in dark suits stood in front of a modern, familiar business building on K Street. All three men were smiling at the camera as they stood next to a large sign that read BAXTER & BAXTER INVESTIGATIONS.

She nearly broke the frame as she replaced it on the mantelpiece. Her breath became shallow as she stared at another frame. This frame held a newspaper article. The article was about how a priceless artifact had been recovered for the Smithsonian by

Clarence and Justin Baxter, the owners of Baxter & Baxter Investigations.

Lana slowly turned to face Justin, who continued to watch her from his position near one of the windows. She reminded herself to breathe as she stared from the newspaper article to him.

"Now we all know," Frank said matter-of-factly from the hallway as he walked into the living room, biting into a peanut butter and jelly sandwich.

"Shut up, Frank," Justin said harshly, his eyes never leaving Lana.

"Who are you?" Lana whispered, staring at him, as if seeing him for the first time. Seeing everything about him that never would have been like an art thief.

Justin said quietly, "My name is Justin Baxter, and I'm a private investigator."

"You're a . . . a . . . what?" she whispered, shaking her head.

"He's a private investigator," Frank said helpfully.

Justin glared at Frank once more, then turned to Lana and said quietly, "I was hired by the Smithsonian to find Frank."

"But you work with my father?" she said, confused.

"No, I don't, Lana," he said softly.

"I always knew, but I felt he needed the fees from the Smithsonian," Frank said, with a shrug.

"You found Frank. Why is he still free? Why are you still . . ." Her voice trailed off because she wasn't certain what she wanted to say. She wasn't certain of anything anymore. She was in love with a man who didn't exist. She had made love to a man who didn't exist. She crossed her arms over her chest, suddenly feeling violated, feeling like she was the punch line in a cruel joke.

"Thanks, Peanut," Frank said dryly.

Then Lana saw the guilty expression on Justin's face. She whispered accusingly, "Lattimore."

Justin finally looked at her, his expression a blank mask. "I think Frank is right about Xavier Lattimore. For a long time the Smithsonian has been looking for an inside leak, and I think it's him. He's close to high-ranking museum employees, he has access to the acquiring list, and he has the money and arrogance to get the pieces he wants."

"You're no better than Frank," she said, surprised by how calm she sounded, even when she thought of Justin kissing her in the cabin, making love to her, making her feel loved and special. "You did this for the money. All of this . . . All of this is for the money."

"I'm sorry, Lana. I should have told you the truth before . . ." His voice trailed off, but they both knew what he meant. Before they made love. She darted a glance at Frank, more embarrassed by the somber expression on his face. As if he suddenly realized this wasn't a joke anymore, that his daughter's pain should be taken seriously.

"Yes, you should have," she finally said to Justin.

She glanced from her father to Justin. She didn't have the energy to be angry, to scream like she knew they expected her to do. She didn't have the energy to make a sharp retort. For the second time in her life, her heart was breaking, and the only people responsible for both times stood in the room with her.

"I'm going to sleep. Is there a bedroom I can use?" she asked, looking away.

"Up the stairs. Second door on your left," Justin said, sounding confused.

"Peanut, are you hungry?" Even Frank sounded concerned as she began to trudge up the stairs. "You haven't eaten anything since lunch and—"

"I'm just tired." Neither man said another word, and she walked into the dark bedroom and closed the door.

And even though she had vowed not to, she slid to the floor and buried her face in her hands and cried.

CHAPTER SEVENTEEN

Justin was having the most delicious dream he'd had since he was fifteen years old. Except now his dreams were more detailed and didn't center on a movie star or Janet Jackson but starred one woman. Lana. Her mouth traveled down his chest to his stomach, her tongue darting into his navel. Justin shivered and clutched the sheets.

Her mouth went even lower and Justin moaned. Then one of her hands wrapped around him. She stroked the length of him, slowly and sensuously. Justin opened his eyes because the feelings that raced through him were too real and powerful to be a dream. He sat up in the sofa and found Lana straddling him, her hand on his length, a seductive smile on her face.

Justin's hands clamped on her shoulders as he inwardly cursed. He could see the revenge gleaming in her eyes. She wanted to make him pay for betraying her, for making her trust him.

"Lana—" He choked as she gently squeezed him. His eyes involuntarily closed as sheer pleasure wracked his body. If she continued to touch him, his vow to be a real man and apologize to her would be lost because he would slam into her and never let her go.

Justin cursed, then quickly disengaged himself from her grasp and jumped from the sofa, where he had been banished since Lana had taken his bed.

"What are you doing?" he demanded, placing his hands in front of his hardness.

Her gaze rested on his hands for a moment; then she met his eyes and smiled. That smile that told him he was in big trouble.

"I know you want me, Justin. It's *hard* for you to hide it from me," she said in a silky whisper.

Justin glanced up the stairs toward the closed doors where Frank slept. "Your father is—"

"I'll be quiet," she promised, then stood from the sofa and sauntered across the floor toward him, the picture of pure seduction. She wore one of his old, worn T-shirts, but he had never looked like that in them. She stopped only inches from him and placed a finger on his bare chest.

"Stop it, Lana," he said quietly.

"Stop what?"

"Stop this seductress routine just to prove to me that you aren't hurt."

A hard glint entered her eyes and she said coldly, "And why would I be hurt, Justin? I know what you want from me. You weren't shy about it. We're both adult enough to admit it was good and I want to do it again. Does that surprise you?"

"I didn't mean to hurt you," he said, silently pleading with her to understand. "Everything after the metro happened so fast. And I should have told you before we . . . before we made love—"

"We didn't make love. We had sex. It's simple. You picked the right girl, Justin. I don't care about emotions or feelings; I just want to have sex."

"I never thought that about you, Lana."

"Of course you did," she said, her cool voice still in place. "And it's all right, because that's what I am. I never pretended anything different and you never pretended to think anything different."

"Lana—"

She walked toward him again and her voice lowered to a whisper as she said, "So do you want me to rock your world or not?"

Justin knew that if he made love to her, if he touched her, he would never see her again.

He placed his hands on either side of her face and said softly, "I'm sorry, Lana. I should have told you, but . . . I'm a coward, and I thought that if I told you, you would look at me like you are right now. And I didn't want that. You're the only person who's really *seen* me for me in the last three years and I guess I didn't want to lose that."

For one moment the two stared at each other through a weighty silence. He could have sworn that a tear glistened in her eye before she pulled away from him. She said with a nonchalant shrug, "Your loss."

She walked up the stairs, the hem of the T-shirt barely skirting the tops of her thighs. He cursed when he heard the bedroom door slam. He stared up the stairs for a moment longer; then he couldn't resist any longer. He walked up the stairs. He didn't knock on the door but instead opened it and walked inside.

Lana sat up in the bed, her mouth opened in speechless shock. Then she slowly smiled and tossed her hair over her shoulder. She reached to pull the shirt over her head, but Justin walked across the room and sat on the bed and gently held her hands, stopping her. She stared at him, surprised, and then he kissed her on the lips. A soft, gentle kiss that could have been given in preschool from a little boy to a little girl. He kissed her again in the same manner, but this time he placed one in the center of her forehead. He skimmed his hands along the soft skin of her jaw.

Lana grabbed his ears and plunged her tongue into his open mouth. Justin's body felt electrified from the contact and his hands dug into her shoulders. Her moan made him grab her hair. Their tongues mated and fought and they lay back on the bed, with Justin in between her legs.

He moved on top of her, his thighs pressing against hers as his tongue pushed inside her mouth. Kissing Lana was like a never-ending erotic dream. The sensations built and continued until he couldn't lie still anymore. His hands roamed over her body, feeling the warmth and the softness of her body through the clothes she wore, feeling the surprising strength in her hands and arms as she wrapped her arms around him. Her tongue battling with his.

He resisted the urge to tear off her clothes, to pound himself inside of her heat like he wanted to. He wanted to go slow with her. Really slow. Like a week's-worth-of-lovemaking-in-bed slow. He couldn't pull from her lips just yet, and he groaned at the feel of her tongue lazily running through his mouth, as if they had all the time in the world.

A small part of Justin's brain that remembered he had come in here to show Lana how much he cared about her, not about sex, made him pull back.

"What's wrong?" she whispered, her lips swollen.

Justin licked his own lips and said, "You were so brave tonight at the hotel. You amaze me, Lana. Every day something else about you amazes me."

Her expression softened and Justin kissed her then. Not the hard, passionate kisses full of lust they always shared but soft and deep and full of emotion. He pulled from her and she stared at him, her eyes wide with surprise and an unrecognizable emotion.

"When you move, all I can think about is kissing you, being inside of you even while listening to you talk about what imbeciles men are," he said, with a slight laugh. "I don't think I've ever been insulted so creatively as I have been by you. And maybe I'm not smart enough to know exactly how much you're insulting me, but you make me laugh, and I haven't laughed in a long time."

Lana stared at him, her expression becoming more and more troubled. She tried to move from him, but Justin refused to allow her to leave. He kissed her again and felt her melt into him, move against him and into him again.

He ran his tongue along her lower lip and she sighed, her breath hot against his mouth. "And know that tomorrow night, while you're dancing and laughing with Longfellow, I will have to restrain myself from bashing in his overinflated head when he touches you. I know you'll think I'm an overbearing man for thinking this, but you're mine, Lana, and I don't want anyone touching you, looking at you. No one but me."

"Justin," she sighed, then kissed him again, but there was no rush in her kiss now. Only the need to give and to receive.

When she had gone to the living room, the only thoughts on her mind had been conquering him, proving to him that she could sleep with him with no strings attached, that she could experience these emotions with him and not care. But her plan had been stupid, she realized. She couldn't do that with Justin, no matter how he lied or why he lied. And she didn't know if it was his touch or his words that had made her completely defenseless. She would berate herself tomorrow morning, but tonight she would enjoy the feel of him, of knowing that one man wanted her for herself, not just for her body or what he thought she could do.

The contrast of his hard, different skin against the

skin on her body that never saw the light of day made her gasp and bite her lower lip. Sparks and jolts of lightning flowed through her body with the one touch. He moved too slowly, like lava, slow and destructive with one touch. Through the moonlight that filtered into the room she saw his glittering eyes when he slowly and gently finally pulled the shirt over her head and tossed it on the floor. For a moment he just stared at her and Lana thought the world stopped. His stare could make her feel her heart beat.

He touched her stomach as if he owned her; then he slowly traced her sternum to her breasts, which he squeezed gently before his fingers moved down to her nipples, softly and deftly twirling them.

"Justin," she whispered as he placed his open mouth on her right breast, his tongue flickering and teasing. She could barely hear herself breathe as wave after wave of want and need built inside her from the flick of his warm tongue.

He tugged on the nipple with his teeth and Lana called his name again. His tongue traced across her chest to the other breast and she grabbed his head as he practically inhaled her. She pulled his head closer as he suckled at her breast, pulling invisible strands of pleasure with his tongue. His mouth moved lower and farther down to her stomach, then to the waistband of her underwear. Nerves and pleasure warred in her body as he pulled the underwear down, then gently laid her on the bed. His eyes moved over her entire body, branding every inch of her with his hot stare.

She had never been nervous before under a man's gaze, but she was beginning to realize that everything was a first with Justin.

"You're so smooth," he whispered in a deep voice that made her shudder.

She still hadn't succeeded in catching her breath when he began to kiss her—one of the open-mouth passionate, hard kisses that made her toes curl. She suddenly remembered to touch him and her hands immediately began to stroke his bare chest. He felt rock-hard, much different from her softness, and it made her breathless. She kissed his neck, then his chest, and smiled as he shuddered. She felt powerful and strong, even in her softness, because she could make a man such as Justin Baxter shake with need. That she could make his hand shake even as he tried to move slow and kiss her.

She tried to voice her protest as he moved from her lips. He placed open-mouth kisses down her body, and her legs restlessly moved against the sheets, her legs falling wider apart of their own accord, wishing him and calling him toward her center. She squirmed on the bed as his hot breath touched her in the one place where she wanted to feel him. Lana nearly reared off the bed as his tongue finally touched her, as if she had been waiting her whole life for just that touch. She sighed his name as he kissed her, more intensely and deeply than she had thought possible.

Lana placed her hands in his hair and felt the pleasure wrack her body as his tongue and lips snaked through her body. She was close. She could feel herself at the crest of something beautiful, and with the final swipe of his tongue she tumbled into the abyss of pleasure. She gasped his name over and over. When she opened his eyes, she watched in a daze as he tore off his shorts.

Lana was awed as she stared at his beautiful body. He was a perfect specimen that should have been immortalized in sculpture. She almost felt intimidated by his perfection until his lips traveled over her body, over every inch of her, followed by his strong hands. He left no spot unexplored, even tasting the skin at her ankle and kissing her toes. He took his time, seeming to make time stand still, as he continued his exploration. She forgot about her previous combustion and her body was instantly ready to receive him again, sending small quivers from her toes to the tips of her fingers. While he moved slower, Lana squirmed and grabbed at his shoulders to rush him, unable to go slow anymore, unable to wait. She had never begged a man before, but as she told herself over and over, Justin Baxter was not a normal man.

"Justin, please . . ." She forgot what she wanted to say as his hands traveled to the juncture between her thighs.

"I can't wait much longer," Justin whispered into her ear. "I can't . . ."

"Don't wait," she said, wrapping her hands around his head and pulling him to her neck.

"But I want to make it perfect." She could hear the strain in his voice, the need, and it made her shake. "Not yet. We still have more time—"

She took matters into her own hands and brought him inside of her. She cried out, as he grunted, as the intense pressure flowed through her. She bit her lower lip to restrain the scream of pleasure as he began to move inside her. She couldn't handle the luxurious waves of Justin that raced throughout her body as his tongue plunged inside her mouth. They moved as one on the bed, giving and receiving pleasure. Lana opened her mouth to speak, but no sound came out, and she could only grip his shoulders as it began. And once more, Lana found herself flying over the edge of sensual gratification. A few seconds later, Justin shuddered and moaned her name.

As Justin planted a kiss on the top of her head and pulled her against his body, Lana realized at that moment that she was a thirty-year-old woman who had been told she was loved by numerous men, but she didn't know how to handle this emotion, this much obvious proof that a man cared about her, that he wanted her. And it scared the hell out of her. More than heights did.

CHAPTER EIGHTEEN

Lana opened her eyes and squinted at the sunlight that flooded the bedroom. She groaned in protest, then turned over. Her heart stopped when she saw that the other side of the bed was empty. He had been there when she had fallen into a worried sleep earlier. She rubbed her eyes and silently cursed. Last night had been another mistake. She was in love with Justin, whoever Justin was, and while he may care about her, they both knew he was not in love with her. Because after all his words last night about how much he cared for her, he had never said the three words that no one had ever said to her before.

Lana sat up in the bed when she heard the sound of voices from downstairs. She assumed it was her father and Justin speaking until she heard the soft sound of female laughter. And while she told herself she didn't care who Justin spoke with, she still couldn't allow another woman in this house while she lay in his bed with his clean soap smell around her.

Lana quickly ran into the adjoining master bath-room. She took the quickest shower of her life—which would have surprised any of her friends—then used a packaged toothbrush she found in one of the cabinet drawers. She frowned at her image in the bathroom mirror. She had started carrying a mini–makeup kit in her handbag after being marooned at the cabin, but the makeup and her handbag were in the hotel room that had been turned into a demolition field.

Lana cursed and tried her best with a brush she found in a drawer and a tube of lip balm in another. The results were not impressive, but she had worked with less before. She heard the sound of laughter again and she forgot her vanity and threw on her dress and washed-out underwear from yesterday. She looked in the mirror again, then rolled her eyes at her reflection, which refused to suddenly grow beautiful, and raced out of the room.

She had almost set foot on the first step when someone grabbed her arm. She whirled around, her fist raised, and she stopped inches from her father's surprised and delighted face. She resisted the urge to let her fist plow through.

Frank placed a hand to his mouth to signal quiet, then pointed down the stairs. "Justin's partner, Clarence, is here," he whispered, moving her to a vantage point where she could see Justin's bare feet across from highly polished black wingtip shoes.

"Justin has a partner?" she asked, surprised.

"Dead weight," Frank muttered, shaking his head.

Lana heard a deep male voice say, ". . . This has gone far enough, Justin. Where is Frank?"

Justin sounded annoyed as he replied, "I told you that I'm seeing this through until the end. Fire me—"

"I don't want to fire you . . . and I checked with our lawyers; I *can't* fire you," the man retorted.

Lana instantly hated Clarence. *She* was the only one who could talk like that to Justin. Frank placed a restraining hand on her shoulder and she realized that she had moved toward the stairs. She glared at her father, but he shook his head and motioned for her to be quiet.

"Can both of you please calm down?" came the soft female voice that must have owned the laughter Lana had heard earlier. Lana instantly hated the woman, too. She didn't like her feminine voice or the fact that her stiletto heels came to stand too close to Justin's bare feet. "Justin, Clarence didn't come here to argue with you or to tell you what to do. He's worried about you. After we heard about the gunfight at the hotel, we both were worried. We just wanted to make certain that you were all right."

"I'm fine," Justin said gruffly.

"And what about Frank?" Clarence demanded. "Is he fine, too?"

"Clarence, please," the woman said quietly.

Clarence apparently ignored her, because he continued, "And Lana? There were reports that a woman broke into a room with two men at the same time that security was alerted about shots in the hotel. Was Lana with you, Justin? Is that who you're protecting?"

Lana glanced at her father, who shrugged, entirely too calm. She shrugged off his hand and moved closer to the top of the stairs.

The woman said hesitantly, "Clarence told me about this woman, Justin. More than anyone, I want you to find the love that I've found with Clarence, but she . . . She sounds . . . You can't trust her. You always told me that you can't trust anyone during an assignment."

Lana gasped softly in outrage and almost started down the stairs to defend herself, but Justin's sharp tone stopped her. "I trust Lana Hargrove with my life. I can only count two other people I've ever said that about in my life, and neither one of them is in this room."

Tears filled Lana's eyes. It was the first time that anyone had ever defended her.

"This is insane," Clarence muttered. "I told you it was useless to come here, Caroline. Justin finally gets some and he's lost all objectivity. It would actually mean something if she didn't give it to anyone who walked by—"

Whatever else Clarence was about to say was interrupted by the sound of flesh hitting bone and then a loud crash. Lana ran down the stairs and gasped when she saw Clarence sprawled on the ground, holding his nose, while Justin stood over him, his hands balled into fists. His expression was frozen into a hard mask of rage and anger.

A woman with short dark curls ran to Clarence and shot Justin a look of censure until her dark brown eyes rested on Lana. A strange look crossed her face before she turned to Clarence.

Lana touched Justin's shoulder and he looked at her. His anger melted away and he looked more sad than anything. She touched his scarred face and whispered, "Are you all right?"

He nodded silently, then directed a grunt at Clarence: "Get out of my house."

Justin stroked Lana's hair, then walked out of the living room and into the kitchen. Lana watched Justin's ex-wife help Clarence to stand as he moaned and touched his nose. She noticed their matching wedding rings and shook her head in disgust and anger.

Clarence froze when he saw Lana. He appeared on the verge of saying something, but then he glanced in the direction of the hallway where Justin had disappeared and kept his mouth shut.

"You must be Lana," Caroline said, with a nod of greeting.

Lana crossed her arms over her chest and said coldly, "And you must be Justin's ex-wife . . . or should I say his cousin's present wife?"

Caroline's expression remained impassive, while Clarence had the decency to look guilty.

"Let's go, Caroline. Obviously, nothing we'll say will be listened to," Clarence mumbled as he limped toward the door.

Caroline continued to stare at Lana, and Lana held the woman's gaze. She expected Caroline to defend herself or curse at Lana. Lana never had many pleasant interactions with other women. She often wrote it off as jealousy, but she knew it was because she was a hard woman to get along with.

Caroline surprised her when she said gently, "He's a good man, and he needs someone to love him as much as he deserves to be loved, as much as he'll love her in return if she can get him to."

Lana nodded slowly. She wanted to ask Caroline about Justin's love, if he would give it to anyone again. But Caroline turned and helped Clarence out of the house. Lana looked up the stairs at her father, who stood in the middle of the staircase. He rolled his eyes skyward, then turned and went to his room, obviously the events of the day too much for him to waste energy caring about.

Justin couldn't believe that the sight of Clarence and Caroline together still made his chest hurt. He now realized as he stood in his small backyard, staring at the tree that he and Caroline had planted together five years ago, that it wasn't because he wanted Caroline or because he hated his cousin for having the courage to love a woman who loved him in return. He was jealous of their closeness, of the fact that they had each other.

He heard the back door open and close, and he prayed it wasn't Lana. He didn't know how long she had listened to the conversation with his cousin and

Caroline, but he didn't want to see the pity in her eyes that inevitably came when someone realized that he had lost his wife to his cousin. Especially after last night when he had laid his cards on the table, when he had told her how he felt and gotten nothing in return. He had gotten mind-blowing sex, but besides that . . .

Since his prayers were never answered, Justin was not surprised that it was Lana. Her bright smile was forced as she walked toward him.

"So now you know the truth," Justin said, laughing dryly. "Caroline left me for Clarence. Clarence told my aunt that they didn't sleep together while Caroline and I were married, that they got close while I was in the hospital after the fire, but I don't believe them."

"Justin—"

"I really don't want to talk about this," he interrupted her angrily.

"Caroline and Clarence . . . they have nothing to do with you," she said quietly.

Justin glared at her, then averted his gaze because he couldn't stand to look at her. Not after what she had heard, what she had seen.

"I have a lot of prep work to do tonight," he muttered. "So do you. We should both get ready. Nothing can go wrong tonight."

She stared at him for a moment; then her gaze suddenly grew cold. She said tightly, "It must be hard for you to feel sorry for yourself all the time. Your face,

Caroline, you can't even properly apologize to me for your lying; you have to seduce me with words and kisses. You told me that you want to live life on your own terms, but if that includes being scared of everything and everyone who may judge you or tell you that you're wrong, then the only terms you're living by are fear. And even though you can probably make me forgive you each and every time, you're an ass, Justin. You should have told me the truth before. I deserved that much. Any chance we could have had at something deserved that much, but maybe that's why you never said anything. Because you didn't want the chance. Because what if it had actually worked?"

Justin stared at the ground, refusing to acknowledge that every word she said was true. Without another word she walked into the house, slamming the door behind her. He groaned when he heard the door open and close again.

He almost smiled in relief when he saw Frank struggling down the back steps, with his injured leg at a straight angle. He came to stop beside Justin.

"That's gotta hurt," Frank said simply. "Losing your wife to your cousin, especially if that cousin is a wimp like yours is."

Justin rolled his eyes and muttered dryly, "Thanks, Frank. You always have that knack of making me feel better."

Frank shrugged and sat on the top porch step. "That's life," he said, then sighed as if he had imparted some great wealth of knowledge.

"What's life?" Justin snapped, annoyed. "Having your face destroyed in a fire? Having your wife leave you and marry your cousin and business partner? Having your family feel sorry for you and tiptoe around you because of it? Having everyone feel sorry for you? Is that life, Frank? Well, I have some news for you: life sucks."

Frank just stared at him and Justin rolled his eyes. The man was infuriating. Justin was beginning to see the merits of Xavier Lattimore's vendetta to destroy him.

"Those scars on your face really bother you, don't they?" Frank asked, sounding surprised.

"Yes, Frank, they do," Justin snapped. "Looking like a circus freak tends to bother people. In fact, it tends to wreak havoc on your life. I'm the prime example. Before fire, I had a great life. After fire and circus freak resemblance, I have . . . I have this life."

"That's funny," Frank finally said, sounding amused. "But, that's not how I see your life."

"How do you see it?" Justin muttered.

"Well, I see that you have a cousin and an ex-wife who love you enough to check on you after hearing about a gunfight at a hotel you may or may not have been staying at. I see that you're a healthy guy who doesn't have to watch his cholesterol yet. I see that you have this house here; that's pretty damn nice. I see that you're not wanted in a few dozen countries for some crimes you did commit but for a bunch that you didn't. I see your loving family, like your uncle and your father and your mother, who makes that damn good apple cobbler that I just finished in the kitchen. And I see that you're still young enough and brave enough and dumb enough to have a chance to do something great with your life if you want to."

Justin glared at the older man for a moment, but Frank calmly returned his gaze. He finally muttered, "Then you're blind."

"When I was younger, I thought having a great life meant having the most money or the most things, giving my wife things. Then when she died, I thought having a great life meant paying back the people who hurt me and hurt the people that I love. And you want to know what I think now?"

"No, but I'm sure you'll tell me."

Frank laughed softly, then said, "Now I think that having a great life would be to own a house like this, go to work every day, drive the kids to soccer practice, change the oil and rotate the tires, take out the trash, and stare at a woman who would stare at me the way my daughter looks at you."

Justin lost all his anger and looked at Frank. "I'm so scared," he admitted. "I don't know what to do."

"First we're going to catch that Lattimore bastard. Then you're going to open your own agency, because no matter how big a man you are, it can't be good for your psyche to be around your cousin and ex-wife. And then you and Lana are going to live happily ever after."

"Lana is never going to speak to me again."

"We Hargroves have to throw temper tantrums every once in a while. She'll come around."

"I wish I had your faith."

"She loves you, Bubba. If she didn't, you would have been eating your gonads for breakfast after she found out about the Larkin–Baxter distinction. *Capisce?*"

Justin smiled at the distant prospect of it all, then said, "And what about you?"

Frank winked and said, "Let's take this one art thief at a time."

Justin laughed and shook his head.

Lana froze with milk dripping from the spoon halfway to her mouth as Frank limped into the kitchen, then plopped across the table from her. He ignored her as he stacked black rope on the table. He cheerfully began to coil it. Lana dropped her spoon in the cereal and milk and pushed the bowl away.

"Lost your appetite?" Frank asked, glancing at her.

"Must be the company," she replied coolly. Frank laughed in response, then continued to coil the rope. Lana asked coldly, "So, as your daughter, can I ask where you've been for the last twenty years when you weren't stealing and getting your name in the paper?"

"You'd be surprised."

"Try me."

"I have a cottage in a small beach town in California. Only surfers and health nuts and ex–art thieves live there. People wave to each other, say hi. We have a pumpkin fair every fall. I have a view of the ocean, and a rose garden that your mother would have loved. There's a bakery I go to every weekend and they make the best carrot muffins I've ever tasted."

"It sounds too good to be real," Lana said sarcastically. "In fact, I think I got a cavity just from listening to you describe it. I was waiting for the part where little Mary Sue comes around every morning to deliver the newspaper on her blue bicycle because her daddy can't work since the mill closed down."

There was a pause as he looked at her and she sent him a challenging lift of her eyebrow. He grinned proudly, then said, "You're a smart-ass, you know that?"

Lana glared at him in return, but she couldn't resist laughing at his bright smile. "Only you would consider that a compliment."

"Your mother had a mouth on her," Frank said as he focused on the rope. "She could curse like a sailor. It was the first thing that attracted me to her. That and the fact that she wouldn't give me the time of day . . . at first. Then she was worn down by my charm."

Lana smiled in response to her father's statement, then frowned when Frank looked at her. She told herself to just get up, wash out the bowl of cereal, and walk out of the kitchen. She had to go to Pauline's house so she could find a dress to wear that night, since her own dress had been destroyed, but for some reason she didn't want to leave. Besides, she was hungry.

"Do you remember her?" Frank asked, the casualness in his tone making her see how truly serious he was.

She didn't have to ask who he meant. "No, I can't remember anything."

"She was fun. She could make going to the dry cleaners an adventure. And sometimes she could make us laugh so hard that our stomachs would hurt," he said, his gaze unfocused as he lost himself in the past. "She had the most beautiful smile I've ever seen. And she was gorgeous, like you. She worked at a hospital in administration and she loved her job. On her breaks, she would go to the pediatrics ward to read to the children or she would go to the pre-natal ward and hold those babies that had been abandoned or born on one drug or another."

"She sounds amazing," Lana whispered, not bothering to hide the tears in her voice.

"She was," he said, then continued, "She loved gardening. We had a beautiful garden in the front of our house that she loved to work in on the weekends. And there were so many plants inside the house that I would tease her about starting a rainforest in the middle of Los Angeles. But you know what she liked to do more than gardening, more than anything?"

"What?"

Frank focused on her and his smile was gentle as

he said, "Spend time with you. She loved you so much, Lana. You were her best friend, her sun and her moon. She told me that she hadn't known it, but when the doctor placed you in her arms, she realized that she had waited her whole life for you. Watching the two of you together, it made my heart feel full."

A tear slid down Lana's cheek, which she quickly wiped away. "I wish I could remember her."

"You do, Peanut. How you walk, talk, flip your hair, even your weakness for designer bags and shoes, it's all Bea."

"It is?"

"She would have been proud of you."

"You think so?" Lana asked, hating the hope in her voice.

"All she wanted was for you to be happy."

"I am happy," she said, then wondered why she felt like she was lying, especially when her father pinned her with that look that she imagined a father who cared about his daughter would do. "Why wouldn't I be? I have my own business that's becoming more and more successful every day. I love what I do. I had one of the best town houses in the city before one of your friends burned it down. I have a fabulous social life, I'm invited to every party that means anything, or I was before this week. And I'm dating a fabulous man, who didn't give me too much trouble for standing him up for dinner."

"This fabulous man . . . That's Bruce Longfellow?"

"Yes."

Frank studied her for a moment, then said, "Your life does sound . . . fabulous."

"It is," she said firmly. She tried to ignore his doubtful expression as he went back to coiling the rope, except for some reason she found it almost impossible to do so. She inwardly cursed. She hadn't known her father for more than two days and already she sought his approval. "What?" she demanded more peevishly than she intended.

"Nothing."

"Frank."

He shrugged. "Nothing, Lana. I'm just glad that you're happy and that after this is all over, you can go back to your happy life with all of your happy friends and happy boyfriend."

Lana didn't like his facetious tone, but she didn't make a sarcastic retort. Instead, she pushed around the remaining Cheerios in her bowl. She didn't feel very happy at that moment.

"Do you remember when we went to the Angels game for the Fourth of July when you were seven years old?"

"I remember," she said blandly.

"You ate three hot dogs. You didn't even get sick," he said, laughing. "You loved baseball. You wanted to be Reggie Jackson and, damn it, I believed you could have done it if you hadn't discovered makeup."

"June third, 1983."

He grinned. "The date that shall live in infamy."

She laughed. "You were one of my first experiments.

If I remember correctly, CoverGirl's Rogue Red matched your skin tone perfectly."

Frank grinned. "Did Grandma let you experiment on her?"

"Only when she thought no one would see her."

Frank smiled and Lana found herself smiling in return. The only other person who could understand her grandmother—the annoyance and love for the difficult and opinionated woman—was her father.

"Mom wasn't the makeup type," he said, shaking his head in amusement. "She was a tough old bird. Did she make you go on the hikes with her?"

"Every Sunday at five in the morning," she said, grinning.

"I miss those hikes," he murmured.

Lana's smile slowly faded. "You didn't make it to her funeral. Even after all those years when you were gone, she never said a bad word about you. She never let me say a bad word about you. She deserved better—"

"I was there," he interrupted her, the amusement gone from his face.

"No, you weren't—"

"Yes, I was. I saw the dozens and dozens of pink tulips. Mom would have liked that."

Lana stared at him in surprise. Her grandmother's casket had been surrounded by the flowers. Everyone in the neighborhood had shown up at the funeral, surprising Lana because her grandmother had been such a loner. Or that's what Lana had thought, but it had seemed as if everyone had thought they had a special connection with Harriet Hargrove.

"You were there?"

"I talked to Mom at least once a week," he said, not meeting her gaze. "She was my best friend, Lana, and she had you."

"Why didn't you talk to me at the funeral?" she asked, tears filling her eyes. "I was so numb, I couldn't even cry."

Frank placed a hand on top of hers and said quietly, "Me, too, Peanut. Me, too."

And that's when Lana saw all the love in his eyes for her grandmother and maybe even some for her. And she couldn't handle it. She couldn't handle realizing that her father was not the devil-may-care man that she had always imagined him to be. She stood abruptly from the table and carried the bowl to the kitchen sink. She took a few seconds to collect herself, because crying would never do; then she turned to her father. He was back to coiling the rope, a cheerful expression on his face once more.

Lana moved to leave the room and Frank said quietly, "Thanks."

"For what?" she asked, turning to face him.

He shrugged. "For finishing your bowl of cereal."

Lana didn't want to, but she sent him a hesitant smile; then she walked out of the room.

CHAPTER NINETEEN

"Thank you for the dress, Pauli," Lana said as she stared at her reflection in the full-length mirror in the corner of Pauline's bedroom. She smoothed down the front of the strapless black ankle-length dress. It was simple, elegant, and understated. In other words, not a dress she would pick out for herself. But at least it had a slit on the right that slashed to her thigh. She frowned as she took one step and barely an inch of skin showed.

Pauline applied blush to her high cheekbones and looked at Lana in the dresser mirror. "What happened to your dress again?"

"I decided that it wasn't right for this occasion," Lana lied.

Pauline turned to Lana, smiling. "You look beautiful, Lana."

"So do you," Lana said truthfully. Pauline had graciously loaned Lana a dress for that evening in exchange for an invitation to the party. Pauline was a good friend, but she also took what she could. "And thank you for the dress again. I don't know what I would have done without you."

"I get to ride in a limo with you and Bruce." Pauline's smile faltered and she abruptly became unnaturally focused on the lipstick tube in her hands. "I just don't think things are going to work out with Ethan and me. We got invited to Xavier Lattimore's party and he'd rather play tennis with his brother. How ridiculous is that? You would never stand for a man to do that to you."

Lana thought about Justin and said softly, "Maybe I'm . . . I'm not saying this is a total change in my attitude, but maybe sometimes—occasionally—every so often, I'm too hard on men. We all make mistakes, even men do, and I guess I don't recognize that as much as I should."

Pauline's mouth dropped open and she was speechless long enough for Lana to laugh.

Pauline placed a hand on her chest. "Did I just hear what I think I heard? Did Lana Hargrove just suggest giving a man a break?"

Lana sat on the bed to buckle the spaghetti straps on the stiletto heels that Pauline had loaned her for the night as well. At least, Pauline had good taste in shoes.

"And I think you're serious." Pauline sounded amazed and amused. She laughed abruptly and shook her head. "What's the cause of this new attitude?"

"Pauli, I'm just being logical."

"Being illogical has never stopped you before in your irrational views of men," she said.

"I've gone through a lot in the last few days and it's made me rethink things. Maybe I treat men like objects because that's how I've always felt they treated me. And maybe when I find one who likes me for me, who looks at me like I'm more than just a set of parts for his enjoyment, and who touches me like I'm special and not just a one-night stand, I'll find a man who deserves my respect."

Pauline looked as if she had suddenly seen a pig fly as she fell onto the bed. She audibly gulped, then said quietly, "I know Bruce, so I know you're not talking about him. Lana, is this Mystery Man responsible for your new attitude? Are you in love with him?"

Lana forced a too-loud laugh and shook her head. "Of course I'm not in love with Justin, Pauli. I don't even like him. He's a liar—he's everything about my father that I hate. And he doesn't love me, which I think should be the number one requirement before you love someone."

"You can't control who you love or when you love them, Lana."

"I can," she said firmly.

"You're in love with him," Pauline said softly. "It's a good thing."

Lana ignored Pauline and glanced at the clock on the nightstand next to the table.

"The limo should be here soon. How do I look?"

"You know you look beautiful," Pauline said, with a short laugh. She stood and walked across the room until Lana was forced to look at her. She hated the serious look on Pauline's face because she knew it could mean one thing—Pauline was going to tell her the truth. "You could have everything you want with Bruce, Lana. Respectability, stability, and financial security for the rest of your life. Now is not the time for you to develop a streak of romanticism. You can have Justin; just don't let Bruce know."

Lana recognized her own words coming from Pauline's mouth. She didn't know what else to say, so she smiled. Gratefully, she heard the sound of a car pulling up to the house. She peered out the window and smiled in relief when she saw the gleaming black limousine and Bruce, wearing a black tuxedo, walking toward the front door. She was relieved because she didn't have to continue this conversation with Pauline, not because Bruce was there.

"Lana, are you all right?" Pauline asked softly.

"I'm fine."

"Well, if nothing else, tonight will be interesting."

Lana watched Pauline leave the door and she muttered to the empty room, "You have no idea."

"She looks beautiful, doesn't she?" Frank said from his position in the passenger seat of the black van.

Justin squeezed the steering wheel, then glared at Frank, but his gaze was drawn back to Lana as Bruce helped her into the black limousine parked across the street from the van. He recited the names of the presidents of the United States under his breath to keep himself from running across the street and pummeling his fist in Bruce's face when he placed his hand on Lana's back.

Justin started the engine, then pulled into the street several cars behind the black limousine.

"Sometimes when I look at my daughter, I wonder how someone that beautiful and that ferocious could come from a man like me."

"Do you think she'll be happy with Bruce?"

"No," Frank said simply.

"You obviously haven't heard her talk about Bruce the Wonderful. To hear her, you would think that Bruce shits gold bricks."

"If you haven't noticed, Lana doesn't talk to me," Frank said, with an amused laugh. "The marriage won't last more than a year, if there is a marriage, but Peanut is smart, too smart to let herself be that miserable for long."

"I don't know, Frank. She wants the name that Bruce can give her."

When Frank didn't respond, Justin glanced at him. Frank looked thoughtful. Justin knew that a thoughtful Frank was usually a dangerous Frank. No one would ever know what Frank Hargrove thought, even when he claimed to be saying exactly what he thought, but when Frank had time to think about it, Justin itched for a pair of handcuffs.

"What are you plotting, old man?" Justin asked warily.

"I know how you feel about her, Justin," he said quietly. "And I know that you'll treat her well. I know that you won't let her walk all over you, that you'll make her be soft, and that you'll protect her even when she pushes you away. And Lana needs you, Justin. Don't let her make you think anything else, no matter what she says."

"Lana doesn't need anyone. Besides, after last night—"

"What happened last night?"

Justin cleared his throat when he remembered that he was talking to Lana's father. Not just his friend Frank. "I just doubt that Lana will talk to me again. I wouldn't be surprised if she didn't."

"Tonight, Lana lets you in and then she returns to the party," Frank abruptly switched the subject.

"That's the plan."

"And the police will be here as soon as we find the obelisk?"

"That is also the plan."

"You still have that childhood friend with the police?" Justin stared at him, surprised, and Frank winked. "I even know your third-grade teacher's name."

Justin smiled, then answered, "Barnie Paulsen. We went to elementary school and junior high school together."

"Are you two still on good terms?"

"Last year, he got me released when one of his colleagues caught me breaking into a suspect's office. I should have been arrested, but Barnie cleared it up."

"He sounds like a good friend."

"He is, even though I haven't been much of a friend to him since the fire. I haven't been much of a friend to anyone since . . ." Justin glanced at Frank and asked guardedly, "Why twenty questions, Frank?"

"I just like to have all of my ducks in a row. That's how I've lasted this long," Frank murmured, then whistled as the towers of Lattimore's mansion came into view. "I have to give him credit. Lattimore has good taste."

"Why would he risk all of this?"

"Men like Lattimore are never satisfied. Not with women or money or things."

Justin passed the mansion and pulled onto a hidden service road where he parked the van. He pulled a black ski mask and gloves from the glove compartment as Frank moved into the backseat with a grunt to sit in front of the computer equipment that would monitor the mansion.

Justin moved to get out the car just as Frank grabbed his arm. Justin turned to him, surprised.

"Take care of Lana," he said quietly.

"She won't be in any danger. After she opens the closet, she—"

"I don't mean just for tonight, Justin. She's my baby, and you may be the only person left who loves her almost as much as I do, or as her mother and grandmother did." Justin nodded, mostly because Frank expected him to, since now was not the time to once more explain to the older man that Lana would probably never speak to him again after tonight; then Frank smiled, satisfied, and patted his shoulder. "Good luck, and remember, don't get caught."

"Thanks for the advice," he said with a laugh.

Frank winked, then slid the van door closed. Justin pulled on the mask and gloves, then ran through the trees behind the mansion to wait for the appropriate time to break into the house of one of the most powerful men in DC.

CHAPTER TWENTY

"You wear that dress well," Bruce whispered in Lana's ear as he handed her a long-stemmed glass of champagne.

The two stood in the middle of the large library. The room held shelves and shelves of books, with a ladder in one corner that had tracks around the shelves. There were two brown leather sofas and a colorful and obviously expensive plush rug. The lamps were turned on and cast a romantic glow across the room, although romance was far from her mind as Lana stared at Bruce.

Her job had been to get into the library and to get the security alarm turned off. A few well-placed smiles and coos with Bruce and her mission was accomplished. She had pleaded with Bruce to take her from the party and the string quartet and numerous contacts that she should have been making and into the library that she had heard so much about. Bruce had found a Lattimore employee and complied, like the arrogant Bruce Longfellow that he was.

As Lana stood in the library pretending to care about the books, she realized that she was excited about tonight, that she looked forward to stealing the obelisk from under Lattimore's nose. She suddenly realized that she was Frank Hargrove's daughter and that she didn't regret the fact.

And as her first—and definitely last—act as an international art thief, she had get rid of Bruce.

"Did you hear me, Lana?" Bruce asked, moving closer to her. "You and that dress are the center of attention at this party. I'm glad that we left the crowd; I had a feeling that I was going to have to start fighting off men with a stick."

Lana didn't smile or laugh like he obviously expected her to, and she didn't think the excuse she had previously thought of involving her menstrual cycle would work, either, to drive him from the room; instead she tried the one thing that neither Justin nor Frank had thought about: the truth.

"Bruce, I need to tell you something."

"Anything."

"My father is a thief," she blurted out.

Bruce fell instantly silent and took one step back from her. "Excuse me?"

"He steals things, very valuable, very pretty things, from museums and art galleries and homes, homes like yours. I'm not bragging, but I have to give him his due—he's one of the most infamous art thieves in the world."

"Your father?" Bruce said uncertainly. She nodded and tried not to laugh at his horrified expression. He stared at her for several moments, unspeaking, as the murmurs and laughter of the party drifted down the hallway and into the library through the open doors. As if he suddenly had come to a decision, he nodded and said, "We can work around that, Lana. My father has always counseled complete and total denial. Clinton's only problem with the Lewinsky thing was that he gave in and admitted it. If anyone finds out and asks us about your father, we'll deny it. There must be hundreds of thousands, if not millions, of Hargroves in America—"

"I'm not denying my father," she interrupted him. "He's the last living relative I have. He's the only person in this world who loves me even if he doesn't know how to show it. I'm not denying that."

Lana realized that it was the truth. She couldn't deny her father, who had held her in bed when she had chicken pox and who had made her mother laugh.

That would have been the perfect moment for Bruce to say that he loved her, too, except he didn't. Bruce glanced around the room to make certain that no one was close enough to hear them, and then he quickly turned and closed the library doors. The room was completely silent as the two stared at each other.

"You should have told me this earlier," he snapped.

"Like before I brought you to this party. People have seen us together. . . ." His voice trailed off; then he snapped his fingers together and smiled. "On the other hand, an art thief isn't like a rapist or a pedophile. An art thief is almost . . . almost gentlemanly, kind of like Cary Grant, right? This could work—"

"Bruce, this isn't going to work between us," she said, shaking her head.

His mouth dropped open and he took several visible gulps of air before he asked in disbelief, "Are you breaking up with me? Women do not break up with Bruce Longfellow, Lana."

"Do we have a relationship to break up from?"

His eyes narrowed as he said accusingly, "People warned me about you, warned me that you might have a different definition of relationship than I would. I didn't believe them. I should have."

"Be careful, Bruce; I don't want to have to slap you at this party. It wouldn't be a girly, feminine slap. It would be hard and it would hurt and, best of all, it would leave a mark."

His jaw clenched, but then he took one step from her. "I'm going back inside."

"I'll be there in a few minutes," she said, then glanced at her watch.

Bruce nodded stiffly, then turned to leave, but he hesitated at the door. He slowly turned to face her again.

She turned to him, surprised to see the remorse in his expression. If she didn't know better, she would think that Bruce Longfellow was actually heartbroken.

"We're good together," he said softly. "I could even overlook the dad thing. I'm a Longfellow; my name makes up for a lot. Think about it."

Lana smiled and patted his face. "You're a good guy, Bruce, and you're going to make some woman a great husband. It's just not me."

He nodded and gave her that Longfellow smile that had attracted her in the first place; then he turned and walked out of the library, closing the doors behind him. Lana noticed that whatever rejection he felt faded the moment he walked through the threshold and straightened his shoulders.

Lana lifted the hem of her dress and ran toward the closet. Justin was right on time. She saw the blink of two flashes of light through the ceiling and ran to the door and unlocked the closet.

Lana watched Justin spray a circle on the glass ceiling; then he suctioned the circle of glass with another machine. A thin black rope lowered through the skylight, then he slid down the rope. He landed on the floor with an athleticism that made her swallow the lump in her throat. She took one step from him. He looked intimidating and dangerous in the all-black outfit and black ski mask and black gloves. And she did still hate him because he was something worse than a thief—a liar. But, her heart was still pounding against her chest at his nearness. He pointedly looked at his watch, then at her, although she couldn't see his eyes in the darkness of the mask.

"Is Bruce gone?" he asked in a soft whisper.

"He went back to the party."

"Good job. You go back to the party, too, and I'll see you—"

"I'm coming with you."

"That was not the plan," he snapped, sounding annoyed.

"That was not your plan or Frank's plan, but it's been my plan all along. If you think that I'm going to make conversation with people I don't know while you find proof to bring down the man who may have killed my mother, you're mistaken."

Justin ripped off his mask and glared at her. She tried not to sigh. She wondered if she would always lose her breath at the sight of him.

"You cannot come with me. You'll slow me down and someone will notice your absence—"

"No one will notice," she said, frustrated. "They'll notice that my body is not there, but they won't notice that I'm not there. That's the problem with my life, Justin. No one notices *me*. No matter what clothes I wear or how I act, no one notices the real me." She didn't add the most important part—Justin was the exception.

She knew that she surprised him because he had no sharp retort. He stared at her for a moment; then he averted his gaze.

"We can talk about this later—"

"We're talking about it now," she snapped. "I'm coming with you."

Justin groaned, then took several deep breaths before he said, "Lana, please. We don't have time for this. Not here. Go back to the party, play the dutiful girlfriend to Bruce, and after we have the obelisk and we talk to Lattimore and Frank, we can talk about whatever else you want."

"If I don't go with you, I will scream so loud that the people in the next county will hear me," she said simply, crossing her arms over her chest. "I'm not going back to the party, especially not when I have to watch Xavier Lattimore act like he's not a cold-blooded bastard."

Justin's jaw clenched as he stared at her, as if testing her resolve. When she didn't budge, he muttered a vicious curse, then said, "Fine, but if we get caught . . ."

He walked out the closet door, his pace long and hurried. Lana picked up the hem of her dress and followed. He opened the library door a few inches, then peered through the crack. He stiffened for a moment, then motioned to her to follow him.

They sprinted across the empty foyer toward the stairs that led to the second floor. Justin grabbed her hand, and the two ran up the stairs and disappeared around the corner just as Lana heard voices moving across the foyer. Justin stopped at the edge of the long, carpeted hallway. He pulled an object from the small bag strapped to his back and pointed it toward the opposite end of the hall, twenty feet away. He pressed the button and there was a small whizz as a dart, attached to a thin, black wire, shot out along the length of the hallway and landed on the opposite wall. He pressed the other end to the wall next to him.

"There has to be an easier way to get across the hallway," Lana whispered. "Like walking?"

In response, Justin pulled a small can from the backpack and sprayed a fine mist towards the floor. A criss-cross of red laser wires was suddenly visible a foot from the floor. Lana gulped in surprise.

"Will you leave now?" he said, the annoyance obvious as he turned to face her.

Grandma Harri had always taught Lana that the best thing a woman could know about herself was her weaknesses. Hanging from a tiny wire several feet in the air was definitely a weakness for Lana.

"The moment you find something, call me on my cell phone," she said, abruptly. "I won't answer, I'll just leave the party."

"You should leave now," Justin said, suddenly worried. "I don't like the idea of you hanging around here by yourself."

"I'm not by myself, there are over one hundred people here."

"I still don't like it," he muttered.

"I'll wait. You may need me." On impulse, she planted a soft kiss on his lips and said, "Be careful."

Justin nodded and turned, but at the last moment, he turned back to her and said, "I'm sorry, Lana. I should have told you the truth about my identity."

"You should have," she agreed, then kissed him again. For some reason, this kiss was sweeter.

He grinned at her, then grabbed the wires and gracefully swung his legs until his feet were entwined at the ankle around the wire. He began to slowly move across the wire, moving his hands and feet in unison like a caterpillar. Lana forced herself to walk down the stairs, and she almost screamed when she bumped into Xavier Lattimore.

The older man automatically grabbed her arm to steady her as she wobbled on her feet. She instinctively looked over her shoulder to make certain that neither Justin nor the rope were visible from the stairs. She faced him and forced a bright smile. Xavier smiled in return.

"How are you, Lana?" he asked, cheerfully. "I've been trying to talk to you all night."

"You have?" she asked, surprised, placing herself between Xavier and the stairs.

"I wanted to talk to you about your father."

"What about him?"

"I have old pictures of him and of your mother that I want to share with you."

Lana's hands grew clammy as she stared at the neutral expression on Lattimore's face. Too neutral. Then she realized that he had not released her arm. When she tried to pull her arm from his grip, his hand tightened, but his smile remained the same as a trio of partygoers walked across the foyer and said their greetings.

"Maybe another time, right now I should return to my date—"

"I know Frank is here, Lana," Xavier said, through the smile that she wanted to wipe off his face.

"I don't know what you're talking about," she said, pretending annoyance rather than fear.

"Yes, you do, and we're going to talk about it upstairs in my office," Xavier said. His grip tightened to the point of pain as he said, "And don't even think about trying any of the black belt shit on me."

He led her up the stairs and Lana half-expected to see Justin still hanging upside down in the middle of the hallway, but there was nothing. No Justin, no black rope. Xavier stopped at a covered panel at the top of the stairs and opened it. He punched in a code, then led Lana down the hallway. She hoped that Justin found the obelisk soon.

Justin wiped the sweat from his brow as he entered the master bedroom. He didn't turn on the lights but felt his way through the darkness to the glass walls that doubled as the door to a walk-in closet large enough to house a small family. Justin pushed open the door and walked inside. He walked to the rows and rows of shoes lined up on built-in shelves and felt along the edges of the shelves until he felt a button. He pushed it in. Just as Frank said would happen, another door slowly opened in the back of the closet.

Justin cautiously walked through the door and found himself in a smaller room. There were several glass cases filled with expensive watches and jewelry, all lined up with the precision of a marching band.

Justin ignored all of that and headed straight towards the safe built into the wall.

He pressed his hand against the earpiece and said into the transistor in his collar, "I'm in, Frank. Do you have a visual of the safe?"

Justin tapped his earpiece as only silence came through on the speaker. He tried again, even as his stomach sank. "Frank? Do you read me, Frank?"

No answer. Justin cursed and ripped the earpiece from his ear. He had forgotten Rule Number Three— never trust a thief. He slammed his fist on the safe door. He couldn't open the safe without Frank. Justin was only the hands, Frank had to break the code with the computer equipment in the van.

Suddenly, the dark room became bright as day. Justin whirled around to see two men in the dark, ill-fitting suits of Xavier's security force standing behind him.

Justin forced a smile and said, "This isn't how it looks. Honest."

The two men responded by grabbing him and dragging him from the room. Justin decided that the moment he was bailed out of jail, he was going to hunt down Frank and kill him.

CHAPTER TWENTY-ONE

The farther the security guards dragged Justin from the voices and other signs of life, the more angry he became. The men obviously weren't just planning to turn him over to the police, they were going to teach him a lesson. Most security guards did that because they knew the criminal network was full of gossips, and if one guy was caught attempting to steal and received broken ribs or broken fingers for his efforts, few other men would try.

Justin was on his way to being pulverized by the Mike Tyson clones, while Frank was stealing the obelisk at that very moment. Justin cursed himself for leaving Frank alone, for trusting Frank.

"There's been a mistake, guys," Justin tried friendliness as he glanced from one large man on his arm to the other one.

"Shut up," the man on his left growled, his mouth barely moving.

"I'm not trying to take anything from Mr. Lattimore," Justin continued.

"That's why you're wearing the I'm-a-thief outfit. And is your face part of the costume, too?" the man on Justin's right said with a bark of laughter. The other man joined his colleague in laughter.

Justin felt their respective grips loosen slightly with their sheer amusement at Justin. He tore his arms from their grips and rolled from between them. They both turned around at the same time that Justin got to his feet and landed a fist in one man's face. The man grunted and staggered from the impact at the same time that Justin whirled around and placed a kick in his partner's chest. Justin ducked a fist from the first man at the same time that he squatted and swung his leg around to take the feet out from under the opposite man.

Blood flooded in Justin's mouth when the first man's hard fist connected. He tried not to focus on the stars circling overhead from the force of the blow and instead swung one fist, then the other in rapid fire. The man fell over unconscious just as Justin heard the click of a gun safety being disengaged.

"Impressive," the second bodyguard said lightly. "Now turn around—" His voice abruptly trailed off and then his expression went blank before he crumpled over, unconscious. Clarence stood behind him, holding a vase in his hands. Justin stared, amazed, at his cousin, in his tuxedo looking like the waiters who had been circulating around the party with trays of drinks and appetizers.

"Clarence?" Justin said, confused as he moved his jaw around to make certain it wasn't broken. It hurt like hell, but he didn't think it was broken. He demanded, annoyed, "What are you doing here?"

"Apparently saving you," Clarence grumbled in reply, then added dryly, "You're welcome."

"I was doing fine on my own."

"Which explains why you're here and why Frank is somewhere stealing the obelisk."

Justin rolled his eyes, then demanded pointedly, "But what are you doing here, Clarence?"

Clarence sighed heavily in impatience and said, "I knew you would try something like this, something completely ill-prepared and not planned, and controlled by Frank, and I knew you would look to the city planning department for the plans to Lattimore's mansion, but the plans that Xavier Lattimore submitted to the city of this mansion were incomplete. There's another room. In the basement. A room with no windows."

"The real safe," Justin said, then spat out a curse. "Frank knew about it."

"Of course he knew." Clarence glanced at one of the unconscious men on the floor, who groaned and rolled his head. Clarence took a careful step from him, then pulled a cellular telephone from his inside jacket pocket.

"What are you doing?"

"Calling the police," he said. "We have Frank and the obelisk in one location—"

"By the time you call the police, Frank will be gone with the obelisk. I know him. Then you know what will happen? No obelisk. No Frank. No more fat contracts with the museum."

Clarence appeared to mull over Justin's retort, then said reluctantly, "I know that I'm going to regret this, but . . . what should we do?"

Justin muttered another curse, then said, "Find Frank."

Clarence nodded; then the two ran down the hallway and toward the bottom floor.

The two ran around the large ballroom where the guests still mingled and laughed. Justin shook his head in disbelief, then followed Clarence into the silent and dark library, the point of entry. There was a door that was part of the paneling, and Clarence frantically turned to Justin. He pulled a small computer from his backpack and attached it to the security alarm.

"Where did you get that?" Clarence asked while glancing at the entrance to the room.

"You'd be surprised what a man like Frank has access to."

"Justin . . ." Clarence hesitated when Justin looked at him. He awkwardly smiled, then said in a rush, "I'm sorry about yesterday—"

"Clarence—"

"I had no right. I shouldn't have brought Caroline there, but she was worried about you, and I know we're not supposed to go near you—"

"I never said that," he protested, horrified.

"No one in the family ever said that, but it's known. I took Caroline from you—"

Justin sighed heavily and forced himself to say, "You didn't take Caroline from me. We had been drifting apart for a long time."

"Justin, for the record, Caroline and I . . . we didn't . . . while you two were married . . ."

Justin put the man out of his misery, saying, "I know."

Clarence sighed in relief, then said seriously, "I guess since I'm confessing, I should tell you that you were right. I didn't want you to succeed on this assignment because I'm scared of what will happen if you do."

Justin forgot about the code as he asked, confused, "Why?"

"You're a detective. You're a good detective, like my dad. I'm not. I like sitting in the office, scheduling appointments, going over the books, coming up with advertising plans. If we get bigger, if we get more clients, then all of that will change. Dad will expect me to . . . He'll expect me to actually detect. Caroline will expect me to detect. And I just don't want to."

Justin did something that he probably wouldn't have done last week. He took his cousin's hand and said quietly, "You're a good detective, Clarence. You found this room. You found me. Don't underestimate yourself."

They both turned at the sound of loud voices on the other side of the closed door drawing closer and closer.

"I'll stop them," Clarence said, then ran out of the room, closing the door behind him.

The code engaged and the door clicked open. Justin glanced at the door that Clarence had disappeared behind, then went through the door. He cautiously descended a dark, narrow stairway to a cool room with a smooth floor and every sort of treasure an art aficionado could imagine. There were paintings, gold, marble, tapestries, wood sculptures, and any other sort of precious jewel and object. Since Justin was not an art aficionado, his gaze swept past all of that to the man dressed all in black standing in the middle of the room with a small, round ball of gold encrusted with jade in his hand.

CHAPTER TWENTY-TWO

"What are you going to do now? Torture me?" Lana demanded, attempting to sound bored, as a security guard closed the door to the large and opulent study, leaving her alone with Xavier Lattimore.

Xavier laughed, amused, then moved to the mini-bar, where he poured dark liquid into a tumbler. "If torture includes champagne or any other type of liquor you want, then consider yourself tortured. What would you like to drink?"

"Nothing, but if we're going over what I'd like, then I'd like to leave."

"That's not going to happen." Her heart began to pound against her chest as the fear flashed across her face. Xavier abruptly smiled, then said, "Not yet."

"You're not going to kill me?" she asked, furrowing her brow in confusion.

"What kind of monster do you think I am?" he asked, laughing. He grabbed a tumbler, then walked across the room to sit next to her on the sofa. He sounded deceptively casual as he asked, "What exactly did Hargrove tell you about me, besides the killing your mother part?"

When Lana refused to answer, Xavier stood and walked to the desk in the corner of the room. He picked up a framed photograph off the desk and returned to the sofa. He sat next to her and handed her the picture. Lana looked at him suspiciously, then finally stared down at the framed picture. She gasped when she recognized the beautiful woman's face in the picture. Her mother in a wedding dress standing next to a beaming Xavier Lattimore.

"This is my mother," she said, glaring at him.

He smiled gently as he stared at the picture. "She's your mother and she was my wife."

Lana's hands grew numb as she stared at him, willing herself to respond with something sarcastic. Except she couldn't. She could only stare at him and remember to breathe.

Xavier placed a hand on her face and Lana knew she must have been shocked, because she didn't pull away.

"Beatrice is your mother, and I'm your father."

"No," Lana whispered, shaking her head in disbelief.

"Yes, Lana," he said firmly. A flash of pity crossed his face and his hand dropped from her face as his gaze focused on the picture again. He began softly, "Frank Hargrove hates me. He always has. From the time we were children until I finally moved away. But he followed me here—"

"No."

"When I moved to DC, I met a woman. She was beautiful and kind and she loved me—"

"I don't believe you," she whispered, her voice weaker than she would have liked.

She jumped to her feet and walked toward the door. Xavier didn't stop her. Instead she was the one who couldn't go any farther. She waited several seconds for him to speak. When he didn't, she turned to face him. He watched her carefully.

"I loved Beatrice, and she loved me," he said quietly. "We got married. We had you." Lana covered her mouth with her hand as tears filled her eyes. The sincerity in his eyes was more than she had ever seen from Frank, and for that much, she wanted to believe him. Xavier continued, his voice toneless and hard now, "And I thought that Frank Hargrove was out of my life, but I was wrong. He wanted Beatrice for himself. He took her and you from me. When she died, he raised you as his own, never telling you the truth. He wanted to destroy me, and he did."

"I just . . . Frank may be a lot of things, but he's not capable of something like that," Lana said, shaking her head.

"I don't expect you to believe me now, not without proof, but at least keep an open mind," Xavier pleaded.

His gaze was drawn to the picture still clutched in Lana's hands. "I loved her so much."

Lana stared down at the picture and couldn't deny that the woman in the picture looked happy, looked loved. She also couldn't deny that all of that love was directed towards the tall, serious man at her side, Xavier.

"How long were you two married?" she asked hesitantly.

"Two wonderful years."

"And then what happened?"

Regret ravished his face as he explained in a halting voice, "I can only imagine that Frank created some lie to make Bea hate me, to make her leave me and take you. She wouldn't even accept my calls. When she died, Frank hid you from me. He knew I would never have separated Bea from her baby, but with her dead, I wanted you—a reminder of her—with me. I had given up on ever finding you until last week when I saw you at the museum. You look so much like Bea, I knew you were our daughter."

"That's not what Frank says happened," she said.

"I can only imagine what lies he's come up with," Xavier said bitterly. "But they are lies, Lana. And I'll prove it to you. We can get blood tests, DNA hair samples, whatever you need to prove that I'm your father."

Lana stood abruptly from the sofa and walked to the window that overlooked the lights of Georgetown.

She didn't know who or what to believe. She briefly closed her eyes and prayed that her mother and Grandma Harri would help her. And strangely enough, Frank's familiar face floated through her mind. It was a strange time to realize how much she truly loved the lying thief.

"You bastard," Justin snapped, balling his hands into fists while trying to avoid plowing a fist into Frank's face.

"I can explain everything," Frank said, not moving a muscle as he smiled at Justin.

"I actually bet you could," Justin said dryly. "But I'm not going to listen, because I may actually believe you."

Frank's smile faded when he saw the anger on Justin's face. He said hesitantly, "Justin, no hard feelings. This is strictly business. Remember?"

"Give me the obelisk." When Frank didn't move, Justin said through barely restrained fury, "Now."

Frank moved across the floor. After one brief moment of hesitation, he handed the miniature obelisk to Justin. Justin rolled his eyes, then stuffed it into the small bag he held.

"All of this for this thing," he muttered as he zipped up the bag. "Your daughter is not business, Frank. She's your daughter. And I know you think that she's hard and independent, and she is, but she needs you. She still needs you."

"She was never in danger," Frank said simply. "Lana is at the party with her boring-but-safe date. And once you tripped the safe in the bedroom, Lattimore's security would catch you and just call the police and your cop friend would bail you out."

"While you sneak into this room and take the obelisk."

"A perfect plan, if I do say so myself," he said, grinning. "No one gets hurt, and I get the obelisk."

"And you disappear?" Justin asked through clenched teeth. "What about Lana? I thought you wanted to have a relationship with her, be her father for the first time in twenty years. That's what you said. It was all a lie, wasn't it? Everything has been a lie since the day I met you."

Frank actually looked momentarily uncomfortable before he finally muttered, "She doesn't need me."

"She needs you," Justin said, frustrated.

"Her life is going good now. She doesn't need her old man to mess it up for her."

"News flash, Frank: You *have* messed up her life. Her home has been destroyed and her business destroyed—all because of you. Not to mention her childhood. She was just a kid, and law enforcement agencies were regular visitors at her home because of you," Justin said angrily.

Frank suddenly looked like a beaten-down old man as he sagged on an ornate cement bench in the corner of the room.

"I couldn't do it without Bea, Justin," he whispered,

shaking his head. "How was I supposed to raise a little girl who had just lost her mother? How was I supposed to go on living when I had just lost Bea?"

"I don't know," Justin said truthfully, because for the first time with Lana he was beginning to understand what Frank had been talking about all of these months. How a man's heart could feel full when he was with the right woman, the only woman.

Frank announced, "I met Beatrice through Xavier. She was his wife."

Justin muttered a curse while Frank had the decency to look ashamed. For a moment. "That would explain why he hates you."

"Lattimore wanted to own Beatrice. He wanted to control her. He never appreciated her for the beautiful, independent woman that she was. Beatrice had enough, and one night she came to me. We ran that night. We settled in Los Angeles, had Lana. I should have known something would go wrong because everything was too right."

"Lattimore came to Bea's funeral and when he saw Lana, he had the strange notion that Lana was his daughter."

"Is she?" Justin asked suspiciously.

"Of course not," he snapped, annoyed. Frank took several deep breaths and swiped at the tears in his eyes while clearing his throat. "Lattimore was becoming as obsessed with the idea of Lana as his daughter as he had been with Bea. I had to get Lana away from me. That's why I sent her to live with my mother because Frank could never bring himself to go back to the old neighborhood. He didn't like to be reminded where he came from so I knew he would never find her there . . . Or at least, that's what I told myself. Now, I know the truth. I was scared and alone, and I didn't think I could raise Lana to be the woman Bea wanted, so I didn't try."

"Now you can try," Justin said simply. "We can send Lattimore to jail for a long time. As I'm sure you've noticed, half of the items in this room have been stolen."

Frank stared at Justin for a long moment, then said, "Your job was to find the obelisk. You found it."

"Lattimore goes down," he said firmly.

Justin pulled a pair of handcuffs from his bag. He leaned over Frank and before the older man could protest, handcuffed one of his hands to the pipe in the corner. Frank gaped in surprise, then glared at Justin.

"What are you doing?" Frank demanded.

"Rule Number Three . . . Bubba," Justin said, then winked and ran up the stairs and into the library just as Clarence walked into the room.

"I have the . . ." Justin's excitement trailed off when he saw Clarence's troubled expression. "What is it?"

"Don't get excited—"

"Dammit, Clarence, what?"

"I heard some of the guards talking about the woman Lattimore has in his study."

Justin's heart skipped a beat as he whispered, "Lana."

"Don't worry, I know where she is," Clarence said quickly.

Justin followed his cousin, wondering if it was too late.

CHAPTER TWENTY-THREE

"I called the police," Xavier said, replacing the receiver on the cradle on his desk.

Lana sighed in relief, then sipped the glass of champagne. Lana had realized around the second glass of champagne that she was throughly confused. Xavier had pulled out a photo box full of pictures of her mother. Lana had begun to pore over the pictures with a thirst that made Xavier smile in understanding. Grandma Harri had had one picture of Bea, sitting on a front porch, her arms wrapped around her legs, wearing an oversized denim dress and a wide straw hat, making a comical fish face at the camera. In these pictures, her mother was smiling, made-up, and sophisticated. Xavier was also in a few of the pictures, and Lana had to admit that her mother's smile had been brighter in those.

But no matter how many pictures Xavier showed her, the truth was that when Beatrice had died, she had been with Frank. Lana didn't know her mother, but she knew deep in her soul—in the part of her that carried Beatrice Hargrove—that her mother left Xavier for her own reasons and not because Frank "tricked" her, as Xavier believed. That small bit of knowledge was the only thing Lana hung onto as Xavier continued to fawn over her, more than Frank had ever done. Lana didn't know why she felt any sense of loyalty to Frank, he had never shown her any, but it was there.

Lana studied one picture of her mother standing in front of a Christmas tree. Beatrice beamed at the camera as she held a small ball of fur, a kitten, in her hands.

"We look so much alike," Lana whispered, more to herself as she traced the woman's brown face in the picture.

"Absolutely breathtaking," Xavier agreed, then he smiled. "I can't wait until you accept me as your father, Lana. I've been waiting for you a long time."

Lana looked at him, inwardly flinching at the hope and expectation brimming in his eyes. "You never married again or had children?"

Xavier's gaze drifted to the picture as he shook his head. Lana sighed and tried not to allow sympathy to dictate her thinking, but a small part of her wondered how this obviously heartbroken man could lie to her about being her father. It was almost easier to believe that Frank, whose second nature was to lie, would lie to her. Almost. But a larger part of Lana, the part that had made her cry herself to sleep numerous times after her father had left her, couldn't believe anything but that Frank was her father.

"Don't you remember anything about Beatrice, Lana?" Xavier asked, helplessly.

Lana shook her head. "No."

He shook his head and said, "Frank should have been telling you about her every day. He should have been telling you about me . . . When I think of all the time he's cost us . . ." His voice trailed off and he abruptly smiled. "But that will soon be in the past. As soon as we get the blood tests and Frank is rotting in a prison, we'll start over. I know it'll take you a while to get used to me, Lana, but I want to know everything about you. I want to know my daughter."

Lana thought she was too cynical to react to a statement like that, but she wasn't. She hung her head as the tears filled her eyes. All of her life she had waited for someone to speak like that to her. To want to love her, too.

The doors suddenly flew open and a man flew inside, rolling across the floor and then slamming into the sofa unconscious. Justin and Clarence followed him. Lana jumped to her feet.

"Lana, are you all right?" Justin asked, running to her side.

"Of course I am."

Justin grabbed her arm, then glared at Xavier, who

watched the three calmly. "What have you been telling her?"

"The truth," Xavier said simply.

"Let's discuss this later," Clarence said calmly. "Right now, let's call the police and let them deal with it."

"Xavier already called the police," Lana told him.

Justin glanced at Xavier, anger crossing his face. "This man is crazy, and he's lying to you. We found the obelisk in a room downstairs with a bunch of other stolen objects. Xavier stole them all."

"That is not true," Xavier said to Lana. "He's lying."

"No, I'm not. And I can prove it. I have the obelisk." Justin glared at Xavier, then reached into his bag, but then confusion entered his expression and he frantically began to search the bag. He looked at Lana, surprised. "It's not here. Frank . . . he must have taken it. . . ."

"That's a surprise," Lana said dryly. The strength of her disappointment in Frank surprised her. She should have been used to it.

"All he wanted was the obelisk the entire time," Xavier said, shaking his head.

"That is not true," Justin said angrily. Lana watched as the two men stared at each other. Once more she was reminded of two gunslingers standing outside a saloon in the Wild West, until Justin suddenly smiled and shook his head. He laughed bitterly as he said, "I have to hand it to you, Lattimore. You played us all."

Confusion crossed Xavier's expression as he said, "Who are you? You were at the museum. What are you doing in my house?"

Lana didn't like the look that passed across Justin's face. She said, "Justin, let's just settle this when the police come. Xavier, Justin is a private detective who was hired by the Smithsonian to—"

"He knows, Lana," Justin interrupted her while still staring at Xavier. "He knows everything."

"What are you talking about?" Lana demanded.

"Xavier never wanted the obelisk. He couldn't have cared less about it," Justin said, turning to her. "This is about Frank. He wants to kill Frank."

"Yet another person duped by Frank's lies," Xavier said, with a sigh of disappointment. "I don't want to kill anyone. I'm a respected businessman—"

"It makes sense," Clarence said to Lana, ignoring Xavier. "Somehow, Xavier found out that Frank was after the obelisk for Seth Grimes . . . just like we found out, and Xavier decided to take it first to lure Frank here."

"He found out, Clarence, because Xavier is the one who hired us," Justin said simply.

Lana stared confused as the two cousins exchanged an amused look, then shook their heads.

"Of course," Clarence murmured. "Using his influence, Xavier got the Smithsonian to declare Frank Public Enemy Number One. Then we were hired to find him. All the information we found out about Frank and passed on to the Smithsonian, Xavier got, too."

Justin's voice was quiet as he stared at Lana and said, "Including information about you."

"You're as insane as Frank," Xavier said simply, getting to his feet. He turned to Lana and said carefully, "I don't know who these two men are, but I do know they are unwelcome guests in my home."

Lana was speechless as she stared at the three men. Once more, she was reminded that no matter what her Grandma Harri had thought, there were men in their lives and they were there to stay. Except, for the first time, as Lana stared at Justin and saw the tenderness in his eyes because he knew she hurt, Lana thought that maybe having some men in her life wasn't such a bad thing.

Xavier held out his hand to her and said, "Come on, Lana, let's get out of here before they become dangerous."

Next to her, Justin tensed as if prepared to launch himself in between her and Xavier. Justin didn't have the chance because a deep voice said from the doorframe, "Get away from my daughter."

Lana whirled around to see Frank, wearing all black and walking across the room without the slight limp. There was no smile on his face, no amused coolness in his voice. He was angry and all of that rage was directed at Xavier. And it was at that moment that Lana remembered her mother. Her mother laughing with Frank, teasing Frank and making him laugh, louder and harder than Lana had ever heard him. Lana remembered how much her mother had loved her, how Bea would hug her after school every day and before she left in the morning, how Bea was so proud of her strawberry pie, how there was always laughter in their household. And so much love that Lana staggered against the sofa as she remembered it. Now Lana knew why she had repressed it all— remembering was like losing her mother all over again.

Lana's eyes filled with tears as she looked at Frank. She wanted to cry for him because she could remember how devastated he had been after Bea's death. The only thing that had kept him going all of these years was his vow to destroy Xavier.

"Speak of the devil and he appears," Xavier said with a smirk, no longer bothering to play the role of the wronged accused.

"I've waited twenty years for this moment," Frank said through clenched teeth.

"So have I," Xavier said, grinning.

"Before I kill you, I need to know why." Frank's voice cracked as he repeated, "Why?"

A strange gleam lit Xavier's eyes as he said tonelessly, "She was walking to her car from the grocery store. She saw me and ran. . . . I didn't know she would run from me. I just wanted to talk to her, to bring her home. If you had never brainwashed her against me, she would not have run. If you had never taken her, Lana would be my daughter."

"I didn't brainwash Bea, you idiot," Frank spat out. "I didn't have to. She despised you. For some unknown reason, she did love you when you two first married, but your obsessive jealousy and violence pushed her away. She would have left you whether I came into the picture or not."

"You brainwashed her," Xavier insisted, nearly stomping his feet. "I loved her, and she loved me! And we would have been together forever if you hadn't destroyed it! If she had been with me, she never would have run from me and she never would have been killed."

Justin said quietly, "And since then, you've been trying to destroy Frank. Most of those objects in the basement . . . Frank has been accused of stealing them, but he never did. You did. You've been pinning thefts on him for years."

Xavier shrugged and said, "It's the least I could do. He destroyed my life; I was just trying to return the favor. He had the past. It was easy for the police to believe it was him."

Frank's eyes narrowed, and he started towards Xavier. Lana more than anyone wanted Xavier to pay, but she also knew that if Frank killed the other man, she would lose her father forever. Frank was not a killer, and it would tear him apart.

"Daddy," she whispered, reaching for Frank. Frank froze in place, as if her voice had turned off whatever force had been driving him towards Xavier. He slowly turned to her. "Daddy, he's not worth it. Let it go."

"He killed Bea," Frank said, his voice straining with emotion.

"Please," she said. "For me."

Slowly, the anger faded from Frank's expression and he seemed to deflate. She sighed in relief as Frank took a step towards her. But before he could reach her, Lana saw movement from the corner of her eye as Xavier raced towards his desk and pulled a compact pistol from his desk drawer and pointed it at Frank. Justin screamed Frank's name and grabbed Lana around the waist, throwing her to the floor at the same time that Clarence dove behind a chair. Before Xavier could pull the trigger, Frank dropped to the floor, pulling something from his sleeve. He flipped a small round disc at the ceiling light and there was the sound of glass breaking before the room went completely dark. Wild shots were fired in the darkness.

Xavier used the darkness to run towards the door. He flung it open, bathing the dark study in light, and ran out of the room. Frank jumped to his feet and ran after him, ignoring Lana's calls. Lana started after her father, but Justin grabbed her arm, stopping her. Even in the semidarkness, she could see the worry in his face.

"Lana, no," he said, shaking his head.

"Frank needs me. He's going to kill Xavier." She tried to yank her arm from his grip, but Justin held tight.

"Frank? Xavier has the gun," he said.

Lana grabbed his shirtfront and said quietly, "He's my father, Justin, and he's in danger—not from Xavier, but from himself. I remember everything now. I remember how hurt he was after Mom's death, I remember her. He was destroyed after her death. He could barely take care of himself, let alone me. I need to be with him, I need to show him that the only way we can handle any of this is to take care of each other."

"Lana—" Justin was interrupted as the unconscious security guard suddenly sprang to his feet and tackled Justin to the floor. Clarence flew across the room, joining the fray, and Lana took that opportunity to slip off her heels, hike up the dress to her knees, and run out of the room.

Justin delivered a final punch to the security guard's face and the man fell over unconscious for the second time that night. Justin winced and shook his hand as Clarence pulled off his suspenders and looped them around the man's hands.

Justin waited until the man was secure and then he started out the door. All he could think about was Lana, running after her father, alone. He wanted to shake her for leaving the study or hold her from now until the next morning. But he couldn't do either until he made certain she was all right. If he had had any doubts before, he now knew with a frightening certainty that he was in love with Lana. And instead of feeling scared or worried, he just felt . . . right.

"Where are you going?" Clarence demanded, getting to his feet.

"Where do you think I'm going?" Justin said absently as he continued toward the door. Clarence moved in front of him, bringing Justin to a halt.

"Let the police handle it."

"What police? They don't even know—"

"I called them," Clarence said simply. "You may trust Frank, but I don't. They should be here any moment."

Justin struggled to remain calm as he saw the determination in Clarence's eyes. He would have to fight his way through his cousin. Normally, that wouldn't have stopped Justin, but he didn't have time to deal with Clarence.

"Lana is out there, Clarence," he pleaded.

"So is Xavier Lattimore. The man is insane."

"Which is exactly why I have to find Lana. If Frank wants to finish this vendetta, I can't stop him, but I'll be damned if I allow Frank or Lattimore to hurt Lana anymore," Justin said through clenched teeth.

"You're letting your emotions cloud the issue. If you go after them, you'll get her hurt and maybe yourself hurt, too—"

"If that was Caroline—"

The two cousins stared at each other; then Clarence released his arm and nodded. "I'll come with you."

"No, someone has to stay here and tell the police the truth."

Justin didn't wait for Clarence's response but ran out of the room and down the stairs. He ran past several gawking guests and out of the house to the backyard. He had no idea where they went, until he heard a woman's scream—Lana's scream—coming from the small building in the distance, the garage.

Justin reached the building, slightly out of breath. He bet that Clarence would have counseled a quiet approach, but Justin kicked in the door and walked into the garage.

Lana was standing over Frank, who straddled a struggling Xavier. Frank held a very dangerous-looking knife that glinted in the moonlight streaming through the small windows. Justin saw Frank's murderous expression, the sign that a man was barely hanging on to sanity, as Xavier whimpered and used both hands to attempt to hold the knife back. He was losing.

"Frank, please," Lana cried, shaking her head.

"He killed Bea," Frank said in a strange monotone.

Justin immediately ran to Lana's side. She gave him a helpless look and he nodded in encouragement. She was the only one who could break through Frank's blood lust. And if Frank killed another man, Justin couldn't help him.

Lana stared at her father again and said, "No, he didn't. It was an accident. Mom wouldn't have wanted this. I don't want this." When Frank ignored her and continued to push the knife against Xavier's hold, Lana's voice grew angry, "Dammit, Frank, for once think about me. I need you. I've needed you this whole time. I lost you for twenty years over some quest for revenge, but now it's over and you've won. Xavier will go to jail for all the things he's stolen, Justin will make certain of it. Don't leave me again."

Frank suddenly screamed in outrage, then slammed the knife down, only inches from Xavier's face. Xavier promptly fainted. Frank stilled, then abruptly rolled off Xavier and stared at the floor. Lana dropped to her knees and wrapped her arms around Frank, who suddenly began to tremble and shake. Justin moved a few steps from the two to give them privacy when Lana held out her hand to him. He had no choice but to move into her arms, where he wrapped his arms around Frank.

"I'm so sorry, Peanut," Frank whispered as he smoothed his hand over her hair. "I'm so sorry."

As if suddenly uncomfortable with his display of serious emotion, Frank finally pulled from her and Justin smiled at the familiar smirk on the older man's face as he looked at the unconscious Lattimore. "I think prison will be more painful for a man like Lattimore than anything I could have done to him."

"He'll be in there for a long time, Frank," Justin said, nodding.

Frank sent Lana a lopsided smile as he said, "See,

Peanut, your old man finally did something beneficial for society."

Lana's smile was uncertain through her tears as she said quietly, "You came back. You could have gotten away. You had the obelisk."

Frank looked bashful for a moment; then he said with a shrug, "Rule Number One, Peanut: Always be ready to improvise."

"That's not Rule Number One," she said, with a slight smile. Frank scratched his head, looking confused, but Justin had a feeling that Frank knew exactly what the real Rule Number One was. She said softly, "Rule Number One is never go back—for anyone or anything—leave with what you have. Remember?"

"I still have time to get away." Both Frank and Lana turned to Justin, who instantly felt the heat fill his face. "Right, Justin?"

Justin resisted every urge in his body to grab Frank by the arm and drag him out to the police. He kissed the bonus good-bye, then muttered, "I'll give you a head start." Frank grinned, then stood to leave, but Justin grabbed his arm and said, with a slight smile because he had to give the old man credit for his persistence, "The obelisk, Frank."

Frank smiled, then handed it to Justin. "You would have lost all respect for me if I hadn't tried."

"I'll tell the police about Seth Grimes," Justin promised as he helped Lana to stand. "You won't have to worry about him. He'll be too busy worrying about the rest of his empire to care about the obelisk."

Frank glanced at Lana once more and said hesitantly, "I know I haven't been the best father . . . and I probably never will be. Even without Lattimore and what he's done all these years, I still would have been awful at it. I just wish that I hadn't let your mother down—"

Lana placed her hand on his mouth to quiet him and interrupted him in a soft voice: "Go before the police catch you."

Frank became very still and very silent as conflicted emotions passed across his face. Frank slowly moved his arms around Lana and whispered, "I love you, Peanut."

Through the windows Justin caught the glimpse of flashlights coming toward the garage. He cleared his throat and said, "Frank, you should leave."

Frank nodded, then released Lana and walked away. Lana turned to Justin and he brushed strands of hair from her face. Even after the excitement of the night, she still looked perfect, not mussed, and his, if he could only find the courage to ask her.

"Are you all right?" he asked softly.

"I'm still trying to understand it all," she said, shaking her head. "My dad, Xavier, you—"

Then Justin saw the movement from the corners of his eye. He watched in slow motion as Xavier rose from the ground, the gun in his hands. There was a maniacal grin on his face as he pointed the gun at Justin and Lana.

Then everything happened at once. The door burst open and the garage filled with police, Justin pushed Lana to the floor, and a black blob flew across the room toward Lana. There was a gunshot followed by more gunshots that Justin vaguely recognized as being fired by the police at Xavier. Justin and Lana hit the floor with a thud hard enough to jar his teeth, and then something, or more like someone, landed on top of them, then rolled off.

Police streamed into the room and Justin opened his eyes, not realizing that he had closed them. He stared into Lana's face. She looked shocked and scared as she stared just past his shoulder at whatever was weighing on his back. Justin carefully moved the unmoving weight, then turned to see Frank Hargrove lying next to him, not moving, his eyes closed.

CHAPTER TWENTY-FOUR

Lana stared at her father's still form as he lay in the stark white hospital bed with wires criss-crossing and running from his body. He had been shot in the left arm when he saved her and Justin. The police had rushed him to the hospital, and after a long night of surgery the hospital staff had pronounced him on the road to recovery. The police had pronounced him under arrest as soon as he woke up. Lana hadn't cared. She had stayed by his bedside through the night and into the early morning.

Lana closed the magazine she had been flipping through and continued to stare at her father. He looked so peaceful and so tired. He looked like the man she remembered, the man she once loved and still loved.

Lana felt the tears fill her eyes as she said through clenched teeth, "Damn you, Frank. Damn you for making me cry, numerous times. Damn you for making

Grandma cry and for making her take care of me when she should have been enjoying her retirement. And damn you for not being there at my high school graduation, my prom, my college graduation, when Chad Winslow broke my heart."

She wiped the tears from her eyes and waited, as if expecting his response. Then she said softly, "I remember when I was six years old and you took me to the park one day. And for that day all we did was play. And I remember you were the only daddy who got on the slide and the swings. And I remember thinking that I was the luckiest little girl in the world to have a daddy like you. And I'm still one of the luckiest girls in the world."

She unclasped the sapphire pendant that she had worn around her neck since Justin gave it to her the first day she met him. She placed it in her father's hand and closed his fingers around it. She kissed his hand.

"I do remember when I gave it to you. I do remember you telling me good-bye at Grandma's house that night you left and I gave you this necklace. I told you that no matter where you went, if you had this with you, you could always remember me, no matter what. I love you, too."

There was a soft knock on the door and Lana turned to see Justin standing in the door frame. He wore faded jeans that emphasized his strong legs, and a green t-shirt. In other words, he looked perfect. The tenderness on his face almost made her cry again. She loved this man and, she realized, mostly because he was so much like her father. Brave, kind, and full of love.

"Do you want me to come back?" Justin asked.

Lana shook her head, then stood and walked across the room. She knew he wasn't expecting it, but she wrapped her arms around him and rested her head against his chest. He rubbed her back, then glanced at Frank.

"How is he?"

She reluctantly released Justin and said, "The doctors said that he's going to be all right. He has a long road to recovery, though. The doctors don't think he'll have the full use of that arm anymore. The police say that's a good thing."

"I have faith in the old man," Justin said, with a crooked smile.

She nodded, then grabbed Justin's hand, noticing the discomfort on his face. "Do you want to take a walk?"

He nodded, obviously relieved. "Hospitals . . . bad memories."

She followed him out of the room and to the ground floor, where they strolled through the humidity of the DC afternoon. Lana still wore her rumpled dress from last night, which caused a few stares as people walked by in their suits on the way to work. An awkward silence fell between her and Justin as they strolled down the sidewalk, not looking at each other. Lana had never been nervous in front of a man, and it made her more nervous that she was now.

"How are you?" he asked, breaking the silence between them.

Lana glanced at the wrinkled and stained material
of the dress. She tried not to think what some of the
stains might be, since she had held Frank in her arms
in the garage.

"Pauline is going to kill me when she sees this
dress," she muttered to herself while shaking her head.

"I start a new assignment tomorrow," he said
abruptly, breaking the silence between them.

"What is it?"

"The New York branch of my father's bank had
some artwork stolen from the vault and they want—"

"Your father?" she said, surprised.

"Yeah. I called him last night. To talk. And he told
me about the bank."

"What did you talk about?"

"No heart-to-heart, no you-did-me-wrong, just
how-are-you-Dad. It was kind of nice," he said, with a
shrug. "I thought he was disappointed in me all this
time, but maybe I was disappointed in him because he
wasn't my uncle. And he deserved more than that
from me. He's a good man."

Lana smiled, then suddenly registered the mention
of New York. She stopped in the middle of the sidewalk and glared at him, suddenly angry with this tension between them, with her strong feelings that told
her to hold him while he looked distant and uncomfortable.

"You're leaving?" she asked tightly.

"For a few weeks," he responded, apparently oblivious to the obvious panic in her voice.

Lana resisted the urge to blurt out, "No." She had finally found all the man she could ever need or want, and he was leaving her without a second thought. Maybe he would return from New York and they would have an occasional date until he went on his next assignment, until she faded into his phonebook, but Lana needed more than that. She needed Justin. For always. Every day, every night. And she wanted to tell him exactly that.

Except staring at his beautifully scarred face, Lana choked on her words because it was harder than she had ever imagined to break through the wall she had built around her heart. For twenty years, she had protected her heart from everyone, especially men. She had worn the sexy clothes and adopted the man-eater persona to control men. Now she was on the verge of willingly handing her heart over to the one man who saw straight through her act. Because of that, she would never be able to control Justin like she had controlled the majority of other men in her life, and Lana didn't want to. She liked that he challenged her, teased her, treated her like a friend, instead of a sexpot. By telling him that she loved him, she would be giving him power that no one had ever had over her. He already had the power, but Lana didn't know if she had the strength to let him know that.

"I'm happy for you and Clarence," she said, forcing a bright smile. "With all the positive press Baxter and

Baxter Investigations has gotten from cracking open the Lattimore case, the agency is going to be one of the most well-known in the field."

"That's what Clarence said this morning. Of course, he was close to tears when he said it," Justin said, with a wry smile. Her smile was genuine, then she stared at her hands, at a loss for words.

"What are you going to do now?" Justin asked.

"Pauline has offered me her spare bedroom until I find a new place. With all the help she's been giving me this past week, I'm going to owe her my first-born child once all this is through." Lana smiled to herself as she thought about Pauline. Pauline had proven to be a true friend—family, and it felt good. "I still have several work commitments that I can't ignore, not to mention phone calls to return—"

Before she could continue, Justin abruptly grabbed her shoulders and slammed her against his body as his mouth covered hers in a drugging, punishing kiss that made Lana cling to him for life. She bathed in the pleasure his tongue wrought as it dug through her mouth with an almost bruising ferocity. And she loved every minute of it.

"I'm so sorry, darlin'," he said hoarsely, finally releasing her. Lana was too stunned from that kiss to react to the guilt wracking his expression. He blurted out, "That wasn't supposed to happen. I meant to take this slow. I finally understand what Frank went through when he lost your mother because if anything ever happened to you, I'd lose my mind. So I was going to do this right, give you no choice but to fall in love with me.

"I was going to ask if I could call you while I was in New York and then I was going to ask if it would be all right if I flew back once a week to see you or if I could fly you to New York on the weekends. I was going to tell you that there would be no pressures, we wouldn't have to make love until you were ready, even though it would be cruel and unusual punishment, but I was going to follow your timetable this time. No kidnappings or secrets or anything between us . . . I know that I have a lot to make up for and I want to make it all up to you, if I could talk you into it . . . This is a mess."

Justin cursed and ran a hand over his hair. Lana suddenly laughed and he glared at her.

"I'm sure you're used to undying declarations of love from men, but this is a first for me, and I'm trying to do it right," he said annoyed, obviously misinterpreting her laughter.

Lana sighed in contentment and he sent her a bewildered look. "Are you declaring your love for me, Justin?"

For a moment, he looked nervous, then he nodded defiantly and said, "Yes."

She grinned again and bit her bottom lip to hold in the joy that bubbled from every molecule of her body. She didn't want to release the feeling just yet. "Then you're doing just fine," she finally said.

Any discomfort fled from Justin's expression as he

smiled and moved closer to her. They both ignored
the people who walked past them on the sidewalk,
gawking at the couple who were oblivious to anything but each other.

"Are you ready to accept love from me, a mere
man?" he asked, softly, his gaze intense.

"You make me believe that there's hope for your
gender."

"True words of love there, Lana," he said dryly, but
he laughed, then pulled her into his arms. She sighed,
relieved because it was the best compliment that she
could give. "You just can't give a man a true compliment, can you?"

"I try," she said begrudgingly.

She was surprised when he said, "I was hoping you
would come with me to New York. I don't know about
this art stuff. Clarence doesn't know much, either, but
you do."

She pushed out of his arms and asked, with a grin,
"Are you asking for my help?"

"Maybe," he admitted begrudgingly. "Besides, it's
not like you have anywhere to go right now. Your
town house is destroyed."

"So you're asking me out of pity?" she said in
disbelief.

He didn't respond for a moment and Lana thought
that maybe her insecurity and bitterness had pushed
him too far. She had spent her whole life pushing
men's buttons, so she didn't exactly know how *not* to
push a man's buttons.

"I'm asking because I love you and after searching my whole life for you, I don't want to be without you for another moment." He gently scraped his thumb along her jaw and whispered, "You make me look forward to tomorrow, something I never thought I would do again. You're my universe, Lana."

Lana had never thought she would be the type of woman to fall for sweet words. She had always thought such words were insincere and laughable, but there was nothing insincere about Justin or the way her heart soared and her body shook from the sheer joy of finally finding someone she knew would never leave her.

She tried to answer him, to express how much he meant to her, how he made her feel like she was dancing in the stars, how he made her forget Grandma Harri's warnings about needing a man for anything. Instead, she stood on her tiptoes and threw her arms around his neck to squeeze him as tight as she could.

And for the first time in her life, Lana Hargrove allowed herself to surrender to a man because her heart knew this man was worth surrendering to. She whispered, "I love you, Justin."

He frowned suddenly and she turned to see Officer McCabe, the policeman who guarded her father's room, running toward them. He looked panicked and out of shape as he huffed and puffed when he stopped in front of them.

"Where is he?" Officer McCabe demanded breathlessly.

"Who?" Lana asked, confused.

"Frank . . . I mean, the suspect. He's gone," the policeman announced.

"How can he be gone?" Lana asked while glancing at Justin, who looked, to her surprise, *not* surprised. "He just came out of surgery a few hours ago. He's wearing a hospital gown and he only has the use of one arm. Where could he go?"

"So you haven't seen him," Officer McCabe guessed dryly. When Lana and Justin both shook their heads, he rushed past them while screaming into his radio.

Lana turned to Justin, who stared after the policeman with a small grin on his face. She asked suspiciously, "You wouldn't know about this, would you, Justin?"

"Of course not."

He abruptly grinned, then kissed her, obviously meaning to distract her. She knew he thought that he'd distracted her with the kiss, and the truth was he had. He whispered against her ear, "In case you were wondering, I love you, too, Lana."

"I know," she said confidently, which made him laugh and shake his head. She couldn't resist adding, "I always thought you were one of the smart ones."

Justin roared with laughter right before his mouth settled over hers.

EPILOGUE

One year later

Frank Hargrove had never owned anything in his life. But, now he owned Sweets & Surf, a café housed in a small building on the strip that overlooked the ocean in the small Southern California beach town of Playa Vista. They served homemade carrot bread, banana bread, and brownies, coffee and soft drinks, and sandwiches. No alcohol.

Frank paid his taxes and worked nine to five, almost like a normal man. It wasn't boring like he'd always feared it would be; it was life. Frank still limped from the knife wound, but with his daily two-mile walk from his small cottage to the café his leg was getting stronger and stronger.

Frank inhaled the fresh salt air as he unlocked the door to the café. He walked into the building but didn't turn the sign to read: OPEN. He still had another forty-five minutes before the morning rush, which usually consisted of a few surfers whom he was getting to know by name, and then Max, an old War World II veteran, who had been sitting in one of the chairs set up in front of Sweets & Surf since the café first opened fifteen years ago. Max brought his own coffee thermos with him, and a chessboard, and challenged anyone who walked by. He never bought anything from the shop, but Frank couldn't tell the man to leave. He had owned the shop for five months now, but he was a believer in tradition and Max was something of a good luck charm.

Then there was the lunch rush. And it was a rush. Frank had one of the high school boys help him in the afternoon. The best carrot bread in California brought people from far and wide, especially since Playa Vista sat on a strip of the scenic Highway One in between San Luis Obispo and any other sign of life until one reached San Francisco. All in all, Frank was having a good life.

He filled fresh coffee beans in the grinder and pressed the machine on. He wiped down the counter as he waited for the machine to finish. He hummed to himself. One of the songs Beatrice would hum to Lana when she was a baby. It would always soothe Lana, and it had always worked on him, too.

Frank suddenly felt like he was being watched. He whirled around, prepared to run. But, no one was in the shop except him. A few surfers bobbed on the waves in the distance, but there was no one else around for miles. None of the other shopkeepers on the strip had come in yet, either.

Frank shook his head at his paranoia. He couldn't expect to retire from that life and suddenly be a normal man just because he wanted to. He turned off the coffee grinder and silence once more filled the shop, besides the sound of waves crashing to shore. And then Frank saw it. A small white piece of paper on the counter. It definitely had not been there before. He approached it slowly, as if the paper had the ability to suddenly turn on him; then he carefully lifted it.

In familiar handwriting, he read: *We're getting married. July 15. There will be lots of hidden entrances and exits for retired art thieves, still evading the cops, who have to walk their daughters down the aisle.*

Frank smiled, then looked out the window. There were two people there now. Justin, the son he had always wished for, and Lana, the daughter he had always prayed for. The two laughed as they waved at him. Getting to know his daughter and future son-in-law over the last year had been a blessing Frank knew he didn't deserve, but he was glad that his Bea had pulled a few strings for him in heaven.

Frank grinned and walked out of the shop to his family. It was just May, but he had a lot of planning to do before July. Rule Number Five—always plan ahead.